David Bowie and Philosophy

Popular Culture and Philosophy® Series Editor: George A. Reisch

Volume 1 *Seinfeld and Philosophy: A Book about Everything and Nothing* (2000)

Volume 2 *The Simpsons and Philosophy: The D'oh! of Homer* (2001)

Volume 3 *The Matrix and Philosophy: Welcome to the Desert of the Real* (2002)

Volume 4 *Buffy the Vampire Slayer and Philosophy: Fear and Trembling in Sunnydale* (2003)

Volume 9 *Harry Potter and Philosophy: If Aristotle Ran Hogwarts* (2004)

Volume 12 *Star Wars and Philosophy: More Powerful than You Can Possibly Imagine* (2005)

Volume 13 *Superheroes and Philosophy: Truth, Justice, and the Socratic Way* (2005)

Volume 19 *Monty Python and Philosophy: Nudge Nudge, Think Think!* (2006)

Volume 25 *The Beatles and Philosophy: Nothing You Can Think that Can't Be Thunk* (2006)

Volume 30 *Pink Floyd and Philosophy: Careful with that Axiom, Eugene!* (2007)

Volume 35 *Star Trek and Philosophy: The Wrath of Kant* (2008)

Volume 36 *The Legend of Zelda and Philosophy: I Link Therefore I Am* (2008)

Volume 39 *Jimmy Buffett and Philosophy: The Porpoise Driven Life* (2009) Edited by Erin McKenna and Scott L. Pratt

Volume 42 *Supervillains and Philosophy: Sometimes Evil Is Its Own Reward* (2009)

Volume 45 *World of Warcraft and Philosophy: Wrath of the Philosopher King* (2009) Edited by Luke Cuddy and John Nordlinger

Volume 46 *Mr. Monk and Philosophy: The Curious Case of the Defective Detective* (2010) Edited by D.E. Wittkower

Volume 48 *The Red Sox and Philosophy: Green Monster Meditations* (2010) Edited by Michael Macomber

Volume 49 *Zombies, Vampires, and Philosophy: New Life for the Undead* (2010) Edited by Richard Greene and K. Silem Mohammad

Volume 51 *Soccer and Philosophy: Beautiful Thoughts on the Beautiful Game* (2010) Edited by Ted Richards

Volume 52 *Manga and Philosophy: Fullmetal Metaphysician* (2010) Edited by Josef Steiff and Adam Barkman

Volume 53 *Martial Arts and Philosophy: Beating and Nothingness* (2010) Edited by Graham Priest and Damon Young

Volume 54 *The Onion and Philosophy: Fake News Story True, Alleges Indignant Area Professor* (2010) Edited by Sharon M. Kaye

Volume 55 *Doctor Who and Philosophy: Bigger on the Inside* (2010) Edited by Courtland Lewis and Paula Smithka

Volume 57 *Rush and Philosophy: Heart and Mind United* (2011) Edited by Jim Berti and Durrell Bowman

Volume 58 *Dexter and Philosophy: Mind over Spatter* (2011) Edited by Richard Greene, George A. Reisch, and Rachel Robison-Greene

Volume 60 *SpongeBob SquarePants and Philosophy: Soaking Up Secrets Under the Sea!* (2011) Edited by Joseph J. Foy

Volume 61 *Sherlock Holmes and Philosophy: The Footprints of a Gigantic Mind* (2011) Edited by Josef Steiff

Volume 62 *Inception and Philosophy: Ideas to Die For* (2011) Edited by Thorsten Botz-Bornstein

Volume 63 *Philip K. Dick and Philosophy: Do Androids Have Kindred Spirits?* (2011) Edited by D.E. Wittkower

Volume 64 *The Rolling Stones and Philosophy: It's Just a Thought Away* (2012) Edited by Luke Dick and George A. Reisch

Volume 67 *Breaking Bad and Philosophy: Badder Living through Chemistry* (2012) Edited by David R. Koepsell and Robert Arp

Volume 68 *The Walking Dead and Philosophy: Zombie Apocalypse Now* (2012) Edited by Wayne Yuen

Volume 69 *Curb Your Enthusiasm and Philosophy: Awaken the Social Assassin Within* (2012) Edited by Mark Ralkowski

Volume 71 *The Catcher in the Rye and Philosophy: A Book for Bastards, Morons, and Madmen* (2012) Edited by Keith Dromm and Heather Salter

Volume 72 *Jeopardy! and Philosophy: What Is Knowledge in the Form of a Question?* (2012) Edited by Shaun P. Young

Volume 73 *The Wire and Philosophy: This America, Man* (2013) Edited by David Bzdak, Joanna Crosby, and Seth Vannatta

Volume 74 *Planet of the Apes and Philosophy: Great Apes Think Alike* (2013) Edited by John Huss

Volume 75 *Psych and Philosophy: Some Dark Juju-Magumbo* (2013) Edited by Robert Arp

Volume 79 *Frankenstein and Philosophy: The Shocking Truth* (2013) Edited by Nicolas Michaud

Volume 80 *Ender's Game and Philosophy: Genocide Is Child's Play* (2013) Edited by D.E. Wittkower and Lucinda Rush

Volume 81 *How I Met Your Mother and Philosophy: Being and Awesomeness* (2014) Edited by Lorenzo von Matterhorn

Volume 82 *Jurassic Park and Philosophy: The Truth Is Terrifying* (2014) Edited by Nicolas Michaud

Volume 83 *The Devil and Philosophy: The Nature of His Game* (2014) Edited by Robert Arp

Volume 84 *Leonard Cohen and Philosophy: Various Positions* (2014) Edited by Jason Holt

Volume 85 *Homeland and Philosophy: For Your Minds Only* (2014) Edited by Robert Arp

Volume 86 *Girls and Philosophy: This Book Isn't a Metaphor for Anything* (2014) Edited by Richard Greene and Rachel Robison-Greene

Volume 87 *Adventure Time and Philosophy: The Handbook for Heroes* (2015) Edited by Nicolas Michaud

Volume 88 *Justified and Philosophy: Shoot First, Think Later* (2015) Edited by Rod Carveth and Robert Arp

Volume 89 *Steve Jobs and Philosophy: For Those Who Think Different* (2015) Edited by Shawn E. Klein

Volume 90 *Dracula and Philosophy: Dying to Know* (2015) Edited by Nicolas Michaud and Janelle Pötzsch

Volume 91 *Its Always Sunny and Philosophy: The Gang Gets Analyzed* (2015) Edited by Roger Hunt and Robert Arp

Volume 92 *Orange Is the New Black and Philosophy: Last Exit from Litchfield* (2015) Edited by Richard Greene and Rachel Robison-Greene

Volume 93 *More Doctor Who and Philosophy: Regeneration Time* (2015) Edited by Courtland Lewis and Paula Smithka

Volume 94 *Divergent and Philosophy: The Factions of Life* (2016) Edited by Courtland Lewis

Volume 95 *Downton Abbey and Philosophy: Thinking in That Manor* (2016) Edited by Adam Barkman and Robert Arp

Volume 96 *Hannibal Lecter and Philosophy: The Heart of the Matter* (2016) Edited by Joseph Westfall

Volume 97 *The Ultimate Walking Dead and Philosophy: Hungry for More* (2016) Edited by Wayne Yuen

Volume 98 *The Princess Bride and Philosophy: Inconceivable!* (2016) Edited by Richard Greene and Rachel Robison-Greene

Volume 99 *Louis C.K. and Philosophy: You Don't Get to Be Bored* (2016) Edited by Mark Ralkowski

Volume 100 *Batman, Superman, and Philosophy: Badass or Boyscout?* (2016) Edited by Nicolas Michaud

Volume 101 *Discworld and Philosophy: Reality Is Not What It Seems* (2016) Edited by Nicolas Michaud

Volume 103 *David Bowie and Philosophy: Rebel Rebel* (2016) Edited by Theodore G. Ammon

In Preparation:

Orphan Black and Philosophy (2016) Edited by Richard Greene and Rachel Robison-Greene

The Ultimate Game of Thrones and Philosophy (2016) Edited by Eric J. Silverman and Robert Arp

Deadpool and Philosophy (2016) Edited by Nicolas Michaud

Peanuts and Philosophy (2016) Edited by Richard Greene and Rachel Robison-Greene

Red Rising and Philosophy (2016) Edited by Courtland Lewis and Kevin McCain

For full details of all Popular Culture and Philosophy® books, visit www.opencourtbooks.com.

Popular Culture and Philosophy®

David Bowie and Philosophy

Rebel Rebel

EDITED BY

THEODORE G. AMMON

OPEN COURT
Chicago

Volume 103 in the series, Popular Culture and Philosophy®, edited by George A. Reisch

To order books from Open Court, call toll-free 1-800-815-2280, or visit our website at www.opencourtbooks.com.

Open Court Publishing Company is a division of Carus Publishing Company, dba Cricket Media.

First printing 2016

Printed and bound in the United States of America.

ISBN: 978-0-8126-9921-0

This book is also available as an e-book.

Library of Congress Control Number: 2016940561

Contents

A Farewell to David Bowie

January 10th 2016—The music died again, but ironically not without leaving us a final extraordinarily precious gift of itself. How terribly sad it all is; how beautiful his final testament to his career. How peculiar the title should be *Blackstar* for someone who shone so brightly on stage and off, like the candle in the middle of it all. David Robert Jones left us an album of mysteries as a parting gift, but do we deserve it?

Bowie was sixty-nine, still a young man by contemporary standards and though battling cancer comprised some of his most astonishing music. Where indeed did Monday go? He died on a Sunday.

For five decades David Bowie pursued a passion that shaped our lives in ways we may never fully appreciate. My parents thought that Rock was unhealthy, even dangerous. Reflecting on this judgment I played the other day an old forty-five of Little Richard's "Rip It Up" and actually paid attention to the lyrics. I think my parents may have been correct. "Rip It Up" *was* dangerous and we're better off for it. I couldn't help but wonder, as a father, whom I would censor for the mental and physical health of my own children. All gangsta rap, all death metal, Two Live Crew, GG Allin, Insane Clown Posse, the Sex Pistols, Pantera? But why stop there—we all know it's a slippery slope.

And what about Bowie? Surely he doesn't belong on anyone's hit list, nor my long list (growing ever longer as I consider the "problem"). Wasn't part of the lure of Bowie that he was dangerously different? Face it, in the early 1970s a cross-dressing bisexual whose lineage traced to Mars and beyond was seriously abnormal—dangerous to the soccer mom of the day, the dutiful working father. However, the violent overthrow of the status quo was never shimmering on the surface of Bowie's lyrics, nor obviously just under the surface. The Sex Pistols, on the other hand, in spite of their questionable beginnings, wore their sense on their sleeves. "Anarchy in the UK," clear—"Suffragette City," "Jean Genie," not so much. One about post-Vietnam mindless violence; sure that makes sense. The other about some bloke in New York doing some things, sleeping on his back or something like that; again, not so much, except for the familiar guitar riff. That riff itself will pass muster, never mind the lyrics. But the opening line of "Diamond Dogs" is another story. "Genocide"—I don't think so. Best not to let your father hear that; he was in The War you know—but that sax solo is *catchy.* By the way, honey, what exactly is a Diamond Dog?

And so it went. Oh, and the guitar riff in "Rebel Rebel" was definitely a take. Why, we could even dance to it. But the parents never really appreciated any of it, did they?

And we did? Or did we dance our way through it? Nevertheless if you were sick of disco, techno, punk, hair bands and so forth, Bowie was always there, offering seemingly unlimited possibilities, even to be heroes, if only for a day. And that's really what we all thought we could be, a hero for a day. None of us took seriously, not really, the from-nowhere-to-center-stage story. Some of us merely wanted a new form of drinking music and if the lyrics were a bit dodgy, so much the better. We could concoct stories that Bowie was dead or the end of civilization around the corner or screw The Man.

Such were the early years of our stupidly provincial perspectives. Our former idols died and the groups dissipated or grew old and played the same shit songs over and over in concerts to groups of older and older folks, merely reminiscing. Not Bowie; long after we could bust a move on a dance floor, Bowie still enthralled. What will it be *now*, Bowie?, we thought. Even *Pin Up* was intriguing because we didn't know why he would craft such a piece. Sentimentality? Surely not, not Bowie. Well, Whatever. What's *next*? Why does he have visions of swastikas. Again, whatever—it's Bowie and it'll make sense at some point. Or not.

And then the dancing stopped for us and the music got serious all of a sudden. Rumors were that he had moved to Germany and given up. Little did we know what was forthcoming. Translate: we began to pay attention to the new releases as well as the now oldies with Ziggy and Major Tom. Nothing quite like playing an early Little Richard forty-five—one of the seven-inch vinyl things with the big hole in the middle. Nothing quite like early Bowie either.

Who would have predicted that Bowie would team with Eno? Iggy Pop and Lou Reed made sense and even Mott the Hoople (the name of a Sixties novel), but Eno and the soundscapes of Kraftwerk and others? And to our collective stupefaction, three of Bowie's best albums emerged from the German fling. How were we supposed to predict that the same composer of "Changes" and "Young Americans" would give rise to *Low*? The Beatles, with notable exceptions, were unastonishing. "I am the Walrus" made no sense whatever, but given the changes wrought by *Revolver* and *Sgt. Pepper's* we tried to find something in it besides "Paul is dead." But *Low* made no sense at all musically and therein lies part of its brilliance. Bowie's ability to absorb and transform influences was unparalleled. Transformation. Bowie transforms the way a mollusk takes in the sea and exudes a magnificent shell.

Did Bowie live within his music? Was the transformation reciprocal? From folkish ditties to R&R to Blond Motown to hard rock to fusion and back and forth. But what would make us think that Bowie is the "faker" he claims in "Changes" with the seemingly unquenchable thirst for change? The Beatles changed too, but there was a huge leap at *Rubber Soul* and another at *Sgt. Pepper's*. But Bowie leapt about always—there was never continuity. I think he despised it.

In numerous interviews he repeated how artistically restless he was. The glaring omission is a claim to American, or English, blues. Even so, we can hear a hint of John Lee Hooker in "Rebel Rebel" and "Jean Genie." Thus Bowie was one of the few British artists of the time not to begin by blowing through John Mayall's Bluesbreakers. He stood on his own, and the originality and makeup and costumes helped create and solidify new genres. For a while, Bowie could count as glam rock, but he transformed again, and the other glam groups faded while others morphed and took their place. Garry Glitter was a one-hit wonder, T-Rex lasted a while, though Kiss has endured; but I am not sure that they even count at all. A "10" for makeup, merely a "1" for originality. There were lights and smoke and fire, and I believe a monstrous tongue was involved, but that's about it.

Bowie, however, left a rich and unique legacy, as well as influences too numerous to count. Some of the influences may be in pure spectacle, in an Aristotelian sense. Countless acts from hardcore groups such as the Genitorturers to the pop pabulum of Miley Cyrus and Britney Spears began to incorporate semi-sophisticated choreography to audience "participation," from mosh pits in which young males beat themselves senseless to GG Allin attacking the audience, seriously attacking the audience in his I Hate The Audience tour. He was knifed and hospitalized in the midst of one performance, claiming on Jerry Springer that such a retaliatory act was fine with him since all bets were off during his "performances." I don't suggest that this brainless idiocy traces to Bowie directly. Bowie was sophisticated, stylized and intelligent; Allin was a moron and a junkie who died of a heroin overdose. How original.

Nonetheless Bowie changed the face of rock forever. Every act of theatricality owes Bowie. An exception might be Zappa, who had his own brand of theatrics and audience participation before Bowie. Even Jethro Tull, primarily a Seventies band, owes to Bowie, and the outlandish costumes of

Elton John. The difference with Bowie remains the lack of *mere* spectacle. Ian Anderson of Tull developed no characters such as Ziggy or the Thin White Duke. Off stage, Anderson was a less animated version of himself on stage. Bowie took theatrics to a new dimension. When he distinguished Bowie from Ziggy, while in Ziggy attire, a threshold had been crossed. Unfortunately many of those influenced by Bowie missed the music and the lyrics, while awed by the spectacle. My mind slips to an image of Miley Cyrus swinging about on a wrecking ball, naked. Really? And what does she have to contribute to music? Does she even write her songs, such as they are? Oh, she's given credit for co-composing with four or five other folks. Okay, there you have it.

The comparisons above are mostly appalling, but more clearly distinguish the extraordinary talent of a Bowie from that of a twerking twerp on the Country Music Awards. Ah, but what about a Bowie simulating fellatio with Mick Ronson, his guitarist. In the former we have the mere spectacle of unabashed crassness. No need for that, and I'm no prude. For the latter, Bowie was encouraging his audience to appreciate gender-bending and cross-sexuality and encouraging his audience to appreciate the multiple ways of being in the world. Miley Cyrus was more-or-less saying, in her inimical way, "look what I can do with my ass." Bowie contributed to the rising discussion of gender issues; Cyrus has nothing significant to say, certainly not to women who have been historically treated well only because of their sexual prowess.

As for intellectual prowess, Bowie's lyrics frequently reveal meanings far deeper than those of his contemporaries. I would not toast "Let's Dance," "Fashion," and "Fame," or "Young American" but many of his lyrics contain complex metaphors, stream of consciousness imagery, free verse and in the German trilogy of *Low, Lodger* and *"Heroes,"* symbolist minimalism, a result in part of the seminal influence of Brian Eno. Bowie mostly eschewed simple rhyme schemes in favor of the lyrical equivalent of soundscapes, lyrics that suggest clarity but which diverge into labyrinthine meanings and images that tease the imagination. "Jean Genie" provides an early example, the driving guitar riff overlain with a story that suggests the clarity of intention but which refrains from simply clarity. Even as early a song as "Space Oddity," with the appearance of Major Tom, remains baffling, especially since Bowie abandons Major Tom as a junkie in "Ashes to Ashes." So we must revisit a song whose message was never clear in the first place. We may have thought it an anthem of sorts to the ultimate freedom of suicides, but then Major Tom makes it home, or, to heaven, the loser. Just another junkie who couldn't feel the freedom in his hands and who thought he had it in his arms.

Perhaps Bowie gave himself to cocaine and sex, and squandered some of his own freedom, but a helpless, hapless, hopeless junkie he was not. Periods of burnout fatigue ensued, but that goes with the territory of Rock. Even the Beatles divorced one another and the Rolling Stones have had dry spells. One or two Stones albums you bought simply because that's what you do. And even if Bowie can't give everything away finally, we can do what we can for his legacy. We can play it over and over—even the albums critics panned—and let it inform our thought and musical sensibilities.

January 10th 2016—the music dies again. What about *The Next Day*? *The Next Day* was but a prelude to the dying day. Whom would he become in the USA; what would be his name? Complex questions to which Bowie but hints at answers on what many of us thought would be his last album, a blatant defacing of the album *"Heroes."* But what is negated and defaced exactly? It isn't as if the *"Heroes"* album either musically or lyrically defined an essential Bowie for the ages or as if with *The Next Day* he takes a radically new trajectory. You could argue that the *"Heroes"* album represents a phase of Bowie's life, the time he spent in Germany away from it all—and now we are told "never again." And never again an iconic album such as *"Heroes" could* have been; it was certainly admired by critics. Or never again a meaningless hand gesture allegedly inspired by the German painter Erich Heckel. And there is an odd familiarity, in this photo shoot, of Bowie's hair, angular face, and leather jacket with that of Robert Mapplethorpe. The shocking contrast of a portrait in *The Next Day*—a stark, almost angry pose bespeaks a person shed of all pretense and affectation. A raw undefined Bowie wondering what he will become the next day.

And so one thing he didn't repeat was the tradition of a highly stylized close-up. Aside from the denial of appearances, what about the music? It seems that Bowie did not make a clean break with *The Next Day* from *"Heroes."* The sharper contrast remains that between *The Next Day* and *Blackstar*, but then whatever aesthetic plan Bowie had anticipated was cut short by cancer. A young rock'n'roll star from outer space named Ziggy Stardust, dressed outlandishly so entirely appropriate I would venture. But a sixty-nine-year-old man reprising his years of 1969 might seem a tad dreadful. A tad like Brian Wilson singing "Little Surfer Girl." I surmise that Bowie did what Robert Mapplethorpe did when Mapplethorpe was dying of AIDS; Mapplethorpe recorded himself in a series of stunning self-portraits, unabashedly facing death. I would say Bowie did the same with *Blackstar*—a series of musical snapshots into his psyche as he battled his own version of death.

I

What David Bowie Was Up To

1
The Actor Tells the Truth

George A. Reisch

I was surprised at the news of January 11th, 2016—not just Bowie's death, but the enormous expression of collective grief around the world. Even six days later, the loss remained fresh, shocking, and slightly incomprehensible. The *New York Times* app offered up six articles—the official obituary along with articles about Bowie as an actor, as an inconspicuous New Yorker, the shrewd financial mind behind "Bowie Bonds," and the co-author of the play *Lazarus*. Then came a review of his last album, *Blackstar*, and an essay by philosopher Simon Critchley. In the media and social media, his passing seemed bigger and more momentous than anyone expected. Had you never heard of David Bowie, you might have thought he was a beloved head of state or cultural leader. More John Kennedy or Martin Luther King than Elvis or Frank Sinatra.

There's a reason for all this sadness, I think. But it's not simple. For starters, as everyone knows, Bowie created and inhabited different musical characters as he built his career in the 1970s. While artists like Neil Young and Joni Mitchell established almost personal, confessional relationships with their fans, Bowie had no intention of baring his soul or communing with his fans through music. Even decades later, what he was trying to do remains confusing and easily misunderstood. Consider his interview with Terry Gross (of NPR's *Fresh*

Air) on the occasion of the thirtieth anniversary of *The Rise and Fall of Ziggy Stardust and the Spiders from Mars.*

Gross is famous for her acumen and trenchant questions. Before each show, she reads up and thinks hard about what to ask her guests. But Gross was not prepared for Bowie. Over and over, the Starman blew her mind. He explained, for example, that once he created a character—like Ziggy, Aladdin Sane, or the Thin White Duke, or those he invented for the 1990s album *Outside*—he fast became bored and yearned to move on.

> **Bowie:** I like putting events together. In fact, everything I do is about the conceptualizing and realization of a piece of work, whether it's the recording or the performance side. And kind of when I put the thing together, I don't mind doing it for a few weeks, but then, quite frankly, I get incredibly, incredibly bored because I don't see myself so much as a— I mean, I don't live for the stage. I don't live for an audience. That really doesn't . . .
>
> **Gross:** Can I stop you and say that I'm really surprised to hear that?

She knew Bowie as a singer and figured that he created different characters so he'd have more and different opportunities to sing. But Bowie's agenda was bigger and quite different. Originally a sax player, he explained that he first stepped up to a mic when the lead singer in one of his bands suddenly fell ill. A star was born, you might think. But that's not how Bowie saw it. What he "really wanted to do," he explained, "more than anything else, up until I was around sixteen, seventeen, was write musicals."

> **Gross:** Was write music.
>
> **Bowie:** [*correcting her*] Music*als*
>
> **Gross:** *Oh, musicals*!
>
> **Bowie:** I really wanted to write musicals. That's what I wanted to do more than anything else. And . . . because I liked rock music,

> I kind of moved into that sphere, somehow thinking that somewhere along the line I'd be able to put the two together. And I suppose I very nearly did with the Ziggy character.

According to Bowie, *The Rise and Fall of Ziggy Stardust and the Spiders from Mars* could and should have been something like *Cats* or *Jesus Christ Superstar*. "I don't know why, to this day, I didn't find some other kid . . . and say, here you are. Put the wig on and send him out and do the gigs, you know. I mean, it would have been much the best thing to do. And then I could have moved on quicker to something else."

> **GROSS:** So when you say you wanted to write musicals, did you want to write, like, Rodgers and Hart kind of musicals or *Hair*? I mean, what was . . .
>
> **BOWIE:** No, my point was I wanted to rewrite how rock music was perceived.

"Oh, I see," Gross said. She was beginning to see Bowie in a new light—not a performer but a producer who hired himself to sing.

What was this new perception of rock music? It's not just that Bowie played different roles in different costumes, that he was a "chameleon." But that was the conventional wisdom. "The idea is that every few years he trots out some astonishing new 'character', complete with a fresh musical idiom to match," *The New York Times* explained a propos of 1980's *Scary Monsters* and Bowie's role on Broadway in *The Elephant Man*. True, Bowie *did that* in the 1970s, but the "idea" behind it, what he was thinking about, was something else—not the parade of characters and styles, the musical product on display. Bowie was instead fascinated by the underlying creative process.

By becoming (hypothetically) a spaceman, a schizophrenic rock star named Aladdin Sane, a post-apocalyptic, mutant Diamond Dog, or the Thin White Duke, Bowie looked at music and art from different angles and perspectives, always reaching for a better view and understanding of his craft and its place in modern life and experience. No wonder Terry Gross was surprised over and over. Bowie was not only a performer, not only a writer and producer of music, but a deeply curious mind who aimed to make us think along with him. "Don't you wonder sometimes about sound and vision?"

Whether or not he figured out sound and vision, Bowie knew from the beginning what kind of presence he did not want to be. When he first conceived of Ziggy Stardust, Bowie told Gross, it was because he was "fed up with denim and the hippies." So he wore makeup and glamorized rock not just to be different, and certainly not (as Gross suggested) to "make a statement about postmodernism or a statement about sexuality." Bowie wanted to subvert the idea of *artistic authenticity* that grew up around denim and flower power. "So let me stop and see if I have this right," Gross asked him. "Wearing a T-shirt and jeans seems phony to you but wearing mascara and eye makeup seem right?"

Not quite. Bowie explained again:

> **Bowie:** I didn't say that wearing a glamorization of the rock artist was any truer from the other thing . . .
>
> **Gross:** Oh, okay, right. It's artifice . . .
>
> **Bowie:** . . . It's all artifice. . . . I think my main point would be that the T-shirt and denims thing, in my mind, was *also* an artifice.

Bowie didn't go into it in this interview, but the elephant in the room filled with denim and hippies was Bob Dylan. In "Song for Bob Dylan," from *Hunky Dory*, Dylan gave his heart to every bedsit room, and "sat behind a million pairs of eyes, and told them how they saw."

Bowie was obviously interested in what Dylan was doing in the late 1960s because Bob Dylan was the spectacularly successful creation of a Minnesotan folk singer named Robert Zimmerman. Dylan was his Ziggy, a persona designed to update Woody Guthrie for the new, changing times. But this production was invisible to the millions of fans who hung on Dylan's every word and took him for some kind of prophet or seer. From Bowie's (make that, David Jones's) point of view, this was quite rich and had to be called out. "Now hear this Robert Zimmerman," is the song's first line.

You might think the philosophy behind Bowie's interests and talents, especially his constantly changing musical identity, is about metaphysics. "I watch the ripples change their size, but never leave the stream of warm impermanence" might be read as Heraclitus's eternal flux meets Parmenides's theory of permanent being. But this interest in the "artifice" of public figures points instead to postwar political philosophy. David Jones was born, after all, in 1947, just two years after Germany was awoken from its genocidal dreams of world domination. Its west reinvented itself as a modern democracy while Soviet communism controlled life in the east. From his first memories, therefore, Bowie grew up in the cold war, an age of ideological competition and anxiety about the future of humanity. Modern life seemed to prove again and again that human beings were surprisingly easy to manipulate and control.

So it is that Bowie's album *Diamond Dogs*, with its anthems "1984" and "Big Brother," kicks off with a Nuremberg-sized crowd cheering for their beloved leader. "This ain't rock and roll," Bowie yells to the frenzied crowd, "this is *genocide*!" This is also a connection to the philosophical debates that dominated American intellectuals after the war—*The Age of the Crisis of Man*, as Mark Greif has compellingly described it, in which philosophers, novelists, and literary critics alike urgently asked, What is humanity really made of? Will it ever rise above the totalitarian nightmares it seems to keep creating?

Probably not, *Diamond Dogs* warned. "Because of all we've seen, because of all we've said," Bowie sang chillingly, "we are the dead." With our last breaths, we're weakly calling out for a savior, "Someone to claim us, someone to follow . . . We want you, Bob Dylan." Actually it's "We want you, Big Brother"—but that's the point. Bowie's driving obsession with inventing and inhabiting characters was not just a philosophy of art and music; it was a larger philosophy of life and politics, a critique of modernity fleshed out in songs, concept albums, and performances, that puts Bowie in this postwar conversation about humanity's future. "Man is nothing else but that which he makes of himself," Jean-Paul Sartre said in a lecture from 1945—"That is the first principle of existentialism." It's also the first principle of Bowie. Only through constant reinvention can we avoid being fooled by ourselves or others.

Not that it's easy. Though he proudly called himself merely "the actor" on the credits for *Hunky Dory,* and confessed in "Changes" to be "the faker," Bowie seemed troubled and anguished at the end of *Young Americans*. In "Who Can I Be Now?" he struggles mightily with where all his costume changing has left him—as in, "Can I be real?" Four years later, in 1980's "Ashes to Ashes," he looked back on his most famous persona to report that Major Tom was washed up, scared, mediocre, and hardly original: he had "never done good things . . . never done bad things . . . never done anything out of the blue."

Bowie knew he was a follower, a synthesizer, a producer who often relied on other people's ideas and talents. *Diamond Dogs* is obviously an homage to Orwell (three of whose books appear in Bowie's top-100 list) and Sartre articulated existentialism decades before Bowie applied it (and set it) to popular music. But Bowie was still a "hero" because of his enormous talent and—most of all—because he was honest. He put his creations—his songs, his clothes, and his perfect, otherworldly hair—up front so that we would never forget that he was a performer, not a prophet or a commanding genius.[1]

Screw all that, he said—"Let's Dance." And we did, for decades, knowing and liking Bowie all the more because he never lied to us.

---

[1] My favorite example of this is "The Man Who Sold the World" on *Saturday Night Live* in 1979. Bowie "wore" a stiff, larger than life plastic tuxedo that prevented him from walking on stage. He was carried up to and back from the microphone by his backup singers.

2
You Don't Have to Be Stupid to Be Cool

THORSTEN BOTZ-BORNSTEIN

Wasn't it disturbing to get the news of David Bowie's death on January 10th 2016, when the media were full of reports of terrorist suicide attacks and the deaths of innocent people?

Bowie seems to represent everything the terrorists are opposed to. With his glamour, transgressions, and lust for life, he symbolized that part of Western culture that puritans all over the world can stomach least. However, what did Bowie stand for more precisely? Being a hero for one day, ashes to ashes. . . . In his last video *Lazarus,* he sings "Look, I am in heaven." This forms a contrast, though at the same time a strange consonance, with the new culture of heroic death, all of which is captured by the media.

When I was in high school we were listening to The Clash, Iggy Pop, and Bowie. How did those elements fit together? The Clash and Iggy were punk and neopunk but Bowie was pop. The rationale of this strange synthesis became clear to me only much later. Thinking back to the early Eighties, my friends and I were pegged into the stuffy postwar world of respectable middle-class parents and neighbors. It was a suffocating environment that the preceding hippie movement had not been able to entirely eliminate.

We wanted to be different, but how? The Clash and Iggy Pop were what we wanted to be but knew that we never could. Bowie, on the other hand, was more like us: a thin, white boy, intellectually tempted, and rather awkward. A random television interview now available on YouTube shows Bowie as a seventeen-year-old youth looking like the typical suburban kid caught between submission, modest provocation, and embarrassment. His only answer to the social pressure of his environment is the shy insistence on being allowed to wear long hair. A similar awkwardness is visible in early videos like the original video of "Space Oddity" from 1969.

Simon Critchley asks in his book on Bowie about "the source of Bowie's power to connect with ordinary boys and girls, the ones who felt bored and deeply awkward in their skin" (p. 31). My answer is: he could do so because he had the same kind of awkwardness in himself.

Bowie's Body Control

Bowie was indeed very much like us. The Bromley mock-Tudor houses were similar to the nondescript terraced houses *we* (European teenagers) were living in. He, too must have felt tortured by the hypercorrect, hypocritical behavior of this petty bourgeoisie with its imbecile expectations and interdictions. In an interview in the mid-1970s he said that parents "fuck you up" and called his mother "repressive" and "a snob" (*Starman*, p. 6). Most probably he did not yet know how to respond to this environment.

But here's the thing: Bowie overcame his initial awkwardness not by imitating the toughness and violence of street culture. Instead, he did what we thought we knew rather well: he worked very hard. Very early Bowie took lessons from a mime who taught him how to control his rubbery arms and legs, how to make his gestures less random and more determined. In Bowie's bodily movements we could recognize our own edginess, imposed upon us by a functional and narrow reality so hopeless in both moral and aesthetic terms. However, *his* angular movements had become stylized and aesthetic.

The image control" that has so often been pointed out as Bowie's trailblazing achievement as a pop star, began with "body control." On the other hand, until the end, his body movements remained rather mechanical and robot-like. This even became his trademark. In my opinion, the most fascinating thing about Bowie is his strange hand movements.

Bowie never acquired the natural swagger of the tough ones. There has never been any rhythm in Bowie, but his appearance stands for white and Western theatricality. I guess that's why we could so easily identify with him. In his last video, *Lazarus*, he's dressed like a skeleton while receding backwards into the heavy wooden closet standing in his hospital room. Once again he moves like a robot and disappears into the dark and square-shaped space of his youth from whence he had come sixty years earlier.

For us, who were living in that dark closet, Bowie was light. He was a revelation, he had opened the door for us. Maybe we emaciated, nerdish kids from the continental European suburb could be cool, too? Bowie had overcome the constraints of his petty-bourgeois living space and established a new reality simply by modifying his own body movements. He had managed to control his body, to stylize it, to aestheticize it. And he stylized and aestheticized it very well.

Bowie was like a reincarnation of Nietzsche, who had written that you should always look at the philosophers' feet. Look at how they're walking, look at their body movements. "There is more wisdom in your body than in your deepest philosophy" (*Zarathustra*). The rest—the mind, the intellect—comes only later. For us this meant that you can eat your cake and have it too, because the mind and the intellect will not be entirely forgotten. You don't have to be stupid to be cool. That's what Bowie taught us.

Beyond the Poses

Bowie's world was made of style. Over time, the constructions of his imagination would transcend the traditional boundaries of rock and pop music. The retrospectives of his stylistic world have become important for the world of fashion, visual art, and design. This is only possible because there must have been, beyond the devices of pure stylization, some substance. How can that substance be qualified philosophically?

Isn't it all style, pose, and fakery? Critchley asks how something true can emerge from all this fakery of different characters, pantomimes displayed by Bowie over decades. Any truth is here "inauthentic, completely self-conscious and utterly constructed" (p. 40). I think the truth is contained in this style's coolness. It's coolness as an ethico-aesthetic notion that mysteriously flows out of Bowie's entire stylization project.

To be cool means to remain calm even under stress (see my "What Does It Mean to Be Cool?"). In Bowie's case, coolness cannot be limited to a mannerist imitation of streetwise toughness. He never imitated anything, but controlled his own body movements. There's nothing "fake" about this. Bowie's coolness was always very honest. It was no pose, but had become an attitude, always linked to the boyish honesty that he could maintain until the end. Bowie seemed to be constantly saying: "That's precisely how cool you can get as a thin, frail, shy, white, suburban kid with bad teeth. Not more and not less. Take it or leave it."

Back in the Eighties, we tried to take it. Taking *this* appeared to be easier than taking Iggy Pop or the whole punk thing. Faking punk would have been dishonest. Iggy was tough and, even worse: he was *born* tough. Iggy could be admired from a distance, and we felt that Bowie probably admired him, just like us, from a distance. Still he had managed to get closer to him, but he could do that only because he had been working very hard.

Bowie wasn't born cool but he became cool. That's what makes him rather unique in the landscape of twentieth-century cool guys from Humphrey Bogart to Denzel Washington. Not everybody can be born rich. However, not everybody can be born poor either. The majority of Western youngsters are white, lower-middle class, provincial kids who have to count on their skills to be successful. Something like Bromley of the 1960s is what most modern Western kids are living in. If they want to be cool, they will probably imitate hip-hop styles or try to speak English with a black American accent. Some—though fortunately not very many—flirt with terrorism because they find the cool swagger of the ISIS soldier more tempting than anything else.

Bowie was constantly transgressing: towards punk, towards the feminine gender, and towards fascism when adopting the "emotionless Aryan superman" character of the Thin White Duke, complete with a Hitler salute in 1976 (he later said that he had been completely stoned, which is probably true). Around the same time (the "Berlin time") he also made use of Communist and revolutionary symbolism. It doesn't make sense to pin Bowie down to one or another political position; he is rather the symbol and the idol of a post-political generation mostly interested in aesthetics. It's more important to observe that whatever he did, he did only through theatricality and play. His "transgressions" were never real transgression. He never stopped being a poet, which is the main characteristic of a dandy who is not just wearing clothes but who is wearing them in a certain way.

Kitsch

Bowie was playing with fire, always transgressing, never giving in, to the simplistic, the clearly defined, the obvious. . . . In later years, Bowie abandoned punk and the feminine, but one transgression would remain constant during his entire career: the transgression towards kitsch.

One reason Bowie was cool was because he could manipulate kitsch without being absorbed by it. Bowie was "kitsch-cool," if such a thing has ever existed. In "Diamond Dog" Bowie sings of "just another future song, lonely little kitsch." Well, maybe he mentions it here only because it rhymes with "bitch." Kitsch was part of Bowie's existence from the very beginning. It came with "Starman's" octave leap from "star" to "man" so reminiscent of Garland's "Over the Rainbow." But already here the melodious drama was "cooled down" by provocative or non-conformist showmanship. The same can be said about the whole-tone upwards repetition of the refrain at the end of "Heroes." Whatever was nice and beautiful would be mixed with something else. Glamour was mixed with dystopianism, most obviously in the dystopian metropolis of the Diamond Dogs.

Few people manage to manipulate a dangerous item like kitsch without losing their coolness. Warhol could do it. Jeff Koons could do it. Some hip-hop artists can do it, too. Glam rock was kitsch by definition as it indulged in purple, orange, lime green, and metallic. In "Space Oddity" Bowie brought in tons of more kitsch: futuristic kitsch. But even this was "cooled down" with avant-garde electronic sounds. What became important in this "science fiction" were not the special effects but the shiny space suits, the rockets colored in Bordeaux-red, and the glaring galaxies and protein pills. Those items became the symbols of the "odd" space-age of glam rock. When glam rock was over, Bowie turned towards other kitsch items. His crooning style of later pieces like "Slip Away" from *Heathen* sounds like a parody of the ultimate kitsch song; and this singing style even became his new trademark.

Finally, the nerdy boy from Bromley had outdone everybody. Kitsch became an empowerment of coolness. While tough people like punks are not allowed to show too much emotion, Bowie could indulge in beautiful feelings without being ashamed of it. And his fans experienced those feelings, too. Among them were some of the world's most puritan Western intellectuals who would normally never have come close to such music.

Bowie and Japanese Aesthetics

There is a Japanese aesthetic term called "*iki*," and I have always thought of Bowie when hearing this term. *Iki* means "stylish" and "chic" but with certain specifications.

The Japanese philosopher Shuzo Kuki has placed *iki* within the oppositional tension between "sweet" and "sour" or "astringent," which is exactly what Bowie impersonates. Kitsch is merely sweet but Bowie's astringent facial expression allows all kitsch to become *iki*. For the aesthetics of *iki*, the "sweet" relationship is the conventional relationship that will be questioned and negated by the astringent. Kuki analyzes *iki* in his book *The Structure of Iki*, which the German philosopher Martin Heidegger found of utmost interest ("A Conversation about Language").

Kuki makes amazing suggestions about sexual ambiguity or gender ambiguity with regard to the particular *iki* style. For Kuki, gender ambiguity "is a disruption of our expectations, which embody the mainstream values of the society into which we have been acculturated" (*Structure of Iki*, p. 156). Such ideas would be unthinkable with regard to any western traditional aesthetic concept. According to Kuki, the psychological patterns enabling *iki* to emerge are typically Japanese while Western-style coquetry merely "wiggles the hips around and performs in lewd reality" (p. 73).

Western eroticism does not provide the right amount of astringency: being too sweet, it easily develops towards kitsch. Furthermore, Kuki explains that the appeal of *iki* always comes "through the body and the body is also the barrier to the spirit expressed in *iki*" (p. 156). Together, it is very much like a description of Bowie's most fundamental aesthetic ideology in which an entire world could be changed simply by changing your body movements.

Bowie was a well-known Japanophile. The above-mentioned mime teacher with whom he was studying in the mid-1960s was none other than the British performance artist Lindsay Kemp, who was heavily influenced by the traditional Japanese kabuki style. Kemp experimented with exaggerated gestures, elaborate costumes, and unusual make-up. Bowie later said that Kabuki Theater had taught him "the discipline of movement" of his body.

So Bowie's theatricality was not as Western as we had initially assumed. Kabuki is also famous for its *onnagata* actors, men specializing in playing female roles. Bowie got more than a glimpse of this art. The renowned *onnagata* actor Tamasaburo Bando taught him how to apply traditional kabuki make-up, which excels in highlighting bold features on a white background, and this most probably inspired the drawing of the lightning bolt across Ziggy's face.

Japanese culture represented another field of transgression for Bowie. In 1973, he used explicit Japanese motifs in "Aladdin Sane." It is also within this field of transgression that he could develop his concept of gender ambiguity. In 1971, Bowie purchased a costume made by the Japanese designer Kansai Yamamoto from his London boutique. He had met Yamamoto earlier that year in Japan.

For Bowie, Yamamoto produced the perfect mixture of kabuki costume and futurist space suit; while Yamamoto liked the androgynous aspect of Bowie's appearance. Bowie would repeatedly wear kimonos on stage as well as the shiny black, red and blue "martial arts" space suit consisting of loose trousers similar to samurai *hakama*. Most spectacular is Yamamoto's "Rites of Spring" costume specially made for Bowie. Yamamoto clearly influenced *Bowie's* fashion sense. If glam rock is today seen as a predecessor of the Japanese, androgynous *visual kei* culture, this is due to Bowie's pioneering cross-cultural aesthetics.

Kuki writes that "when sweet dreams are broken, *iki*, which is rich in critical knowledge, awakens" (p. 73). It is worthwhile to stay with this sentence for a while. When dreams and illusions are broken, the initial sweetness will not give in to kitsch but can most conveniently transit towards *iki*. However, the disillusionment and the "breaking of the dreams" should not be too extreme either: "Yet when negation shows ascendancy afresh, and approaches the extreme, *iki* changes into the astringent" (p. 73). A typical source of astringency is "some past wrong, for instance spurned love. Not satisfied with an active engagement of the other . . ., the *iki* relationship takes from the astringent its orientation towards the past" (p. 152).

There must be a "past wrong" or "spurned love." Wendy Leigh devotes several pages in her biography to Bowie's traumatizing childhood experience of being left-handed, which made him the subject of ridicule and violent submission. Leigh concludes that this was "the battle that left him scarred." Bowie narrates the story in his own words as follows: "It put me outside others immediately. I didn't feel the same as the others because of that. . . . So I think it might have been one of those tips of how I was going to evaluate my journey through life: All right, I'm not the same as you motherfuckers, so I'll be better than you" (*Bowie: The Biography*, p. 9). Read this together with his account of the "repressive," "snobbish," and "nutty" input he ascribes to his mother's influence in his youth, and you have a perfect source of astringency.

There's more to say about Bowie and *iki*. *Iki* is a sort of stylish coolness but it does not appear in the form of an essence that can be imitated or obtained by following rules. According to Kuki *iki* remains a "possibility" that should not and will not turn into an actuality. *Iki* is not something real but it remains virtual and can only be guessed: "a certain appeal in the posture, hand gestures, hairstyle . . . that constantly remind us of . . . the possibility that must be maintained as a possibility, rather than being destroyed through conversion into actuality" (p. 156). Again, this matches Bowie's approach of playful transgression. Bowie overcame his initial awkwardness not by imitating the toughness of street culture, but attempted to control his movements using the advice of a Japanese-minded mime artist, finally finding something like a fleeting *iki* expression.

The Uncool Jihadis

In this chapter we've traversed the London of the Sixties and ended up in Japan. Still, I have to come back to the other dead people who fill the news of our time, who are the jihadi-cool people going to Syria to fight for the Islamic State. What is their relationship with the above concept of coolness? They obviously believe they are cool while drifting on their tanks, entirely clad in black, with their long hair flowing in the wind. However, they are not cool at all because they are merely longing for the sweetness of death, for unmitigated heroism, and for "actual" eternity. And this is the worst kitsch ever: it is simplistic, exaggerated, and self-gratificatory. What is lacking is the astringent element as well as the idea of playful transgression that remains potential and virtual by definition. Bowie taught us that you don't have to be stupid to be cool. Obviously, those people did not have the right teachers.

3
The Flux of It All

THEODORE G. AMMON

LGBTQ. This sequence of letters now almost enjoys the same widespread usage and familiarity as WTF and LOL. And that's a good thing—for it implies a healthy change of attitude toward people systematically discriminated against. And the US Supreme Court has even pitched in! Say Halleluiah!

As has frequently been the case, pop culture brought such issues to the public's eye before the public's eye opened. We're quickly reminded of the Fifties and Sixties when the times they were a-changin' in spite of the vicious backlash against minorities, gays, feminists, anti-war protestors and others, anyone with a mere joint of pot.

And certainly change was afoot when Robert David Jones Bowie penned "Changes" and publicly declared himself bisexual. What an affront to polite society, eh? No, he was merely ahead of his time, as they say, in the sense that rock icons-to-be did not usually adorn themselves in dresses and makeup and blur images of their gender and species as a spectacle for those of us who paid attention. As George Reisch observes, young David Jones always wanted to write musicals; is it any surprise that his rock performances became partly theater, whose plays and protagonist morphed seemingly on a whim of the main actor?

The man in a dress who sold the world becomes a rock god from Mars—or is it the other way 'round?—who becomes "a lad insane" and a sort of Motown wannabe, a neo-German something-or-other, a member of a hard rock band with leather and everything, the purveyor of "reality," and ultimately, as if all before had been a frantic coke-fueled day in the life of your basic icon, the cautious reflective persona of *The Next Day.* What to expect next? *Not* death, surely. What to make of it all?

Change, and the apparent necessity, and at least the endless capacity for it, subtends the entire process that was David Bowie, this I believe. A 3-CD *The Very Best of Bowie* was released in 2014 with the title *Nothing Has Changed*, and inside the foldout is written "Everything has Changed." These claims are not contradictory—they are logical contraries: both can't be true but both can be false. If both are false then it follows that something has changed and something has not. But the immediate question is: What is change?

Impossible Change

From the early Greek philosopher Parmenides, we hear that change is movement from where or what something *is* to where or what it *is-not*. The problem for Parmenides was the status of this "is-not." How can something change to what or where it "is-not"? In order to do so, reasoned Parmenides, there must be a state of "is-not" into which it changes, but the very idea of such a state is contradictory and hence impossible in fact. In short there is no such thing as nothing, no place where there is not *being* of some sort, no void, no absolute emptiness, no "is-not." Hence, reasoned Parmenides, there is no such process as change.

His studious pupil Zeno provided mathematical arguments to prove the point to the unbelievers. Remember that you can't cross the room until you cross half the distance first, but you can't cross that distance until you cross one-fourth, and so on to infinity; however, crossing an infinity of lengths is impossible, and so there is no crossing the room.

The problem with Parmenides's view is that ordinary sense experience belies it. You can jolly well rise from your chair and cross the room, or so it appears, and you can see obvious differences among the various incarnations of Bowie. But the lesson to be learned from Parmenides for our purposes is not that Bowie fails to change visually but whether he remains the same fundamentally, underneath the visual changes. Descartes later asks a similar question while watching a piece of wax melt on his hearth. All of the wax's sense-properties change, and so what makes Descartes believe that same wax endures all of those changes? The trans-species Bowie of *Diamond Dogs* is the same Bowie as the suave husky-voiced crooner of "Young Americans" is the same leather beclad pseudo-thug rock'n'roller of Tin Machine? Does it beggar the imagination to believe that David Jones Bowie was a single ordinary bloke who changed images but not self?

How would we know? This question begs the answers to several other questions: 1. that we had access, and knew that we did, to the inner workings of Bowie's identity; 2. that the Bowie-identity and Bowie-self were the same being; 3. that both self and identity can either run indefinitely or stay put indefinitely. The question presumes that changing makeup, hair, britches, dresses, shoes and blouses are *merely* visual changes; whereas we want to know about the Parmenidean-static-*being* Bowie.

If we tripped over Bowie's identity-self would we know that we had? A cautious argument indeed may prove that self = appearance. The better argument might reveal that change of appearance = *evidence* of change of self. Even so, we still need to know when a change affects the underlying self.

The tradition of personal identity and selfhood cuts in two directions: that of the permanent soul-substance on the one hand, and on the other, the flux of experience + continuity of memory over time. The latter provides a more fruitful tree to pluck, for if the self just is an immortal soul-substance then there is really little more to say here. We could merely ask why the soul manifests itself in myriad forms, and with no sensible answers forthcoming then we may as well adopt a version of an empiricist view—a view based on what we can see and touch. And one such view would be that there is no static identity or self; there is only the flux of experience.

Unintended Meaning

Even so we need to beware of committing the "intentional fallacy"—swallowing the mistaken theory that creative artists are the final authority on what their works mean. If Bowie identifies with Ziggy in an interview, and actually distinguishes Bowie from Ziggy then we still have to decide whether to believe such apparent whimsy. Artists don't have the last word on their creations. Regardless of what artists claim about their works, if upon scrutiny the work fails to support the claim then that's that, and vice versa.

The most infamous example of the reverse scenario is Charles Manson's delusional interpretation of "Helter Skelter." Say what McCartney will about the complete absence of predictions of race riots and mayhem in the song, the fact of the matter is that a paranoid schizophrenic was meted out a life sentence in part for thinking so, and numerous other people believed him. And of course people are dead. When interpretations in these matters go horribly awry death usually proceeds as predictably as the same song played for the hundredth or thousandth time. Fortunately Bowie has been spared such insanity.

A more pleasant version of the ramifications of the "intentional fallacy" regards Robert Penn Warren who claimed that the noted critic Harold Bloom pointed to a recurring image of a hawk in Penn Warren's work, a claim Penn Warren denied. Warren denied the assessment but re-read his work nonetheless, thereby finding the recurring image of a hawk that Bloom previously had noted. Warren's response? To write a poem about a hawk.

Bowie's remarks may illuminate his work, but he has systematically given us enigmas, and we remain always in the position that David Hume, the famed Scottish empiricist, warned us against. Anyone can tell us anything, even if it is true, yet we still have to decide whether we believe it. For

Hume, what matter ancient accounts of miracles if there is absolutely no evidence that they happen today? Okay, Bowie's interviews trumpet no miracles, and hence might be dismissed out of hand in a David Humean snit. Nevertheless, at the very least caution is in order when a tremendous rock star proclaims genocide from the stage and reports that rock stars are basically *fascists*. Huh?

Hooray for Bowie for revealing the evil secret of the rock world? I really do not believe so, nor should you—perhaps. Skepticism in these matters is prudent, but curiosity prevails: what on Earth did he mean?

But the philosopher wants to know what meaning is; what does it mean to mean? This matter we can put to rest for our purposes: meaning is use. Once I discover how words and phrases are used in the language then I know their meanings. Meaning is linguistic use. So to return to 'fascist'—what did Bowie mean when he used that term to describe rock stars? Ahh, answering that question here would be far too facile, and furthermore I don't want to commit the intentional fallacy. I have no clue what Bowie meant in terms of the psychic contents of his mind, even though I know how the term is used in the language. The issue requires extended analysis. Keep reading, in short.

The Procession of Selves

Were each new appearance of Bowie to herald a new self—a new Bowie-identity—then Bowie, and perhaps the rest of us, would transmogrify our way through life shedding selves with each new fantasy, or change of clothes. I exaggerate, and speak poorly. But critics *and* Bowie have attributed such-and-such behavior to Ziggy or to Aladdin Sane, as if Bowie is but a poor player upon a stage, merely the polite and cheery chap described by, say, Leigh in her biography. Merely an ordinary chap, until the peculiar clothes, outrageous coiffure, makeup, jewelry—and then a transformation ensues.

Yet, we must make room for the Meryl Streeps and Anthony Hopkinses of the world who adopt a persona so convincing that awards abound and nightmares and dreams vivify. Do Streep and Hopkins change their respective selves or is there such a thing as "merely acting"? Likewise shan't we allow for Ziggy Stardust without implicating the essence of Bowie's identity as Bowie? In short Bowie is Bowie and Ziggy is Ziggy. Too simple? Surely, but the question is to what extent Bowie adorned Ziggy and remained Ziggy, even backstage in the dressing-room after the concert. We discover in a later work that Major Tom is a junkie, and thus one can see Bowie rejecting the earlier personas as just that.

Bowie has stated that he is easily bored with the business of change, *his* business mind you, and so really Bowie is the junkie, a *change* junkie. The dismissal of Major Tom I interpret as an ill-fated attempt by Bowie to dismiss former versions of himself, an attempt undermined by the alleged massive amount of cocaine he consumed and sleepless workaholic days and nights he endured without a psychotic break or heart attack. The rock god survived and returned in *Reality* and *The Next Day* to prophesy again. In truth his lyrics are filled with apocalyptic visions and imagery. Even his first album which ought to be, we assume, somewhat naive and jolly, is filled with wars, pedophiles, overpopulation, and infanticide. So Ziggy extrapolates and expands themes with which Bowie begins from the getgo. Ziggy may name a cluster of early ideas from which Bowie draws, but Ziggy Stardust the character never exits stage right, and thus masks the pernicious reality he has become, lodged securely in the identity of Bowie. You don't cast off a persona any more than you do a first love.

The Constant Self

It doesn't follow that there is an underlying self—besides, even if there were such a "thing" it would be in a constant state of flux. Of course we remember special people and events, but the accumulation of memories is not absolute. We forget far more than we remember and we need to do so. Without the simultaneous processes of acquiring new memories and forgetting details of current and older ones we would be incapable of generalizing. To generalize just is to forget differences among ordinary objects and to focus upon the broad sweep of being. Such forgetting can be accomplished without positing a Platonic essence. The notions of essence, soul, permanent identity—those that imply a fixity—are simply unhelpful.

Can't we forget the differences among our various selves and generalize to a constant self? For the purposes of law and establishing legal guilt perhaps we pretend to do so, even if such attribution is philosophically indefensible. Regardless of what we claim about ourselves as secure thinking things, at any given moment if we introspect we stumble, says Hume, upon this or that particular perception. Even if we lead a roaring life and then settle down in our golden years all of those previous experiences that we can remember constitute the golden years self. We are always an amalgam, or as Heraclitus puts it: a river we can't step into twice.

Philosophy walks a thin line in the consideration of self and identity. On the one hand there is the legal and moral need to hold someone accountable over time. For example, Charles Manson will die in prison. And on the other hand there flows the river of ever-changing selves. Through it all Bowie presents an interesting study, for once again, how many Bowies are littered by the wayside of his work—critics have noted four, five, maybe six—depends upon who or which one counts. Yes Bowie ditched the elaborate theatrics, but then who is the Bowie of the German Years? Of *Low, "Heroes,"* and *Lodger*, and the Bowie who fairly recently seemed to nullify the entirety of *"Heroes"* with *The Next Day* album? Did he finally arrive, again, by circuitous and Bacchanalian excess, to the dutiful husband, father, and pleasant chap?

We encounter no problems pigeonholing a Bowie who wears makeup and simulates fellatio with his guitarist, for these matters are the stuff of mere appearances. I have not considered yet the change of musical styles, and the albums considered artistic flops. If there are such flops, are they comparable to hitting the wrong typewriter key? The *Never Let Me Down* and the *Tin Machine* eras (errors)? If I hit a wrong typewriter key I doubt anyone would proclaim a new me has emerged. I would have to write sentences and paragraphs and chapters misbegotten as well. And then an interview to explain myself, should anyone care, would be arranged immediately.

Bowie didn't merely hit a wrong key, he changed with the *Tin Machine* albums. He became a member of a group, relinquishing considerable control over the musical product, and as a result experienced his music from an entirely new perspective. A new Bowie flowed with and through these albums, critics be damned. Do I subtly imply that Bowie was generally dispassionate and aloof from his own creations? Not at all, but I say his work came from the head, not the heart. Some would blame, or applaud, Brian Eno for the Berlin trilogy, for example.

Which David Bowie?

Even the forlorn apathy of failing to distinguish bullshit from lies (*The Buddha of Suburbia*) appeals to the head over the heart. Followed by "Sex and the Church," a song weary of social mores, is equally weary of composing songs that speak to the times. I would say that Bowie could not care less about whatever conflict existed at the time between sex and the church. Which church? There is no "the" church. No matter, Bowie was not on the front lines in the street, as it were, of sexual liberation, in spite of influences in those directions. "Sex and the Church" is followed by a seven minute jazz-rock fusion piece that dispenses with lyrics altogether. Just as well. The piece for all of its attempts at random complexity is nonetheless formulaic. The bass line pleases well enough, but the rest of the instrumentation is weary. 'Weary' is the word that comes to mind. On to seven minutes of Brian Eno and Kraftwerk-inspired sonic drivel.

In truth the album is more than tolerable, but who is responsible for it—which Bowie? As an early album it is inconceivable, but even post–*Low*, *"Heroes,"* and *Lodger* the album makes little sense. More jazz-rock fusion that repeats 'shine' over and over interspersed with the sort of rap we might expect of a white English man. Isn't it all clever, this melding of influences? Well yes and no. No, because the album at first blush is listenable, almost singalong-able, but nevertheless deeply cynical upon closer inspection. But yes, because several of his best lines are penned—"can't tell the bullshit from the lies" and "strangers when we meet." Here is a mixture of semi-pop and rock jazz fusion. Pleasant, even catchy at times, but, as stated, deeply cynical upon repeated listenings. And by all means don't forget the reference to Buddha.

So this David Bowie we come to know and love may be a pleasant chap by all accounts but one with a deeply cynical streak that manifests throughout his work.

And therefore, I may be wrong. Not about his being lovable, but about his essential nature. I make a case that our Bowie is many Bowies and that his essential nature is flux: ch-ch-ch-changes. But maybe he doesn't change fundamentally from his first album to *Blackstar*. And if not then, now we have come full circle. How would we know, beyond merely presupposing the fact? And that won't do at all.

We need to look at recurring themes in his works. Dancing emerges as one such prominent theme; the dualism of mind and body, with body the dominant of the two; predictions of doom; apocalyptic visions of dystopias; the untrustworthiness of authority—all of which are intellectually engaging, except perhaps dancing. "Don't Look Down" from *Tonight* seems to advocate an intentional distance between New York and shantytown. Or is the song ironic? The latter interpretation might be preferable if it were the case that Bowie was consistently mindful of social problems in his music; but he's not. You have to dig for scathing social commentary, even in the area of gender issues, which we should expect to be in the forefront of his concerns.

The Continual Undercurrent

Easily the best song on *Earthling* is the blatantly political "I'm Afraid of Americans"—but here Bowie retreats even further from the front line. He's afraid of Americans *and* the world, but can't help it. That's it: a wimpy statement of how he *feels*. There is no call to arms or recognition of the cause of this fear. The song thus collapses in on itself as narcissistic. I, David Bowie, am personally afraid of Americans and the world.

Others were afraid of America as well, notably the fine English playwright Harold Pinter (Nobel Prize for literature, 2005), who publicly stated that the USA is the most hated and dangerous country in history. For Pinter, the problem remains worldwide, and includes a complicit Great Britain. For Pinter something must be done, about the wars, the torture, all of it; for Bowie the issue is a meek personal one, though embedded in an otherwise compelling song.

We need not sift through song after song to tease out those with similar themes. It suffices to concede that the undercurrents are there. This composite of themes remains however a continuous under*current*. Then am I not at least partially reneging on my own thesis, that there is no static Bowie? After all, if there are recurring themes in his work then we should be able to argue on those grounds alone that there really is a fixed Bowie-self. I disagree. Themes in poetry, fiction and lyrics result from the adoption of a persona for the purposes of composing. The persona may bespeak its own consistency up to a point, but once the novel or poem or lyrics are complete then the persona dissipates, leaving the flux of experience and memory in consciousness. What would it mean to say that Bowie is fundamentally and irrevocably a dancer, when all is said and done? Or a purveyor of apocalypses? The idea is incoherent. There is no such enduring self as the apocalyptic dancer.

A version of a question I have avoided is this: Whom do I *want* Bowie to be? Another cliché is that we see what we want to see in people, especially those larger than life. Photos of the Beatles were fairly dependable, Springsteen even more so. But I am avoiding the matter again, for it isn't a matter of how he *looked* at a particular point in his career that addresses my question. I want Bowie to be the shapeshifter, as he has been called; I want him to be the flux of my possible experience; I want him to be just out reach; or the river into which I cannot step twice. I would be fabulously disappointed were my analysis to turn back upon itself and thereby reveal an essential Bowie, a fixed being with an unwavering aesthetic vision of what his music should be and convey, a constant and dependable friend. What if that were the case? After a circuitous route we discover that Bowie is at heart "a damn fine friend" and that's it. Would we accept that answer? I think not. Better a cantankerous aesthete, chronically dissatisfied and self-absorbed. But he isn't that either.

Better still: simply the flux of it all, from Robert David to Ziggy to a Blackstar.

4
Warm Impermanence

RANDALL E. AUXIER

The embarrassing truth is that, back at the beginning, David Bowie wasn't into stuff we'd call cool nowadays. He had an odd affection for Anthony Newley and the sort of pop sound that dominated the late Fifties and early Sixties, and then he also had a dangerous flirtation with the Great Folk Scare. If you haven't ever checked to see where it all started, listen to "The Laughing Gnome" (1967)—it's unmistakably Bowie, but a strange ride.

For those of you who don't recognize the phrase "Great Folk Scare," it was the time when folk music almost became the dominant popular music in the US, but then we managed to avoid that (for the most part) thanks to doo-wop and the British Invasion, and also due to Bob Dylan's eventual boredom with acoustic guitars and banjos (praised and copied by Bowie in the Helm-like drums and Robertson-like guitar and Manuel-like piano in the song he wrote for Dylan). It was a close call for Bowie, and for us all.

But Bowie, well, he sort of liked that campy, silly stuff. He even became (gasp) a folk singer and songwriter, of the Donovan stripe. He also wanted to be like Dylan. (And don't we all?) But by the time Bowie penned that tribute to the Troubadour of Highway 61, the Scare had abated and the effect was very post-Newport. In fact Bowie never sounded or wrote much like Dylan apart from the one song. The point is: either way, it was really quite a stretch from folk pop to Ziggy Stardust and glam. It happened gradually, move by move.

How do you do that? And why? Part of it has to do with Bowie's peculiarities, of course, stuff no one else would have seen or done. But the journey has more to do with the Art World than you might think at first, and especially with Andy Warhol. That's what I want to talk about—the changes that led from David Jones, folksinger, to David Bowie, dominant among the creators of glam rock—and maybe to David Bowie, artist. We shall see.

The Philosophy of Art

In the second half of the twentieth century, Arthur Danto (1926–2013) was the most important philosopher of art in the world. There's a big difference between the "philosophy of art" and "art criticism," and neither one is the same thing as "aesthetics." Danto wrote in all three areas.

In art criticism he was among the foremost, and this is the activity of reviewing, comparing, adjudging, documenting, and organizing critical ideas about art. The audience is generally the interested public, but it includes artists and gallery owners and museum curators and anyone else who wants to consume or promote art. Good art criticism imparts information, judgments, and experiences of art to those who want to *read* about experiences of art. If the criticism is well written, the reader may have an aesthetic experience of the art of writing, but that isn't the primary aim of art criticism, according to most people. (I think art criticism should be art, but that leaves me in a small company.)

Aesthetics is the study of feeling and sensation and their relation both to the world and to perception, and even to knowledge. Art is often the featured subject matter of aesthetics because it is thought (and rightly so) that in the *experience* of art we find exemplary cases of how sensation becomes highly organized feeling, and then such feeling becomes not just perception but *heightened* perception. Art perks us up, makes us notice our senses and perceptive powers, goads us to refine them. (It's good to remember that perception involves the combining of *all* our senses into one experience of the world, including how it smells, looks, sounds, tastes and its tactile and kinesthetic character.)

Perceptions are created by our bodies, as a *synesthesia* of many physiological processes—and perception occurs just a bit later than the sensations that are received and processed by our bodies. What you are perceiving happened less than a quarter of a second ago, or so, but it's over before you perceive it. That's why humans cannot hit a baseball by perceiving it. They only see the ball leave the pitcher's hand and the spin and anticipate where it will be as it gets to them. There isn't time to perceive and then swing. It's the same with releasing a bowling ball or squeezing a trigger in target shooting. Aesthetics, as a discipline, is as much concerned with that sort of experience as with art.

Our senses are heightened in the presence of visual art, and of beauty (whether in nature or artifact), and of other sorts of highly organized stimulation, such as we find in music and painting and sculpture, prepared for the kinds of senses and feelings *we* have. We do not create art for non-humans. A symphony written entirely in tones below 16 Hz. would not be for humans, since we couldn't hear it—elephants, however, might enjoy such music quite a lot. The study of aesthetics could well include such a symphony, since it is not limited to merely human perception and sensation and feeling. And aesthetics does not have to study art at all. It just usually does.

Art, however, belongs to the human world exclusively, Danto believed. Even Bowie would not bother with a subsonic song for the elephants, all tones vibrating below 20 Hz. Of course, *someone* actually might have *tried* something like that (John Cage or Philip Glass), had anyone thought of it, but it would have been more for us to enjoy *the idea*, as a piece of art, than for elephants to enjoy the actual music. Philip Glass did take Bowie's compositions entitled "Low" and "Heroes" as the bases for his own Symphonies #1 and #4 respectively, but was this not Glass making art of what had been, perhaps, better described as "commodity" or, more sympathetically, as "song"? Was this not analogous to James Harvey and Andy Warhol—one designed the Brillo box, but the other created *Brillo Box*, the sculpture? One was known only as a commercial artist; the other was the greatest artist of the second half of the twentieth century.

And so we might note that "Subsonic Symphony (for Elephants)" is really not Bowie's domain. You can't sell such a thing, or its sequel, "Supersonic Symphony for Dogs," written entirely above 20 kHz. If Glass writes this stuff now, I should be credited—and given a Warhol *Brillo Box* as compensation. Even if I only had the *idea*.

Ideas can be art, Danto thought, so long as there is at least some *embodiment* of the idea, and assuming that there was some *meaning* thus embodied. Since my writing has embodiment (and that is how you can read it), it could be art, even if it probably isn't. On the other hand, if I only *imagined* this chapter, it couldn't be art. Embodied meaning is what art requires, Danto argued. It may require *more* than that, of course, but not less. Not everyone agrees with Danto, but I think he's right. And this definition of art belongs neither to aesthetics nor to art criticism, but to the *philosophy of art*.

The philosophy of art, apart from asking and answering the question "What is and is not art?" also pursues various other mysteries, such as why do humans create art? Does art exist in every culture? Is art essential to our humanness? Is there a universal art recognizable to all (such as music)? Is beauty indispensable to art? Is there sublime art? What is the "artwork" itself? Does the artwork involve the process of its creation or is it only the product? Does the artist's intention determine the meaning of a work of art?

There are hundreds of other questions and shades of questions connected to the philosophy of art, and this is what Arthur Danto did best. Danto had been an artist himself (his specialty was wood block prints, very nice ones) and also eventually he became a critic. But initially he was just a philosophy professor who happened to have a degree in art history as well. It can be a potent combination, if you're at the right place and time and if you seize the moment.

The Art World

There is a sort of social universe of people who care about art, and their motives are varied. Some produce it, some buy and sell it, some collect and display it, some regulate, promote, censor, lobby for or against it, and some just write and think and talk about art all the live long day. When we take this cross-section of civilization that is concerned with art, we have what Danto calls "the Art World." This is a highly interactive and dynamic cultural conglomerate; its edges are ragged and vague. Art trails off into commerce or kitsch, or commodity, or mere entertainment, or politics, or mere pastime, or hobby, or even religion, at its numerous edges.

At the center of the Art World are places like New York and Paris where large numbers of art people are concentrated and whose doings and makings are enviously noted by others in lesser locations. Where art serves some form of culture apart from itself, it's not "the Art World." Casual Bowie fans who have an album or two and who can tolerate an elevator-music version of "Rebel, Rebel," with an oboe carrying the Ronson guitar line, are not part of the Art World. It takes a willingness to aestheticize your life in order to fit in. This movable feast of culture called the Art World is of huge concern to serious Bowie fans, whether they realize it or not, for it's the Art World, in Danto's sense of that term, that *gave* us Bowie. Take your protein pills and put your helmet on, and I will explain.

Looks a Scream

Danto had something in common with Bowie, since both were pretty close to being obsessed with Andy Warhol, but in Danto's case, it wasn't just because he was a fan—in fact, at first he really *wasn't* a fan. But Danto became convinced that Warhol's vision and work had changed the world, irreversibly. Danto made the astonishing claim that Warhol's exhibit at the Stable Gallery in New York City in 1964 marked the *end* of art history. It was over. From the cave paintings of Lascaux, some 17,000 years ago up until April 1964, art had a history, and then, poof, Warhol ended it. Or perhaps it would be more honest to say that Danto ended it in Warhol's name.

Here's what happened. Danto went to the Warhol exhibit and saw the *Brillo Box* sculptures Warhol had made—and *make* them is what he *did*. Yes, they looked like ordinary Brillo boxes we could buy at the supermarket, but they were not. It was not like Marcel Duchamp placing a urinal in the art exhibit and calling it "Fountain." This was Warhol painstakingly constructing plywood boxes and creating the silkscreens to paint them, and then touching them up by hand after they were silkscreened, and installing them in a pyramid in the Stable Gallery as a sculpture.

We all know, by this late date, that Warhol was the progenitor of "pop art" and that a part of his aim was to hand us back in the form of art (with whatever glib critique it may imply) the images, colors, forms and figures that fill our overfilled lives and whose "art" we would not notice were it not for the activity of the artist in framing, repeating, installing, presenting, and otherwise calling attention to what we would normally ignore. Everyone also knows that he said "in the future everyone will be famous for fifteen minutes." This was not so much prophecy as simple observation carried to what it clearly portends. Time has tended to bear out the expectation in spirit if not in exact quantity.

In the process of ending art history—which he didn't know he was doing—Warhol achieved something that was to replace art: celebrity. The art he made was, after all, desirable, but that fact was mixed, inextricably, with the fact that it bore *his* name. Indeed. It was good, whatever *that* means. I sure wish I had one of those *Brillo Box*es in *my* collection. I'd give my entire Bowie LP collection for one. Or for anything Warhol touched. Or anything he mass produced himself. Or anything he endorsed. I think I'm in good company here. *You* want a Warhol. You know you do. Don't pretend you don't. But the unintended consequence of this celebrity, on these terms, is that Warhol realized that his celebrity *was* the essence of his art, and he theorized it thus. If Andy wrote a book, the book was art because of Andy. If he made a movie, the movie was art because of Andy. If he took a walk, the walk was art because of Andy.

Andy even made art out of philosophy, with his book *The Philosophy of Andy Warhol (From A to B and Back Again)*. The book contains no philosophy to speak of; it is an autobiographical something or other—what? Mémoire? Not exactly. Aphoristic ejaculations? Well, there are many of those, and many blurted out opinions, but precious little philosophy—except that in calling it philosophy, Warhol exercises his considerable celebrity upon the meaning of that word.

And if Andy Warhol looked a scream, the look was art, as was the scream, because of Andy. I have read in several places that Warhol hated that line in Bowie's song because Warhol was self-conscious about his appearance. I have no idea what to believe in the piles of tripe written about either Warhol or Bowie, but every time I read that Warhol hated the song on account of that line, I smile. I *have* to. It's perfectly ridiculous to imagine that Andy Warhol cared how he looked *in that way*, that is, the normal vanity of normal people, leading to normal self-consciousness. Even if he said what was reported, it doesn't mean he actually felt that way. But maybe Andy did care about that.

Something prevented him from becoming Bowie's mentor. Maybe Bowie's song for Andy was too much too soon and contained an unforgivable faux pas. Great though Bowie became, he never approached Warhol's importance to the Art World (and I'll come back to this point). It may be a good thing that Bowie and Warhol were not close friends. It might have ruined them both, or at least Bowie. I doubt anything could have changed Andy apart from Andy.

Your Face Is a Mess

It was obvious to Bowie that Warhol, whether intentionally or not, had created an art form that could be picked up and built upon: the art of celebrity. It could be sold as art without being cheapened thereby. The key was continuous reinvention of your persona *as* artist, endowing upon whatever you do the status of artwork, or if not that, in the highest sense of "art," then at least artsy-cool. But to maintain such celebrity beyond fifteen minutes, the choices have to be just right—they have to be like Warhol's choices. There must be an artistic importance about the choices that drags the public up to and into what they wanted but didn't yet *know* they wanted. Part of the secret to making the public *desire* the work (or at least the new album) is that it carries the mystique of the artist's persona. But that alone would never be enough to bring the public along. The art also has to be, well, *good*.

Music never was Bowie's only artistic form of endeavor, but it was always his bread and butter. The stylings he took on, one after another were also art. He certainly never could have known that his different-sized pupils (the result of a fist fight with a friend over a girl) would be so important to him, but that was how we recognized the man through the ch-ch-ch-changes. "Is that Bowie?" Well, check the eyes. They're weird, you know? In a cool way. Still, the effort was more conscious and more Warhol-influenced than many folks realize.

After seeing a London production of Warhol's play *Pork* in 1971, Bowie hired the principal cast members, including Cherry Vanilla, Wayne (now Jayne) County, Anthony Zanetta, and Leee Black Childers—all from Warhol's Factory—to create an image for him. The result was Ziggy Stardust, and in succeeding related personas—Aladdin Sane, the Diamond Dogs persona, the Man Who Fell to Earth, the Thin White Duke, and, moving from one creative crew to another, it went on to Lazarus, his final persona. If Bowie and Warhol had become closer friends, it's possible to conjecture that

Bowie might not have been quite so independent. Warhol cast a huge shadow.

The End of Art

What Danto believed and wrote after visiting the Warhol exhibit in 1964 is that after *Brillo Box*, *anything* could be art, in principle at least. What Warhol had done was to inform us that the difference between art and non-art resides in what the Art World does *now*, in the present and for the future, *not* in what art history tells us. Art is no longer determined by a tradition or schools of painting or dance or architecture. Rather, it is the theories that are proffered and which dominate the Art World that provide us with Art. Since we will no longer be able to trace the history of movements in art by studying the characteristics of the art works, we shall have no further art history. What we have after April 1964 is an imperative to learn the theories uppermost in the Art World and then we can know what is and is not art.

Danto also expressed the opinion that art was only the first cultural form to come to the "end" of its history. He expected others, philosophy in particular, to come to a point where, for example, the Philosophy World determines what is and isn't philosophy, but Danto believed we were some ways short of that point. Art, however, has reached an end.

But the "end" is a sort of spiritualization, almost, of the forms that a cultural activity may take. It means that we're liberated from the strictures of the various stages we endured along the way, in which art must first be, say, classical and then romantic, and then realist and then impressionist and then cubist or pointillist or Dadaist, and so on, *rejecting* whatever it *had been* in order to become what it *will be* next. It is this historical dialectic Danto pronounced to be "at an end" in 1964. All of those stages are now available for the making of art, without the expectation that there must be a "next" in the way there was before 1964.

Art had, at the hand of Andy Warhol, rejoined the world of change and life and conversation and was now in the hands of those who make it, sell it, criticize it, exhibit it, buy it, even destroy it. We now see art's possibilities in Andy Warhol himself, Andy walking, Andy tired, Andy snoozing, and not being able to tell the silver screen from the artist. This is clearly not art history, whatever else it is. As audacious as Danto's pronouncement sounds, there is something to it, and it is something David Bowie understood, with or without any help from Danto (Bowie read a lot, and I'm betting he read Danto, but I don't know). In any case, the central insight of Bowie's song about Warhol reports an inability to distinguish Andy from his screen—this is as much his silkscreen as the surface upon which the films are projected, and any other surface you please.

Time May Change Me

It's not easy to distinguish the autobiography from the manufactured myth in Bowie's case, but the people who knew him insist there was no serious effort at misdirection on his part. He wasn't different from you or me—except that he got to have sex with whomever he pleased and, well, most of us don't—on that point, it's impossible to know what to believe, but if there wasn't just tons of sex, well, the storytellers sure say a lot of the same things. For one such see the biography by Wendy Leigh, called, appropriately enough, *Bowie: The Biography*.

The mystique and the masks are surely products of planning and intention, but not designed to keep us from learning who the man was. As he said at the end, in "Lazarus," his deathbed piece of performance art, "everybody knows me now." It's show biz, and that's about all it is. And it's all in good fun, even the part about dying at the end. Life's a warm impermanence, after all. Why waste energy trying to sell us a performer we aren't interested in—the *real* David Jones—when it's so much more fun, and more profitable, to imagine what *does* interest us, and sell us *that*?

It's easy to imagine it, but it isn't easy to do. Such a plan requires that the performer guess what would interest us when *we*, ourselves, don't know it yet. Do we want the man who sold the world? Well, we weren't sure. There came a moment of decision for Bowie, a moment when he decided to dive into an unknown water and try a hand at something that hadn't been done before—although we're familiar with it now. This is the celebrity whose persona shifts over and again to become a new artwork, and to enjoy another fifteen minutes of fame for going to the trouble to re-invent. Long before Hannah Montana morphed from Disney Sweetheart into the raunchiest pop singer in history, and long before Stefani Germanotta put on a dress made of raw meat, and even before Madonna became Marilyn Monroe, Bowie foresaw what it meant to trade in your person for a persona.

For some celebrities (Michael Jackson comes to mind), the psychological cost of reinventing yourself every five to seven years seems to be pretty high. It isn't easy for them to endure the isolation, whether self-imposed or a condition of their safety, and perhaps also the trials of "not being known" by anyone. Is it any wonder that Jackson could make common cause with Lisa Marie Presley? Jackson once complained that whether he told the truth or lied about himself made no difference, since people would believe what reporters said before they'd ever believe the man himself. For Bowie, however, it appears that his ego-strength (and I mean this in an entirely admiring and positive sense) was enough to keep him sufficiently grounded and creative and imagining and, if such a speculation is allowed, happy and well-balanced after about 1980, to all appearances.

How can someone so strange be so grounded? Well, Bowie wasn't strange. But he had strange fascinations. Tony Zanetti said that it was just about being adored, for Bowie. He was willing to be thought strange in exchange for that, and to keep changing if he could only guess what *we* wanted next. Was it Ziggy? Apparently it was. We didn't know it until we saw and heard it, but we definitely knew it then.

I Can't Trace Time

The song "Changes" documents Bowie's decision to adopt the life of shifting personas, while "Queen Bitch" and "Andy Warhol" from the same album explain where the momentum would come from, musical and artistic. The first verse of "Changes" (and indeed of *Hunky Dory*) is a soliloquy, Hamlet-esque, filled with gnawing questions portending ominous answers—like fleas the size of rats feeding on rats the size of cats. What was I waiting for? What of all those dead end streets? How was I losing so much time? And what kind of success would taste sweet enough? And, by the way, what now—now that I'm so acutely aware the others don't see the faker, but neither can I?

"We" can't dwell on these things, we can't take that test, Bowie advises himselves. We sweep all of it away in our changes, if we can face the strain. That includes the people who are no longer useful or inspiring to us—the band, the entourage, the business people, all quite dispensable. "We" have to become comfortable with the idea that we never really see ourselves as others do, and yet others won't know when we're faking. I can't trace time, but then again, neither can you. There's a space that we can fill with our imaginations, if we so choose. And we resolve to do it.

What brings Bowie to this pass? His first two albums (I'm thinking of *David Bowie* and of *Space Oddity* as the same album) had songs that occasionally betrayed moments of self-doubt, of self-reflection in the sense of self-undermining. These hesitancies had to be conquered. Somewhere between *The Man Who Sold the World* and *Hunky Dory*, Bowie became what Andy Warhol could not become—Bowie read the augurs and became whatever *we* wanted him to be. He painted, acted, wrote, strummed, pranced, sang, and transmogrified. Look out, rock'n'rollers, the folksinger has become self-aware. Indeed, he's out of this world. He'd like to come and see us but he thinks he'd blow our minds. When we had enjoyed and applauded Ziggy, Bowie retired him and became whatever we needed next.

But was it art? Performance art would be the easiest category to cover all the activities. By Danto's criteria, it certainly was embodied meaning. The Art World was a bit less enthusiastic about calling Bowie's creations art, however, and in Danto's world, they hold sway. Philip Glass was enthusiastic enough, and many artists bought their Bowie albums and listened, but in a way, that is exactly what you don't do with art.

An interesting fact is this: the popular world, filled with people like you and me, and with rock critics and the full weight of the recording industry, and people who shop at Wal-Mart, and people who definitely do not shop there, we all want the Art World to say of Bowie: "this was art, and this was an artist." They don't, however, treat Bowie as a performance artist, or indeed as an artist of any kind. Warhol is one of their darlings while Bowie is, well, a folksinger on cocaine and a magnificent showman, or something. He surpasses Elton John, sure, but not in a way that would turn anyone's head.

You Can't Trace Time

How, then, can we, the public, resist the urge to strangle the Art World? We want to say that Bowie was *better* than Warhol, don't we? But it also isn't true, is it? Bowie has endowed the world with priceless memorabilia. Warhol has given the world the art it will pay more for and hold to its breast more closely than anything Bowie ever did. I know you love Bowie. You're reading this book. But if I gave you a choice between, say, an original multi-track tape, a one-of-a-kind out-take from the *Diamond Dogs* sessions, or a *Brillo Box*, which would you take? Or if you don't like my example, choose whatever you would like from Bowie's *oeuvre*.

Here's the thing. That *Brillo Box* changed the world. The Bowie piece, whatever it may be, only showed the world how it had *already been changed*. After the *Brillo Box*, well, the days flow through my eyes, but still they seem the same. Give me the *Box* and accept my apologies David. And I'll put on some music, your music, and admire my *Box*. Which music will I choose for my admiring? Well, dear reader, what would you recommend? Have you heard *Blackstar* yet? It's awesome. It's about being dead. I never realized I was interested in that until recently, but then, I can't trace time.

II

Soundings of Bowie

5
Squawking Like a Pink Monkey Bird—What?

GREG LITTMANN

David Bowie is an alligator. He's a mother *and* a father, and he's coming for you. He's a space invader and he'll be a rocking rolling bitch for you. What the hell?

Bowie has written many of history's greatest and weirdest songs. I love "Moonage Daydream" (*Ziggy Stardust and the Spiders from Mars*, 1972), paraphrased above, but I don't understand it. I get that Bowie is wooing his "bay-beh" in space, but that's about all I'm sure of. For example, he orders, "Keep your mouth shut. You're squawking like a pink monkey bird." But I don't know what a pink monkey bird is or what it sounds like. I'm even more lost interpreting "Bewlay Brothers" (*Hunky Dory*, 1971), "Watch That Man" (*Aladdin Sane*, 1973), and so many more of Bowie's compositions that rank among my favorite pieces of music. From *The Man Who Sold the World* (1970) to *Scary Monsters (and Super Creeps)* (1980), Bowie barely composes a comprehensible lyric, while crafting a string of albums that I want to classify as great works of musical art. But how can we even begin to evaluate Bowie's songs as art if we don't know what they *mean*? How can we possibly appreciate words we don't understand?

The Making of an Incomprehensible Rock Star

David Bowie's more surreal lyrics can be classified as a form of "nonsense literature." Nonsense is characterized by the use of dream-logic and idea association, and by the use of meaningless, uninterpretable, or apparently random lyrics. Traditional folk songs frequently employ nonsense. For instance, "Hey Diddle Diddle" opens with gibberish ("Hey Diddle Diddle") followed by a sentence fragment ("The cat and the fiddle"), followed by a tale of a cow jumping over the moon and cutlery eloping. In England, nonsense literature underwent a revival in the nineteenth century, producing writers like Edward Lear, popularizer of the limerick, and Lewis Carroll, best known for the novel *Alice's Adventures in Wonderland* (1864). Nonsense remained a part of English culture in the twentieth century and comic nonsense songs were popular in Bowie's childhood. For instance, the comedy team *The Goons* had hit singles with the meaningless "Ying Tong Song" (1956) and the bizarre "I'm Walking Backwards for Christmas" (1957).

However, the roots of Bowie's "nonsense" extend far beyond the nonsense tradition itself. For a start, he draws on rock-'n'roll tradition, which has always permitted an amount of meaninglessness or obscurity in lyrics. Little Richard, Bowie's childhood idol, rocketed to fame with a cry of "A-wop-bom-a-loo-mop-a-lomp-bom-bom!" ("Tutti Frutti", 1955). Other musicians would mask sexual innuendo by disguising it as gibberish, as in Chuck Berry's "Roll over Beethoven" (1956): "Go get your lover, then reel and rock it / Roll it over and move on up just / A trifle further and reel and rock it, Roll it over" ("Roll over Beethoven", 1956). Elvis Presley even took Jerry Leiber and Mike Stoller's surreal prison fantasy "Jailhouse Rock" (1957) to number one in the US and UK alike.

Distinctively, Bowie also draws on poetic and theatrical tradition. In the 1950s, Bowie's beloved American Beat poets, like Allen Ginsberg and Jack Kerouac, couched their rejection of conventional society in dense, cryptic verse. In a foretaste of Bowie's tales of weird social outsiders, Ginsberg wrote in "Howl" (1956) of the "angel-headed hipsters burning for the ancient heavenly connection to the starry dynamo in the machinery of night."

In the 1960s, Bowie was heavily involved in avant-garde theater, studying under Lindsay Kemp and eventually forming his own troupe. Lyrically, he was influenced by expressionist theater, which prioritized conveying feelings over making sense, and by expressionism's offshoot, absurdist theatre, which deliberately avoided making sense to emphasize the senselessness in life. For instance, the Irish absurdist playwright Samuel Beckett felt free to introduce characters who live in trash cans (*Endgame,* 1957) or who are slowly being buried in sand (*Happy Days*, 1961), for no reason other than that these conditions reflect the characters' inner lives.

The Sixties output of Bob Dylan was enormously influential on Bowie, so much so that Dylan remains the only composer about which Bowie has written a musical fan-letter, the bitter "Song for Bob Dylan" (*Hunky Dory*). It was Dylan who first proved that an album could be both cryptic and commercial. He dived into folk surrealism in 1963 with *The Freewheelin' Bob Dylan* and reached peak weirdness in 1965 with the folk-rock albums *Bringing It All Back Home* and *Highway 61 Revisited*. His songs of this period are wrapped so deeply in symbolism that they are impenetrable without outside information. When a blind commissioner in a trance with one hand tied to a tightrope walker and the other in his pants wanders down "Desolation Row" (*Highway 61 Revisited*), the listener can only guess at what it all means.

Dylan is difficult to understand, but like the Beat poets who inspired him, his lyrics always mean something specific, at least to him. Even this level of sense was discarded when the flowering of psychedelia in the late 1960s produced a renaissance of lyrical nonsense. In place of tightly crafted riddles like Dylan's, there were kaleidoscopic visions and torrents of idea association. In England, The Beatles wandered among plasticine porters with looking-glass ties in "Lucy in the Sky with Diamonds" (*Sgt. Pepper's Lonely Heart's Club Band,* 1967) and Pink Floyd tripped out on sounds of lime and limpet green as they floated underground in space in "Astronomy Dominae" (*The Piper at the Gates of Dawn,* 1967), while The Yardbirds and Cream had their own weird adventures. Meanwhile, in the US, Jimi Hendrix kissed the sky while in a "Purple Haze" (1967); Jefferson Airplane dived down a hole while feeding their heads in pursuit of a "White Rabbit" (1967); and The Byrds, The Doors, and The Grateful Dead each bloomed with idiosyncratic strangeness. Bowie's "Memory of a Free Festival" (*David Bowie*, 1969) exemplifies his early experiments with psychedelia as he searched for his own sound.

Bowie was also highly influenced by the New York protopunk scene, becoming friends and collaborators with Lou Reed of The Velvet Underground and Iggy Pop of Iggy and the Stooges. Both were writers of cryptic lyrics. For example, in Reed's "White Light / White Heat" (*White Light / White Heat,* 1968), a song regularly performed by Bowie on stage, Reed sings of the unexplained white light that is messing up his brain, driving him insane. Likewise, in "TV Eye" (*Funhouse*, 1970), Iggy is being stalked by a cat with a "TV Eye" on him.

Bowie has been a weird composer at least from the time he wrote the pop/music-hall single "Rubber Band" in 1966. But while this tale of lost love and elastic orchestras in the 1910s is strange, it isn't unclear. We can follow the story easily enough, as we can in Bowie's early character studies of eccentric outsiders, like the single "I Dig Everything" (1966), and "Uncle Arthur" and "Please Mr. Gravedigger" on the self-titled album *David Bowie* (1967). Yet enigmatic lyrics are in full force in Bowie's second self-titled album *David Bowie* (1969). The quirky lover in "Janine" can't explain what's tormenting him, while the quirky lover in "Unwashed and Somewhat Slightly Dazed" explains what's wrong with him in a torrent of gibberish. "Memory of a Free Festival" becomes a hallucinogenic trip and "Cygnet Committee" a hallucinogenic nightmare. Things only get more indecipherable on the next, and first truly great, Bowie album, *The Man Who Sold the World*. With the exception of the odd but straightforward "Running Gun Blues" and "Savior Machine," the entire album is written in cryptic verse. From the moment Bowie sits "in the corner of the morning in the past" in the opening track, "Width of a Circle", to the concluding "strange, mad celebration" in which "softly, a super-god dies" in "The Supermen", we receive a barrage of fragmentary ideas.

Having achieved peak incomprehensibility, Bowie maintains it through *Hunky Dory*, *Ziggy Stardust*, *Aladdin Sane*, and *Diamond Dogs* (1974). He lapses into being relatively understandable in *Young Americans* (1975), but returns to baffling form for *Station to Station* (1976), his "Berlin" trilogy—*Low* (1977), *"Heroes"* (1977), and *Lodger* (1979)—and *Scary Monsters* (1980). *Scary Monsters* marks the end of Bowie's greatest period of nonsense writing. In the 1980s, he becomes more conventional, and much more commercially successful, with the multi-platinum *Let's Dance* (1983) and *Tonight* (1985). However, Bowie would never lose his touch or interest in nonsense composition, continuing to delight with weird albums and strange songs.

There's no clear line between nonsense literature and literature that is simply difficult to understand. Writers have traditionally couched their meaning in similes, as in "If you would fall into my arms / and tremble like a flower", and metaphors, as in "For here / am I sitting in a tin can." When the similes and metaphors get sufficiently complex, they can make a poem or song hard to penetrate, as in the case of the Beat poets or Dylan. Yet the Beat poets weren't writing nonsense, because their words were intended to convey certain meanings. If you don't understand what the poem means, you can't appreciate it. Dylan's work, on the other hand, is often effectively nonsense, since it is pitched at an audience who are not expected to understand what he means. As for Bowie, he makes no secret of the fact that his lyrics may lack a specific meaning to him, or that he may interpret them differently now from when he wrote them. Even when his cryptic words do have specific meanings, the audience isn't expected to decipher a song before appreciating it, any more than in the case of Dylan. As Bowie says, "The piece of work is not finished until the audience come to it and add their own interpretation—and what the piece of art is about is the grey space in the middle" (Paxman interview). So, for example, while I *think* it's possible to follow Bowie's train of thought in "Life on Mars" (*Aladdin Sane*) enough to translate the lyrics into ordinary English, you don't need to be able to translate it like that to appreciate the song. After all, "Life on Mars" is intended for an audience who will put their own interpretation on it.

Turn and Face the Strange (Loving the Alien)

That's my take on what Bowie's doing. But how can it have artistic value? How can value attach to lyrics that aren't intended to be understood?

We might start by noting that since a song is a form of music, it might be valuable because of the sound of it alone. After all, the sounds made by a musical instrument don't have meaning in themselves. When Bowie breaks into the guitar solo on "Space Oddity", the individual guitar notes don't represent specific ideas, like the phrases in a sentence do. A voice can likewise be treated as a musical instrument and used to make sounds that serve no purpose other than being pleasing to the ear.

This in itself is traditional enough. Perfectly serious opera has always been peppered with gibberish, such as Wagner's *Die Walküre* (1870), in which Valkyries sing their battle cry of "*Ho-jo-to-ho.*" Jazz even adopted the "scat" technique of nonsense syllables, like Cab Calloway's "Hi-de hi-de hi-de hi" in "Minnie the Moocher" (1931). When Bowie concludes "Starman" (*Ziggy Stardust*) by singing the meaningless syllable "la" over one hundred times, he's doing nothing groundbreaking. The use of words as music likewise traditionally justifies distorting them. Words or syllables may be elongated, as in "For heeere / Am I sitting in a tin can / Faaar above the world" ("Space Oddity", *David Bowie*, 1969), or new syllables may be added, as in "Turn and face the strange—ch-ch-changes" ("Changes", *Hunky Dory*) and "I'm happy, hope you're happy too-oo-oo" ("Ashes to Ashes").

Obviously, though, Bowie is doing a lot more with his lyrics than making vocal music. After all, even at their least cohesive, lyrics in a Bowie song will still follow general themes. For instance, "Moonage Daydream" involves lust in space, "Heroes" (*"Heroes"*) involves love under political oppression, and "Scary Monsters (and Super Creeps)" (*Scary Monsters*) involves discomfort with other people. In some way, Bowie is harnessing vague meanings even while avoiding explicit meanings. Why?

One advantage of lyrics without fixed meanings is that they can paint a complicated setting in a few obscure strokes, leaving it to the listener's imagination to fill in the details. When Bowie tells us in "Drive In Saturday" (*Aladdin Sane*) that "It's hard enough to keep formation with this fallout saturation / Cursing at the astronette / Who stands in steel by his cabinet," or in "We Are the Dead" (*Diamond Dogs*) that "It's the theater of financiers / Count them, fifty 'round a table" he's suggesting much more detailed worlds than he would be capable of explicitly presenting in a three minute song. Likewise, in songs such as "The Supermen" (*The Man Who Sold the World*), "Oh! You Pretty Things" (*Hunky Dory*), "Five Years" (*Ziggy Stardust*), and "Diamond Dogs" (*Diamond Dogs*), Bowie suggests exotic settings with a few cryptic comments.

Bowie also uses obscure suggestion in this way to convey the weirdness of very weird people. Sometimes, these are weird fictional performers, as in "Lady Stardust" and "Ziggy Stardust" (*Ziggy Stardust*), and "Aladdin Sane (1913–1938–197?)" (*Aladdin Sane*). More often, his subjects are weird social outsiders, as in "After All" (*The Man Who Sold the World*), "The Jean Genie" (*Aladdin Sane*), and "Joe the Lion" (*"Heroes"*). As in the case of setting descriptions, Bowie conveys more strangeness with his obscure lyrics than he would have been able to just by describing the characters.

Drawing on expressionist tradition, Bowie also often uses a fractured style to convey the point of view of a character with a fractured mind. For instance, he uses surreal lyrics to convey the disorientation caused by drugs, as in "Memory of a Free Festival", in which LSD turns the sun into a machine, and "(Segue)—Baby Grace (A Horrid Cassette)" on *Outside* (1995), in which Baby Grace complains that since she's been put on "interest drugs", "I'm thinking very too, bit too fast like a brain catch."

Bowie likewise uses surreal lyrics to indicate mental illness. For example, in "Unwashed and Somewhat Slightly Dazed" (*David Bowie*, 1969), he interrupts his love-song to announce that he has "eyes in my backside / That see electric tomatoes / On credit card rye bread." "All the Madmen" (*The Man Who Sold the World*) ends with a refrain of "Zane zane zane, ouvrez le chien" ("Sane, sane, sane, open the dog"). In "Rock'n'Roll Suicide" (*Ziggy Stardust*) when Bowie tells us that we're suicidal, he assures us that "The wall-to-wall is calling / It lingers, then you forget." In "Jump They Say" (*Black Tie White Noise*, 1993), the suicidal man has "A nation in his eyes / Striped with blood and emblazed tattoo." Similar use of nonsense to indicate mental fragmentation is found in "Breaking Glass" (*Low*), "Blackout" (*"Heroes"*), and "Scream Like a Baby" (*Scary Monsters*).

Most strikingly, Bowie has frequently used surreal lyrics to convey alienation, indicating a person out of place with words out of place. Examples include "Janine" (*David Bowie*, 1969), "The Man Who Sold the World" (*The Man Who Sold the World*), "Life on Mars?" (*Hunky Dory*), "Ziggy Stardust" (*Ziggy Stardust*), "Aladdin Sane (1913-1938-197?)" (*Aladdin Sane*), "We are the Dead" (*Diamond Dogs*), "Fame" (*Young Americans*), "Station to Station" (*Station to Station*), "Sound and Vision" (*Low*), "Heroes" (*"Heroes"*), "DJ" (*Lodger*), "Ashes to Ashes" (*Scary Monsters*), "Where Are We Now?" (*The Next Day*, 2013), and "Lazarus" (*Blackstar*, 2016). In "Space Oddity", Major Tom is distanced from us by his dreamy association of ideas: "Planet Earth is blue and there's nothing I can do." In "Ashes to Ashes", he's distanced from us by the absurdity of his reported problems: he's stuck with a valuable friend, little green wheels are following him again, and so on.

But this still leaves plenty of songs unaccounted for. Only on *David Bowie* (1969), Bowie's first album containing true nonsense, does nonsense always have a clear explanation, whether it be LSD or mental illness. Starting with *The Man Who Sold the World,* Bowie stops feeling the need to explain. "The Width of a Circle", for instance, is a phantasmagoria for no reason hinted at in the song. Bowie meets himself and possibly God, and is tempted by a demonic, homoerotic creature, but how he ended up on this wild trip, we don't know. There are songs with "nonsense" that is just as inexplicable on every album to come, such as "The Bewlay Brothers" (*Hunky Dory*), "Moonage Daydream" (*Ziggy Stardust*), "Watch That Man" (*Aladdin Sane*), "Candidate" (*Diamond Dogs*), "Young Americans" (*Young Americans*), "Golden Years" (*Station to Station*), "Subterraneans" (*Low*), "Sons of the Silent Age" (*"Heroes"*), "Fantastic Voyage" (*Lodger*), "Up the Hill Backwards" (*Scary Monsters*), and more recently, "The Next Day" and "If You Can See Me" on *The Next Day,* and "Blackstar" and "Girl Loves Me" on *Blackstar*.

In general, Bowie uses nonsense lyrics to establish a mood, feeding us evocative words and ideas while leaving it up to us to give the lyrics meaning. "Moonage Daydream" may be baffling, but the romantic mood is blatant. Likewise, "The Bewlay Brothers" expresses a sense of loss, and "Up the Hill Backwards" a sense of frustration. Obscure lyrics have the advantage that we can fill in the details of the song in ways that resonate with us, matching the basic mood that has been set. Is Bowie's lost "Bewlay brother" a literal brother or an old friend? The fact that that song doesn't tell you allows you to make the character anything that touches you.

Importantly, we don't generally actually fill out all of the missing details in our head. I don't have a clear mental story to explain "The Bewlay Brothers," I haven't assigned any particular identity to the "Starman" (*Ziggy Stardust*), and while I know that The Jean Genie parties wildly, my conception of his specific debaucheries remains vague. (I can't speak for you, of course. Perhaps you have crystal-clear images of the Jean Genie letting himself go and of Bowie's Bewlay brother being a chameleon, comedian, Corinthian, caricature.) Still, even if actually filling in the blanks with specifics is not necessary, the way that such songs leave interpretation to us might still allow easier identification by not forcing an interpretation that we *can't* identify with. If "Ashes to Ashes" had been a clearly written account of the life of an alienated Englishman in 1980, the specific details of his life could get in the way of our identification with him. It may be no closer to our own experience to be strung out in heaven's high and followed by little green wheels, but if we aren't going to interpret the lyrics literally anyway, then no such detail is ever particularly jarring.

It seems that at the most general level, the value of serious nonsense lyrics is that they act as a spur to our imaginations. Rather than simply enjoying the ideas conveyed by the song, we enjoy the ideas the song evokes in us. But this makes nonsense particularly difficult to evaluate as art. If nonsense relies for its effect on the subjective associations applied by the audience, what exactly is coming from the artist? Of course, strictly speaking, all music relies on the subjective audience response for its effect. No melody is intrinsically catchy and no story has intrinsic emotional power. To be catchy is to be catchy *to* some audience and to have emotional power is to be moving *to* some audience. But lyrics like Bowie's make far more demands on audience imagination than more traditional lyrics. Even when Mozart presents a fantasy world of sorcerers and magical beings in the opera "The Magic Flute" (1791), he presents a more or less clear and coherent description of events for the audience. Bowie frequently offers almost nothing coherent at all.

Bowie's reliance on audience response doesn't in itself mean that he's a lesser artist than Mozart. Toying with people's associations in a way that they will find satisfying is not easy, a fact demonstrated by the number of musicians who have failed to find commercial success while trying to follow in Bowie's footsteps. But the more that a song relies on audience input, the harder it is to evaluate as a thing in itself, because audience input will vary so widely. Maybe Bowie's lyrics only appeal to us so much because he got lucky and happened to write in a style that we would respond to. "Moonage Daydream" has lasted three generations, but what associations will it have for someone who works on the moon?

Future Legend

Our best clue to what Bowie's lasting appeal will be is his extraordinary lasting popularity so far. Almost forty-five years since he first achieved mainstream success with *Ziggy Stardust*, he remains the iconic rock star, with massive worldwide sales of his back catalog, with 2013's *The Next Day* hitting Number One in the UK and Number Two in the US (his highest ever US ranking), and with 2016's *Blackstar* apparently poised for similar success. Rising on the tide of glam rock in the early 1970s, Bowie remained popular when glam faded, taking with it the popularity of one-time giants like the fey Marc Bolan, the hard-rocking Slade, and the excremental Sweet. In the mid-1970s, his experimental "Berlin" albums made a poor showing in the charts compared to those of contemporary superstars like the cheerful Swedes' ABBA, the falsetto Bee Gees, and the tartan-clad boy band, The Bay City Rollers, but Bowie kept selling as the tides of fashion swept other bands away. And so on. Bands and acts ruled the charts for a time, then fell from grace. But Bowie's music refuses to fade. No other solo artist in popular music, not even Elvis, has demonstrated such enduring appeal. It seems a good bet that in another forty-five years, few people will listen to Taylor Swift, Katy Perry and Ed Sheeran, but a proportion of the kids will get into David Bowie.

While Bowie's words may be difficult to penetrate, the emotions he cultivates are universal: love, lust, isolation, stress, loss, confusion, fear, longing, and even anger and disgust. These won't be going away in the future. What's more, it is possible that the cryptic nature of Bowie's lyrics will make them more accessible than other lyrics from our era, since new generations can read into them whatever they like, bringing whatever associations make the lyrics relevant to them.

I don't think that lasting appeal is the same thing as artistic value. Micky Mouse and *The Three Stooges* are both healthy franchises that continue to move merchandise, though there is not much to them as art. Still, at the very least, Bowie's ability to infect the minds of generations of music lovers suggests that his success is not simply a fluke, but reflects something special and valuable in his work. If, as I predict, his music is still popular in forty-five years, it will be hard for even the most conservative philosopher of music to deny its artistic value.

The question of why Bowie's bizarre art is so effective will be thornier. Nonsense defies rules, making the task of finding the rules of nonsense tremendously difficult. Bowie's been called an enigma so often, it's become a cliché, but from the perspective of philosophy of art, understanding his work is a slog up the hill backwards through quicksand while wondering "Where are we now?" (possibly while beset by flocks of squawking pink monkey birds, packs of diamond dogs hiding behind trees, and the occasional iron lion on his way back from the bar).

It ain't easy and I really don't understand the situation. Not that it stops me enjoying the songs, of course. Philosophy of art is a means to cultivate our joy in art, not to kill it, even when we are left in perplexity. I'm happy. Hope you're happy too!

6
Bowie the Buddhist

MARTIN MUCHALL

The fingerprints of Tibetan Buddhist philosophy are to be found all over the Bowie song "Quicksand"—in spite of its allusions to Crowleyan magic and the Nietzschean ideal of the Superman. The best way to understand this song is in a wider Buddhist context.

Bowie was by no means flirting playfully with Buddhism at this point in his career, and the long-term influence of the Buddhist faith has also surfaced elsewhere, for example in the lyrics to "Where Are We Now?" which marvelously heralded Bowie's sudden emergence from occultation in 2013.

When Bowie sings, "Don't believe in yourself" at the outset of the chorus to "Quicksand," he is clearly alluding to the Buddhist teaching of *anatta*. How can we be sure of this? Because several biographers and commentators on Bowie have drawn attention to his familiarity with Buddhist teaching prior to the recording of *Hunky Dory*. In his study of the album *Low*, Hugo Wilcken suggests that Bowie might have been introduced to Buddhism by his older half-brother Terry, possibly via the medium of Beat Generation writers like Kerouac and Ginsberg. Peter Doggett confirms this, as well as informing us that Bowie was a self-proclaimed Buddhist with a fascination for both reincarnation and Tibet and was also familiar with the popular guide to Zen Buddhism by Christmas Humphreys.

The early song "Silly Boy Blue," for example, references "Lhasa" (the Tibetan capital), "chela" (a Tibetan Buddhist term for a religious disciple), and "Potala" (the former residence of the Dalai Lama), while the saffron robe–wearing eponymous subject of "Karma Man" is clearly a Buddhist monk. Most tellingly, Bowie spent time studying and meditating with Chime Rinpoche (and possibly Chogyam Trungpa), two prominent Tibetan spiritual teachers at the Samye Ling monastery in Scotland, and seriously contemplated becoming a monk himself.

Trungpa was later to become a highly controversial and prominent spiritual teacher who shocked many who came into contact with him. Unusually for a monk, he attained notoriety for divesting himself of his Buddhist robes, eating any food he liked, smoking and making use of psychedelics, sleeping with his students (apparently of both sexes), and his eventual premature death was reputedly attributable to complications arising from alcoholism.

Leaving aside his tarnished reputation, a constant theme in Trungpa's writing is to do with "ego." This term, for Buddhists, refers to our constant tendency to place an "I" at the center of our experience. Descartes's famous declaration, "I think therefore I am" is therefore considered to be an illusion. All that Descartes demonstrated, from a Buddhist point of view, was the existence of thought. And just because we all have a lot of thoughts about ourselves does not mean that we actually do exist. Although the formation of ego is an inevitable consequence of our cognitive development, the process through which we eventually separate ourselves from the outside world is ultimately revealed to be no more than a false mental construct.

Don't Deceive with Belief

In his most famous work, *Cutting Through Spiritual Materialism*, Trungpa particularly emphasised the pernicious consequences that result from a predilection for interpreting reality from the vantage point of ego. According to Trungpa, "It is ego's ambition to secure and entertain itself, trying to avoid all irritation. So we cling to our pleasures and possessions, we fear change or force change, we try to create a nest or playground" (p. 6).

Furthermore,

> We adopt sets of categories which serve as handles, as ways of managing phenomena. The most fully developed products of this tendency are ideologies, the systems of ideas that rationalize, justify and sanctify our lives. Nationalism, communism, existentialism, Christianity, Buddhism—all provide us with identities, rules of action, and interpretations of how and why things happen as they do. (p. 6)

Concepts and ideologies therefore "screen us from a direct perception of what is. The concepts are taken too seriously; they are used as tools to solidify our world and ourselves. If a world of nameable things exists, then 'I' as one of the nameable things exists as well. We wish not to leave any room for threatening doubt, uncertainty or confusion" (pp. 6–7).

It is probably impossible to know whether Trungpa's particular take on egoism was this fully worked out prior to his reputed acquaintance with Bowie, and how much of it rubbed off on Bowie, assuming, as is very likely, that Bowie was acquainted with Trungpa's thinking. However, it's not unreasonable to think that Bowie absorbed a version of this outlook, as there is evidence for this elsewhere in the lyrics to "Quicksand."

Firstly, we should note Bowie's complaint that he is *sinking* in the quicksand of his thought and is powerless to resist this process. Against this backdrop, he confesses, amongst other things, to being "immersed in Crowley's uniform" (obsessed with the occult), preoccupied with nationalistic fantasies ("Himmler's sacred realm") or, at the very least, delusions of grandeur, as well as declaring himself unable to shake off the trappings of conventional human rationality and "bullshit faith."

In this and other ways, Bowie is recognizing the fact that—as Trungpa famously put it—"ego is able to convert everything to its own use, even spirituality." Hence the first two lines of the chorus, which implore the listener (and also probably the singer) to dispense with belief in the self and not to allow oneself to be seduced by ego-reinforcing beliefs and belief-systems.

Buddhism from the Beginning

It may be a mistake to see Buddhism as either a philosophy or a religion. As Rupert Gethin has pointed out in his primer *The Foundations of Buddhism*, Buddhism is essentially a skill, a "practical way of dealing with the reality of suffering" (p. 64). In cultivating this skill, Buddhists do make claims about the nature of reality in the same way that philosophers do. This is because in India, the birthplace of the Buddha, a particular philosophy is referred to as a *darsana*, a "way of seeing" reality. The idea is that if you see reality clearly you will no longer be deceived by it.

For Buddhists, however, this involves lots of meditation, as the Buddha's claims about reality were all based on meditative experience. Buddhism is something that you have to *do*. You have to practice the skill of meditation to discover what is really going on, to get the necessary insights, which is a lot different from simply sitting in an armchair and engaging in philosophical speculation about the way reality might possibly be. The famous Buddhist scholar Edward Conze put this rather amusingly:

> There is ultimately only one way open to those who do not believe the accounts of the yogins. They will have to repeat the experiment-in the forest, not the laboratory—they will have to do what the yogins say should be done, and see what happens. Until this is done disbelief is quite idle, and on a level with a pygmy's disbelief in Battersea power station, maintained by a stubborn refusal to leave the Congo basin, and to see for himself whether it exists and what it does. (*Buddhist Thought in India*, pp. 18–19)

The Buddha of Suburbia

The Buddha lived between 566 and 486 B.C.E. or 480 and 400 B.C.E. (the dates are uncertain). He was born in Kapilavastu which is now on the border between India and Nepal. He was not a Prince as the traditional stories suggest but the son of a powerful, local chieftain in what was then a republic. "Buddha" itself is a title meaning "Awakened One." The Buddha's actual name was Siddhartha Gautama. Although wealthy, well-educated, and expected to eventually occupy the same role as his father, the Buddha grew disillusioned with worldly life and turned his back on it at the age of twenty-nine.

India at this time was a fairly affluent place to be but the religion of the period (known as Brahmanism) had become stale. Power was invested in a priestly hierarchy called Brahmins who through elaborate ritual and sacrifice were thought to be able to control and manipulate the gods. Your place in this hierarchical and rigid society was decided by birth, and the most privileged group at the top of the tree were the Brahmins. Below the Brahmins were the warriors or *Kshatriyas*, then the *Vaishyas* (merchants and traders), and finally the *Shudras* (servants). These four groups formed the caste system and the Buddha was born into the *Kshatriya* or warrior caste.

A religion based on sacrifice rather than religious experience and one in which a select group enjoyed a monopoly of power eventually caused people to consider other religious possibilities. Theodore Roszak has pointed out that circumstances like this can result in the emergence of a counterculture (where a significant minority challenges the prevailing system of values). Countercultures tend to occur during historical periods of affluence combined with population shift. Both of these factors seem to have been at work in the Buddha's India. The "shift" in this case was a move from village to town and city, which produced a sense of social dislocation. During such times people tend to experiment with alternative lifestyles (just as the Beats and hippies of the 1950s and 1960s counterculture did, and as did Bowie during the latter decade).

The equivalent of the Beats and the hippies in ancient India were the *sramanas*, the spiritual dropouts, "wandering philosophers" or "walking corpses" (depending on which translation you prefer) who had turned their backs on mainstream society, rejected the social hierarchy of the caste system and its religion of sacrifice, and embraced a homeless, wandering lifestyle. It was this way of life that the Buddha adopted at the age of twenty-nine.

The traditional stories describe the Buddha as having been prompted to turn his back on worldly life because of his encounter with an old man, a sick man, and a corpse, which evoked within him a profound awareness of the impermanence and inevitable suffering that is part and parcel of this earthly life. This all happened when he took a trip out of his opulent place of residence, where we are asked to believe that he had spent all his previous adult years up to that point, living a life of luxury and pleasure without ever seeing things that caused him to think about old age, suffering, and death. An inspirational further encounter with a becalmed *sramana* then caused him to seek out a solution to the problem of the human condition.

And so the Buddha became a dropout and spent the next six years learning how to meditate whilst practicing rigorous asceticism, an attempt to master suffering through a life of severe self-discipline and self-denial. But just as his earlier life of hedonistic self-indulgence did not bring him lasting happiness, neither did a life of self-denial and near-starvation. Finally, at the age of thirty-five, Siddhartha had exhausted the material and spiritual possibilities of life in this world.

Then he recalled an experience from his youth when his mind had settled into a state of deep calm and peace while he was sat in the shade of a tree. This prompted him to investigate this state of mind further. Having increased his food intake in order to maintain a state of meditative awareness, the Buddha resolved to once again sit under another tree, and to remain there until he attained complete awakening. Having done this, Siddhartha did awaken; he finally achieved Nirvana, the cessation of suffering, and spent the next forty-five years teaching others how to achieve the same realization. The records of this teaching were maintained and transmitted orally in the first instance but eventually got preserved in the writings of several Buddhist groups. The most complete written record is that of the Theravada ("Way of the Elders") school of Buddhism. Known as the Pali Canon, this body of writing was committed to paper (or rather palm leaf manuscripts) in Sri Lanka in approximately 80 B.C.E.

Reality

The most famous of the Buddha's teachings is the Deer Park Sermon which was revealed to five former *sramana* companions of the Buddha in a park near modern Benares, India. It is a statement of the Buddha's "Middle Way," a practice that puts a stop to suffering without resorting to the extremes of self-indulgence or self-denial. The first part of the sermon goes like this:

> The Noble Truth of suffering (dukkha) is this: Birth is suffering; aging is suffering; sickness is suffering; death is suffering; sorrow and lamentation, pain, grief and despair are suffering; association with the unpleasant is suffering; dissociation from the pleasant is suffering; not to get what one wants is suffering—in brief, the five aggregates of attachment are suffering.

The First Noble Truth of the Buddha essentially declares that life itself is *dukkha*, a word that is rich in meaning and nuance, more so than the usual English translations of "suffering" or "ill" can readily convey. My preferred translation would be "unsatisfactory experience." It is because of this emphasis on suffering that many people have come to the conclusion that Buddhism is a pessimistic religion. But they would be wrong. Buddhism claims to be neither pessimistic nor optimistic but *realistic*. Here's why.

First of all, the Buddha is not denying that there is happiness in life. There is even a Pali word for it: *sukha* or "bliss." But what he is saying is that happiness is transient. It doesn't last. In fact a careful reading of this first paragraph reveals that there are three categories of suffering. The first of these is self-evident suffering. When we're in mental or physical pain there is no question that there is *dukkha*.

Then the Buddha moves on to state that, "association with the unpleasant is suffering; dissociation from the pleasant is suffering, not to get what one wants is suffering." These are examples of suffering produced by change. At the end of a lot of old TV films and dramas with a happy ending the frame freezes with all the characters smiling. This was wonderfully parodied in the series *Police Squad* (from which the *Naked Gun* movies were derived): in one episode the set starts to collapse around the main characters with their fixed grins. In another, all the characters dutifully turn into statues while a chimpanzee runs riot around the set shrieking and throwing stuff around. These are both perfect examples of what the Buddha was getting at: there may be happiness in life but there are no happy endings because reality can never be freeze-framed. We always end up in situations we would rather not be in. Or as the famous Buddhist scholar Trevor Ling once put it, "after the party comes the hangover."

The third type of suffering is arguably the most important (Note the words "In brief," meaning "what this all boils down to is . . ."). Essentially, the "five aggregates" are us. All that we consist of are five things that change. This is the famous teaching of *anatta* or "no self" and is the key to unlocking the significance of that chorus to "Quicksand."

Don't Believe in Yourself

On the night of his enlightenment the Buddha made his third and most essential discovery, namely, that there is no permanent, unchanging self either outside of us (in the form of an eternal God or Ultimate Reality, which in Hinduism is called Brahman) or inside of us (in the form of an eternal soul or what Hindus call an "atman"). When we look inside of ourselves we don't find anything that is unchanging. And when we look outside of ourselves, at the world as a whole, we don't find a God or anything else that is everlasting. All we encounter is an ever-changing reality.

The word "Aggregate" is a translation of the Pali term *khandha* or *skandha*, a word that can also be rendered as "heap" or "bundle." Humans are made up of a bundle of five things, and when we examine these five things closely we will learn that there is nothing remotely resembling a permanent soul or self to be found there. Instead we find:

a. **A physical body normally endowed with six senses (mind is a sense in Indian thought).**

b. **Sensations that are pleasant, unpleasant or neutral.**

c. **Ideas and concepts about what we are sensing.**

d. **Various desires, impulses, and reactions that arise in response to the previous two inputs.**

e. **An awareness of all this.**

In plain English, our body is constantly changing as do the things we perceive with it. Meanwhile, our ideas and responses to what we perceive are in a constant state of flux. Lastly, our awareness of all this fluctuates, depending on how alert or aware we happen to be at any one time.

The constant morphing of Bowie's public personas—from Ziggy Stardust to Aladdin Sane to Soul Boy to Thin White Duke to Man Who Fell to Earth—surely reflect this characteristically Buddhist awareness of the fluidity and insubstantiality of the personality. It's no surprise, then, to learn that in a 1973 interview published in the *New Musical Express*, Bowie admitted, "I'm not very sure of myself when it comes to thinking about me. I try and leave 'me' alone. . . . It's much more of a realism for me to think that this [*points around the room*] is all me, that there's nothing in here. I prefer that way of existence."

We Are the Dead

So that's the fountainhead of Buddhist thinking. To get from that main source to Trungpa, we also have to know about Tantra.

A confection of "lust, mummery, and magic" was how one rather strait-laced Victorian author attempted to categorize Tantra, an Indian tradition of beliefs, meditation, and ritual practices that emerged in the fifth century C.E. and went on to heavily influence the form of Buddhism that eventually emerged in Tibet.

That Victorian assessment is not entirely inaccurate. Tantra is probably the nearest Asian equivalent of the Western occult tradition, and divides itself up into "right-hand" and "left-hand" paths that roughly correspond to "white magic" and "black magic." It's also similarly esoteric, intended to be understood only by a small minority of initiates. Its scriptures are composed in a deliberately opaque style. Special initiations and specific guidance from a guru are therefore required to unlock their meaning. Sexual yoga, elaborate ritual, and the harnessing of psychological forces for magical purposes are all historical aspects of the *Vajrayana* or "diamond vehicle" path to enlightenment, the Buddhist variant of Tantra. So its appeal for Bowie would have been obvious.

But let's not get too carried away. In spite of Trungpa's licentious behavior, the more benign associations evoked by the image of the Dalai Lama are a better guide to what one might expect from latter-day *Vajrayana*. And Tibetan Buddhism is only magical to the extent that it is transformative. The basic principle involved is that of psychological alchemy: the practitioner engages directly with the darker, more neurotic forces that most contribute to reinforcing our ego-driven behavior, in order to transmute them and place these energies at the service of liberation, not just our own liberation, but that of all suffering beings. Of these forces, fear of death is the most powerful, and therefore potentially the most liberating of all.

The opportunity to master this fear and free yourself from the cycle of death and rebirth and all the suffering that goes with it is what the *Tibetan Book of the Dead* is all about. This scripture would typically be read aloud daily in the home of someone recently deceased. It's essentially an instruction manual that enables the freshly disembodied psyche to negotiate experiences encountered in the aftermath of the demise of the physical body, during which time it passes through different planes of existence located beyond ordinary life.

The lyrics to "Quicksand" are, on close inspection, suffused with an awareness of this journey. First of all, Bowie appears to be inexorably sinking into the after-death state as he is powerlessly "drawn toward the ragged hole." Although he remains aware that "knowledge comes with death's release," he's also "frightened by the total goal."

According to the *Book of the Dead*, at approximately the time of physical death, a fundamental or primary clear light is glimpsed by the deceased, and if they recognize this "Great Body of Radiance" as the source of their own consciousness and identify with it, liberation is achieved. However, most mortals don't have the prior meditative training to recognize this, and their lack of understanding and fear of this overwhelming luminosity causes them to continue—like Bowie—their passage through two further planes or *bardos* (a term explicitly referenced in the song) of after-death existence.

A feature of these bardos is the presence of hallucinations that the psychoanalyst Carl Jung considered to be externalized projections of the unconscious mind. "Crowley's uniform," "Himmler's sacred realm of dream reality," "Garbo's eyes," "Churchill's lies," and perhaps the "viper's fang" might all be regarded as manifestations of this type.

Where Are We Now?

When someone is freed from the delusions of ego, enlightenment or *nirvana* is achieved, a state in which psychological suffering ceases. And when Bowie—after a decade of silence—asks "Where are we now, where are we now?" and then adds, "The moment you know, you know, you know," he is reminding us that the present is the only place where life can truly be lived. This is why Buddhist meditation continually returns us to our immediate, direct experience. It alerts us to the fact that right before our eyes, there is a vast, vibrant, endlessly morphing, ungraspable present, and encourages a state of *felt* oneness with it. It invites us to understand that beyond the spinning out of ego's fears and worries, we all participate actively in, and are intimately connected to, a fathomless reality that only appears to be external.

There's also another sense in which the *Book of the Dead* may be understood: it too, is about now. If reality is constantly re-inventing itself, then we too die and get reborn every thought-moment, or as Chogyam Trungpa puts it:

> To realize impermanence is to realize that death is taking place constantly; so there really is nothing fixed. If one begins to realize this and does not push against the natural course of events, it is no longer necessary to re-create samsara [the world of time-bound, ego-fueled delusion] at every moment. (*The Dawn of Tantra*, p. 34)

Pay attention! Wake up! This is finally Buddhism's simple message. We can see in the songs "Quicksand" and "Where Are We Now?" that it's a message David Bowie heeded.

7
David Bowie, Political Philosopher?

R. KEVIN HILL

> And that pose is out too, Sunny Jim. The new thing is to care passionately, and be right wing.
>
> —*A Hard Day's Night*

The idea that there is a political philosopher lurking behind David Bowie's music may not seem very likely. He doesn't talk much about politics or philosophy, and he's not usually thought of as a political songwriter the way that, say, early Bob Dylan was. That said, there are quite a lot of songs with political themes in them, from "We Are Hungry Men" in 1967 to "If You Can See Me" in 2013, and dozens of songs in between, songs criticizing psychiatry, domestic violence, and poverty in the Third World, songs about war, terrorism, the Middle East, religious fundamentalism, surveillance, and much more.

Is there an underlying theme in all of this? I think so. David Bowie's political songs seem to be driven by a passion for freedom. But how is that any different from the passion for freedom that is common to many rock stars and their music? And what is it that makes this a philosophical concern? The short answer is that Bowie was not merely passionate about freedom, he was perplexed by it as well, and in the lyrics of the songs I'm going to discuss, he seems to be trying to work out what the nature of freedom and oppression really are, in a way that doesn't simply adopt the available political options of Left or Right, but tries to think through their roots and their implications.

What's even more interesting, Bowie's attempt to understand what freedom is evolves over time, and in a certain sense, follows a wide circle that begins by criticizing the conception of freedom held by the counterculture of the late 1960s, and ends with a kind of acceptance of it. This whole odyssey takes place under the shadow of World War II and against the backdrop of the Cold War, and the thought of totalitarianism was never far from his mind. Unlike so many rock stars and their fans of the 1960s, Bowie was as troubled by the Soviets as by the Nazis, and while he could not embrace the mainstream culture because of the ways that it limited people's freedom, he couldn't fully support the counterculture either. For his suspicion was that its revolutionary impulse was motivated, not by a desire for freedom, but by a desire for power.

Equating Fascism and Communism

In the song "Cygnet Committee" (1969) the problem Bowie poses is how people who reject a society that cries out for revolutionary change should relate to the movement it takes to bring about such change. In the song three voices alternate, the narrator's, the Thinker's, and the Revolution itself.

In the first verse, the narrator presents himself as a weary and detached observer, who introduces the Thinker, who bitterly recounts how he gave his all for the revolution, which has used him up, draining his very soul dry, and abandoning him once it achieved power. The narrator then introduces "his friends," the voice of the revolution, who admit to exploiting the Thinker to achieve power, which they have now done. "We broke the ruptured structure built of age. Our weapons were the tongues of crying rage." But the voice Bowie gives to the revolution inadvertently reveals that it's fueled by resentment towards the older society's powerful and filled with contempt for the poor it seeks to liberate.

The revolution turns out to be tyrannical and dogmatic. When the narrator returns, we see the extent of the destruction the revolution has wreaked, killing lovers and children, likening it to a murderous robot which has taken on a life of its own, a "love machine" that plows down men and women, "not hearing anymore."

The narrator himself wants to believe in the revolution, but ultimately he and everyone else is imperiled by it. The song ends with the narrator begging the revolution for mercy, crying "We want to live! I want to live!" In the song we see a familiar conservative concern about revolution becoming a source of tyranny in its own right, but from the perspective of someone who rejects the society it destroys as well; it is an "individualist" criticism.

Nietzsche, who was no conservative, had said similar things: "Socialism is the fanciful younger brother of the almost expired despotism whose heir it wants to be; its endeavors are thus in the profoundest sense reactionary. For it desires an abundance of state power such as only despotism has ever had; indeed it outbids all the despotisms of the past inasmuch as it expressly aspires to the annihilation of the individual, who appears to it like an unauthorized luxury of nature destined to be improved into a useful organ of the community" (*Human, All Too Human*, p. 173).

And while the picture Bowie paints reminds us of Soviet communism, the references to "love" and "peace" scattered throughout make it clear that it is the radicalism of the late 1960s which he's talking about. The problem is that the existing social order suppresses the individual enough to make it not worth conserving, but the revolutionary movement required to overturn that order will destroy the individual too. It's hard to hear the song as anything other than a repudiation of revolution. In an interview much later he confirmed this interpretation:

> Politically, I equated Fascism with Communism, or rather Stalinism. On my trips through Russia I thought, well, this is what Fascism

> must have felt like. They marched like them. They saluted like them. Both had centralized governments. It's hard to see that you could get involved with all that and not see the implications of what you were getting into. (*Strange Fascination*, p. 252)

But if that's all true, then what can an individual who wants to be free from the oppression of the existing society do about it?

Big Brother

Bowie's worries about radicalism are by no means confined to "Cygnet Committee." In "Panic in Detroit" (1973) we're presented with an ironic portrait of a narcissistic revolutionary who "looked a lot like Che Guevara" and who appears to be responsible for (or at least laughs at) some sort of terrorist attack. "A trickle of strangers were all that were left alive." The narrator leaves the revolutionary to explore the ensuing chaos, only to find upon his return that the revolutionary has committed suicide, and left behind a note that says "let me collect dust." Revolutionary violence ends in nihilistic self-destruction.

Perhaps even more telling, around this time Bowie started to work on a musical based on George Orwell's *Nineteen Eighty-Four*, and there's no reason to think his attitude towards it was to be ironic or critical; although the rights to *Nineteen Eighty-Four* proved not to be available, the concept album *Diamond Dogs* (1974) contained songs that had been written for it, "We are the Dead," "1984," and "Big Brother."

Orwell's whole outlook seems similar to Bowie's in one respect: Orwell, who was himself a socialist, found much to criticize in present-day society, but reserved his greatest criticism for the likely shape of a totalitarianism that might emerge from its overthrow. Orwell, who was no friend to fascism, focused his attention on the totalitarianism of the Left, and its impact on individual freedom. Where Bowie's song "Big Brother" differs from "Cygnet Committee" is in its focus on the mass psychology of totalitarianism, in the collective yearning for leadership that causes people to willingly renounce their own freedom. Ultimately the problem lies not in systems of government, but in the collective flight from freedom that motivates them.

The Insubstantial Self

All of this would seem to suggest that Bowie's political vision is simply some form of liberal individualism. The basic ideas behind liberal individualism are 1. that society is fundamentally a collection of individuals; 2. that social arrangements (especially political arrangements) exist to serve individuals, not the other way around; and 3. that individuals should have the freedom to make their own decisions and determine the course of their own lives without obstacles or interference.

The main problem with this approach is that individuals being free can have a negative impact on other individuals who are trying to do the same thing; my attempt to determine the course of my own life can interfere with or obstruct your attempt to do the same. Because of this, the liberal individualist holds that one of the primary purposes of political arrangements is to make sure we don't get in each others' way. As the philosopher John Rawls put it, "Each person is to have an equal right to the most extensive system of equal basic liberty compatible with a similar system for all" (*A Theory of Justice*, p. 220). For liberal individualists, restrictions on individual freedom which are not necessary to facilitate individual freedom in some way cannot be justified, and should therefore be abolished. The incompatibility of liberal individualism with both the Nazi and Soviet forms of totalitarianism should be obvious.

But matters are made more complicated when we ask what the nature of this "individual" is. What is this self which people abandon when they flee from their own freedom in order to create totalitarian societies? Bowie seems to think that there is no individual self at all, at least in his own case. All that exists are performances in a social context, performances which only exist by virtue of being seen by others, who themselves are nothing but performers.

The insubstantiality of the self emerges early in Bowie's lyrics. In "Janine" (1969) he tells a lover that if she kills him, she will really be killing someone else—for he has no self to kill. Introspection proves useless for identifying a real self amidst the transitory performances we enact for others. As he says in "Changes" (1971), despite all his efforts at trying to locate a self through introspection, he "never caught a glimpse." Whatever the self may be, it can only be known by others, and as a center from which ripples emanate in "the stream of warm impermanence," it is radically changeable. This notion of the self as radically changeable ultimately comes from Nietzsche. In "Quicksand" (1971), Bowie says that he is "a mortal with potential of a superman." This suggests that the task of the individual is not to liberate, actualize, or express a self, but to create one, or at least get out of the way of those who are in the process of doing so: as he says in "Oh You Pretty Things" (1971) we've "got to make way for the Homo Superior."

We're beginning to get a fix on what the fundamental tension is in Bowie's early political philosophy: each self is a void, an evanescent center, a cluster of ever-changing social performances, but it's up to us to decide who it is that will write our role for us: others, or ourselves. If others create our role for us, then we have no freedom or personal fulfillment; perhaps it's this which produces not only the society that oppresses us, but the revolutionary impulse, born of resentment, that seeks to overthrow it politically . . . only to lead to a new, even more oppressive society. What we should do instead is creatively fashion our own role, giving birth to ourselves as both artists and works of art. To this extent, Bowie is following in Nietzsche's footsteps again, who wrote:

> To 'give style' to one's character—that is a great and rare art! It is practiced by those who survey all the strengths and weaknesses of their nature and then fit them into an artistic plan until every one of them appears as art and reason and even weaknesses delight the eye. Here a large mass of second nature has been added; there a piece of original nature has been removed—both times

> through long practice and daily work at it. Here the ugly that could not be removed is concealed; there it has been reinterpreted and made sublime. Much that is vague and resisted shaping has been saved and exploited for distant views: it is meant to beckon toward the far and immeasurable. In the end, when the work is finished, it becomes evident how the constraint of a single taste governed and formed everything large and small. Whether this taste was good or bad is less important than one might suppose, if only it was a single taste! (*The Gay Science*, p. 232)

Bowie's early interest in mime and theater, and in importing a certain theatricality into rock music, is at least suggestive of such ideas.

A Temporary Self

In *The Rise and Fall of Ziggy Stardust and the Spiders from Mars* (1972), this theatricality breaks out of the space within which it is usually confined. The album presents a fictional character, Ziggy Stardust, who, like Bowie, aspires to become and becomes a rock star. This character is then presented in Bowie's own rock concerts without any theatrical "framing": Bowie as performer playing the role of the performer. And it was this album which led to Bowie's early fame. Through manipulating his audience by performing a role, Bowie had created a kind of temporary self. That this role or self was not contained within any theatrical frame is illustrated by the fact that he stayed "in character" in interviews and other public settings, thus turning ordinary social interactions into performances and other social actors into his audience. For Bowie as Ziggy (or, subsequently, Aladdin Sane, Halloween Jack, or the Thin White Duke), all the world was a stage.

However, this stance generates a political problem. In order to have the greatest possible scope for self-invention, as many others as possible must be reduced as much as possible to spectators. Perfect freedom would consist turning society into an audience and manipulating its perceptions in order to create the self desired. Once Bowie began to be famous, he began to see parallels between the celebrity he sought within a liberal society, and the role of the political leader . . . and at the limit, the totalitarian leader. Anxious reflection on what it is like to be a political leader begins to appear, surprisingly, on his least experimental and most popular (up to that point) album, *Young Americans* (1975). Not only was the album itself an extremely cynical bid for popular success in the American market; it says as much itself. In the title song, Bowie bemoans his own manipulativeness, his own lack of passion, crying at the end "Ain't there one damn song that can make me break down and cry?"

The answer to this rhetorical question is, of course, "No." The song itself is an indictment of the shallowness at the heart of the very America Bowie is courting, which, two years after President Nixon's resignation, doesn't even remember who he was. In the end, what matters is "I've got a suite and you've got defeat." The link between manipulativeness, discussed in "Win" and "Fascination," and political leadership, is made clear in the prescient portrait of a Reaganesque leader in "Somebody Up There Likes Me." In this new portrait of Big Brother, celebrity and political leadership have merged, leaving a moral vacuum at the heart of political power. Instead of choosing our leaders by their values, expertise, or experience, we pick them on the basis of experience alone. This portrait is offered in the third person, but Bowie's anxiety that he might have become indistinguishable from it becomes clear in "Fame," which "makes a man take things over."

The Thin White Fascist

In Bowie's next album, *Station to Station* (1976), the themes broached thus far reach some sort of crisis point. Bowie decides that his next character, the Thin White Duke, will embody fascism itself. The Duke is coldly manipulative, but represents romantic passion convincingly. More important for our purposes, Bowie's Duke began to actually discuss fascism in interviews. When he did it was difficult to tell whether he was analyzing fascism, playing the role of a fascist for some artistic purpose, or actually being a fascist:

> Rock stars are fascists. Adolf Hitler was one of the first rock stars. . . . Think about it. Look at some of his films and see how he moved. I think he was quite as good as Jagger. It's astounding. And boy, when he hit that stage, he worked an audience. Good God! He was no politician. He was a media artist. He used politics and theatrics and created this thing that governed and controlled the show for twelve years. The world will never see his like again. He staged a country . . . People aren't very bright, you know? They say they want freedom, but when they get the chance, they pass up Nietzsche and choose Hitler because he would march into a room to speak and music and lights would come on at strategic moments. It was rather like a rock'n'roll concert. The kids would get very excited—girls got hot and sweaty and guys wished it was them up there. That, for me, is the rock'n'roll experience. (The *Playboy* Interview, September 1976)

Unfortunately, if Bowie's view of the self is that it is a work of art created by social performance, this distinction collapses. Earlier in 1976, he had apparently said "As I see it, I am the only alternative for the premier in England. I believe Britain could benefit from a Fascist leader. After all, Fascism is really nationalism." Had Bowie "passed up Nietzsche and chosen Hitler"? Could he even tell the difference anymore? Was there a difference? Forty years later, with vice-presidential candidates becoming reality TV stars and reality TV stars becoming presidential candidates, it's not so clear to us either.

A Self Imploding

Of course, Nazism as a philosophy of individual freedom is ridiculous, and if this is where the entire project of creating the self as a work of art through social performance leads, then that project has to give way to something else. In the so-called Berlin Trilogy, *Low*, *"Heroes,"* and *Lodger*, Bowie sorted out what that was to be. Initially, it seemed that he had embraced a conception of his work that was not only devoid of theatricality, but devoid of any sense of self at all.

On *Low* (1977) more than half of the album consists of instrumentals, either tracks originally intended for songs for which no lyrics or vocal track were ever developed, or purely meditative music (much of it composed with Brian Eno). What songs there were seem to tell the story of a self imploding.

A Collapse of the Self

In *"Heroes"* (1977) Bowie begins to turn a critical eye on his experience so far, from his rejection of the counterculture as potentially totalitarian, his Nietzschean aestheticist response, and its transformation into a kind of fascism. "Beauty and the Beast" sets an ominous tone by suggesting a world on the brink of a fascist coup, in which there is "slaughter in the air." The song "Blackout" seems to chronicle a mental breakdown, a collapse of the self. Bowie's ambivalence about the Nietzschean notion of the self as a work of art finds expression in "Joe the Lion," a song about performance artist Chris Burden, who is perhaps best known for his work *Trans-Fixed* (1974), which involved being crucified on the back of a Volkswagen Beetle.

"Sons of the Silent Age" seems to criticize the psychology of Nazism itself: the silent age of film ends in 1929, shortly before Hitler's rise to power, and its "sons" are portrayed as vapid, sleepwalking illiterates with "one inch thoughts." But it's the title song which serves as the centerpiece of the album. "'Heroes'" seems to be a celebration of romantic love set in Berlin during the Cold War which had served as the context for all of Bowie's political reflections so far. At the climax of the song, Bowie sings of himself and his lover standing by the Berlin Wall, and of the "shame" that lies on the other side.

The force of the song's romanticism is so great as to almost overwhelm critical judgment, but here too, Bowie's critical reflection on romanticism is still operative. Most notably, the word "heroes" in the title is in irony quotes. The lovers are far from attractive characters, being cruel, alcoholic, and self-deceived, and in a situation which is essentially hopeless. Their belief that love will give them a lasting victory is an illusion, for while the narrator sings that "we can beat them forever and ever" we are repeatedly reminded that their heroism will last "just for a day."

If the "stream of warm impermanence" mentioned in "Changes" is still the fundamental fact about the human condition, then romanticism is nothing but the illusion of permanence through love. What's more, that sense of permanence is intertwined with a political stance, for while Bowie imagines his lovers, like the lovers in *Nineteen Eighty-Four*, defining the value and importance of their love through its opposition to totalitarianism, the overall ironic stance of the song suggests that romantic anti-totalitarianism is itself an illusion. After all, Nazism presented itself as a form of romantic anti-communism. What's more, the people of East Germany were taught that the Germany which lay on the far side of the Berlin Wall from their perspective was a continuation of Nazi Germany, a pure evil against which they could define themselves heroically. This was reflected in the fact that the East German government referred to the Berlin Wall as the Antifaschistischer Schutzwall, the Antifascist Protective Wall. And although John Miller in *National Review* named ""Heroes"" one of "the 50 greatest conservative songs," not only did the irony quotes not come to his attention, neither did the fact that the song never tells us which side of the Wall we are on. This is something the listener brings with them into their encounter with it.

The rest of the album consists largely of meditative instrumentals as with *Low*, though of a noticeably gloomier tone, culminating in "Neuköln," a song named for a borough of Berlin with a large immigrant (especially Middle Eastern) population. It's as if Bowie, in the collapse of his struggles over how to relate himself to himself and his own social world, has suddenly noticed that there is a world elsewhere in which the concern is not with whether one should conform to a socially given identity or craft an identity for oneself, with whether one should be a romantic or an anti-romantic, but with survival.

Survival for these immigrants is eked out against the backdrop of a world already dominated by a European and American culture without which Bowie's prior preoccupations make no sense at all. Although he may not have articulated the point in quite this way, it's as if he had discovered that all his prior concerns were artifacts of a bourgeois individualism and idealism blind to the material conditions within which it operates and against which it is powerless. In short, he appears to be on a journey leading back to Marx.

Full Circle

In the third album of the Berlin Trilogy, *Lodger* (1979) for the first time Bowie's question "How am I to become free?" seems to have given way to the question "How are we to become free?" without any trace of his prior association of the Left with totalitarianism. The freedom Bowie now seeks is devoid of aestheticism and sought with humility. Navel-gazing has given way to observation and documentation. Instead of imaginary landscapes of the future he gives us the real world damaged by and struggling under the weight of colonialism and imperialism.

Instead of constructing a theatrical, androgynous identity, he simply attacks sexism ("Boys Keep Swinging") and domestic violence ("Repetition") head on. Instead of ambivalent reflections on the psychology of leadership, he suggests that our problems may ultimately be structural and economic ("Red Money"). As he says in "Fantastic Voyage," "But I'm still getting educated / But I've got to write it down / And it won't be forgotten / 'Cause I'll never say anything nice again / How can I?"

With this, Bowie had come full circle, to something like the radical political philosophy he had repudiated in "Cygnet Committee." No longer withdrawn within himself, he ceased to be the performer to be observed and had become the observer. And yet there was a kind of strange inevitability to this return to progressivism. As Tom Carson explained,

> Even his most revisionist Seventies work depended for its point and urgency on having those Sixties assumptions constant in the background. It's hardly unprecedented, in any of the arts, for a figure originally perceived as breaking with tradition to be understood in the long run as that tradition's last upholder—which, in relation to Sixties utopianism, was just what Bowie was. (p. 536)

8
The Babe with the Power

NICOLAS MICHAUD

David Bowie was, and in many ways still is, magical. There was always a mystical and mysterious quality to the man that made him both enticing as well as a bit dangerous. That combination made Bowie the perfect man to play Jareth the Goblin King in the 1986 surreal film *Labyrinth*.

Jareth, as depicted by Bowie, was ruthless as well as beautiful, cunning as well as brutal, not to mention powerful, sexy, and a bit terrifying. As one of the two main characters played by actual human beings in the film, which, otherwise, was largely populated by whimsicalities conjured up by Jim Henson's Creature Shop, Jareth was fantastical while being real flesh. Bowie, with all of his mystery, was the perfect casting choice because he bridged the gap between Henson's fantasy creatures and the "real" world.

Because of Bowie's portrayal, the movie *Labyrinth* is more than just a child's fantasy as told by clever muppets. Instead, it's as sophisticated as it is playful, thoughtful, challenging, and perhaps even a bit philosophical. There's a great deal to be learned from Bowie and his Labyrinth. The story teaches viewers about growing up, accepting the consequences of reality, and the value of friendship. It is easy to assume that the fantasy world of *Labyrinth* is just a creative backdrop to those more important lessons. That assumption, though, belies the importance that Bowie's combination of fantastic creature and real world man brings to the movie.

That fantasy world, Bowie's portrayal of Jareth hints to us, is potentially more real than we might think. In fact, that mystical world of goblins, talking caterpillars, dwarves, sword-fighting fox-terriers, and whatever the heck Ludo is, is, perhaps, more possible than we realize.

In Search of New Dreams

In understanding how *Labyrinth* challenges our ideas of reality, it helps to remind ourselves that the movie begins with the protagonist, Sarah Williams, rehearsing a play. That play, the viewer can only assume, is what inspires Sarah to fantasize about, and call to, the otherworldly kingdom belonging to Bowie's Jareth. The play, presumably is fantastical, a dream-like reality into which Sarah can escape from the mundanity of her real life.

In that play, the character of the Goblin King is the man or creature she calls to in asking him to whisk away her baby brother, who is, like most baby brothers, annoying beyond belief. So, from the very beginning, the movie toys with the idea of reality. We don't start in a fantastical world, we start in a world of acting as Sarah rehearses her part. So we, as the viewer, are watching a real actress play a young girl who's rehearsing a part for a fake play about a world where she's going to go adventure in a labyrinth, which is the central world of the real-world movie we are watching. In other words, *Labyrinth* is a story about a fake story in the story that is actually the real story of the play—Sarah's fake world, Jareth's kingdom, is the real world movie!

So what I am really trying to say is that Bowie's film calls us to blur the lines of reality. Sarah doesn't challenge the fantasy world she enters. We don't see her telling herself, "This is my imagination" despite a series of surreal sequences that seem as if they can only take place in a dream. As a result, we might view the movie as nothing more than a child's perspective on reality. She plays an "imaginary game" wishing that her brother be taken way, fantasizes that she must save him, and then wakes up to find her brother still there, of course, because he never left.

The fact, though, that the movie has almost a Hamlet-like quality of a play within a play, which in this case, the fake play that they are playing with is really the world of the real film, should give us pause and ask ourselves, "Maybe the film is saying something about dreams and reality."

What if the "real" world is only a creation of our minds, like in dreams? What if, in fact, the reality of dwarves, Bogs of Eternal Stench, Goblin Kings, and magic is only a matter of letting our minds create a world that we just don't believe is possible? This sounds silly, of course. But think of even the surreal existence of music, like the music of David Bowie. Music has a weird kind of existence, doesn't it? It's not a "thing" but it affects us like a thing. You might say it's like an idea—something that isn't physical but can bring about feelings and thoughts. Yet, music is also physical, existing as vibrations of air. But then again, you can hear music just by looking at written music (if you're well trained) . . . no instruments necessary! So music seems to exist in the mind, yet it's shared by many people. Perhaps the world isn't as clearly physical as we would like to believe . . . and perhaps the mind creates far more of it than we realize, like in our dreams.

The Power of Voodoo

When I see *Labyrinth,* I think of philosopher Bishop George Berkeley (1685–1753). Berkeley had a perspective on reality that meshes nicely with Bowie's fantastic world in *Labyrinth.* That perspective is one that, like the child's perspective of *Labyrinth,* we tend to think is cute, amusing even, but one that we should dismiss in the end as ridiculous.

Berkeley thought the world didn't exist as we believe. He thought that only minds and ideas within minds can really be said to exist. All the stuff that we perceive as "out there" doesn't act as evidence for a real physical world at all.

Berkeley may sound as if he's nuts, but what he says actually makes a lot of sense. Simply, the world we experience we always experience through our senses, right? Let's say I was lucky enough to have met David Bowie (I wish!) Well the person I see, all the colors and textures that make him up, come to me through my eyes. Maybe I shake his hand, which is an experience of feeling textures through touch. Perhaps he wears cologne I can smell, and certainly it's my ears that capture the sound of his voice. If I had no senses, I couldn't know that I was meeting Mr. Bowie. If I couldn't see, feel, hear, or smell, then I wouldn't know he was there. My experience of Bowie, as of all objects, is an experience of colors, textures, smells, and so on. But those experience don't exist outside me; they are creations of my mind!

Okay, no, seriously, take taste for example. There's a point when Sarah eats tainted fruit in *Labyrinth.* Think of where the taste of that fruit really exists. . . . We like to think that the taste of food is *in* the food. But that's just silly. That would mean that fruit is made up of little "fruit flavored" atoms—little fruit-flavored protons, neutrons, and electrons! Not to mention, if the flavor is *in* the fruit, how come we can all disagree about the taste of the fruit? No. The fruit taste is actually created by our brain. That's why as we grow older and our taste buds and brains change the taste of a food can change, though the object is no different. When those molecules of fruit come in contact with our tongues, our taste buds are triggered which send a signal to our brains *which then creates the taste of that fruit!*

The same is true of sounds, colors, textures and all of the other stuff our senses tell us! You probably don't believe me. You might be thinking to yourself, "No that can't be right. When I see a color, that color is really *out there* in the world" but it isn't. Which explains why we can see colors and hear sounds in our dreams. When we dream our brain creates sounds and colors. In fact, the same parts of the brain fire to create those sounds and colors as when we are awake. That's why it is so important that we generally forget our dreams, *because they are confusable with reality.* So, to protect us from having lots of memories that we cannot tell if they are real or not, our brain washes hormones through itself to break down memories created while we sleep. Which is why we often have trouble remembering *actual* things that happen when we are woken up briefly in the middle of the night—our brain broke *all* memories down during that time period, including the real ones. *Why?* Because our brain can't tell the difference between a dream memory and a real memory!

Here is probably some of the best evidence I can give you . . . optical illusions. Specifically, the kind that appear to move. Like this one:

Looking at this image, and other illusions like it, may work because of a delay between the eye and the brain. Basically, it takes a fraction of a section for the eye to tell the brain what it sees. So, to prevent us from being behind all the time, the brain predicts what it *should see* (just like it does with the blind spot in both of our eyes). The result, is, though, that the brain sometimes finds out that it was wrong, so it auto-corrects . . . like when you see a stick on the ground and for a brief second you actually *see* a snake, only to realize it isn't. In the case of illusions like the above, the brain is actually wrong when it makes the correction, so it corrects back only to be told that it is wrong again by the eyes, so it switches back and forth. If this theory is true, the world that we "see" isn't in fact the direct "real" world but our brains' prediction of what the world will be. If this is true, then the world, as we see it, is just a creation of the mind that, with the help of sensory stimulus, tries to predict whatever is "out there."

The Sky within Your Eyes

Okay, I realize I might sound pretty desperate to make the crazy fantasy world sound possible. I'm going through a lot of trouble to say that there isn't all that much difference between dreams and reality, and Sarah's world is just supposed to be a dream, right? Why worry about it? We know, for example, that there is blue out in the world. We've seen it! Maybe the same parts of the brain fire when we see blue in our dream life, but that's only because we saw it, for real, when we are awake, right? Nope!

There are recent studies, and I encourage you to look them up because they are mind-blowing, that suggest that unless we have a word for a color we don't see the color. In fact, the color blue is one we experience only very recently as being distinct from green because we have only needed a word for blue recently since it is a very difficult pigment to actually physically produce. There are still people in the world today who live in cultures that do not use a word for "blue." If you show them objects that are green and blue and other colors and ask them to identify which objects are the same and which are different they will tell you that the blue and green one are the same color . . . as if they can't see the difference.

That seems especially silly, because we have always been around blue, right? Like Sarah in the labyrinth we can just look up and *see* the blue sky. So why would old cultures like the Greeks not have a word for blue and not identify blue? (Homer referred to the "wine-dark" sea in his writing, suggesting that the Greeks saw the ocean as closer to red). If there is so much blue sky over us, we would always need a word for "blue", yes? No. One scientist tried this experiment out when he had his baby daughter. As she grew up, he taught her all the color names, yes even "blue" but they never said to the child, "The sky is blue." So when she was old enough he took her out and asked her what color the sky was on a cloudless day . . . she wouldn't answer. He kept trying, and eventually her first answer was "white." . . . Even though she could identify the color blue on other objects, the sky seemed more white to her. We might similarly all think of it as "white" had we not been taught to think of it as "blue." The sky is, in fact, very close to being "white," when you think about it.

So what's the point? The point is this, if the things we perceive are in fact actually in our heads, colors, textures, tastes, and so on, then *objects really exist as ideas in our heads*. This would be why we have so much trouble telling that our dreams aren't real. Because the objects in our dreams look and *feel* as real as they do when we are awake. And our waking reality is one that is actually created inside our heads. Colors like blue exist only inside our mind, and we can't even be sure that other people's experience of blue is the same as ours, which might explain why some of us like some colors and some of us don't. So worlds that seem impossible, crazy, and dreamlike, like the world of *Labyrinth* might be more possible than we realize. If the world is only a creation of our minds, what's to stop us from believing that we could create, as just as real, any world in our minds?

As the World Falls Down

When we sleep we create a world that looks, tastes, smells, and feels just as real as our waking life. My favorite scene in *Labyrinth* is the ballroom scene, which, really is just a dream within a dream, if Sarah is just imagining the labyrinth in the first place. She dreams of a masquerade ball when she is under the spell of the evil fruit she eats, but eventually realized that time is running out and she must wake up to save her baby brother. The whole world collapses around her as she wakes, leaving only Jareth, there, alone.

I think that the collapse of the world around Jareth is something of a metaphor for death. Which probably makes this the best time to talk about a sensitive subject, the death of David Bowie. If I'm right, Mr. Bowie's experiences were creations of his brain just as Berkeley argued. For example, if he and I had met, Mr. Bowie's brain would have created, inside of his own mind, the colors, and textures, and perspectives that make me up. I wouldn't really know the "Nicolas Michaud" that David Bowie created, and when Mr. Bowie died, that Nicolas Michaud, those colors and textures created by David Bowie, would die too. In fact, the entire world as created by David Bowie, all of its colors, tastes, smells, textures, and sounds, would cease to exist when he passed away . . . the whole world would fall down.

If the world is created by our minds, then our world ceases to exist when we do. That sounds silly, because the world still exists now that Mr. Bowie is dead, and so do I, but *not the world as he created it*. What we have left is the world as we create it, and when we die, that whole world collapses too. No one else sees, hears, tastes, and experiences the world as you do, it is all inside your head, which means that your passing will be the death of an entire world.

The existence of the world as inside our heads would explain trippy experience pretty nicely. Think of what happens when people hallucinate—when they take a drug or do not get enough sleep. They start to see things that we do not see. The world begins to do strange and confusing things, because their brains are creating experiences in ways that it normally does not. In fact, the idea that one might "smell colors" or "see sounds" while tripping on acid is evidence to my idea. What this would mean is that while on that drug, the part of the brain that normally responds when the eyes send it a signal doesn't, and instead, the sound part of the brain responds. So when the person's eyes send the signal, the sound part of the brain creates a sound so they literally "hear colors" much the way people who have synesthesia seem to. But doesn't this also mean that I'm wrong? After all *we know* someone hallucinates because that person sees stuff that *isn't there*. The rest of us can see the world is not like their hallucination, so we know that they are not seeing "real things."

Lost and Lonely

I think the world that Jareth creates for Sarah in *Labyrinth* points to the problem that Berkeley's philosophy creates for us. He talks to her about how he has played with reality, even with time, to give her what she wants, yet that is not enough. No matter how he bends the world, he cannot get her to see it as he wishes. He will remain alone. Like their struggle within the Escher-like world, Sarah and Jared are forever separated by a twisted reality. I see this as a metaphor for our own lives. If it's true that we each create the world in our own minds, then it's not a shared world. Which would seem to be the best evidence against my thesis . . . don't we share our experiences?

I don't think we do. Consider two people in love. They might both be in love. We describe their feeling with the same word, and, yet, if we ask them to describe the feeling they might describe it differently. One might describe how comfortable they are with the other while the other describes their love as a feeling of nervousness "and butterflies in the stomach." Not only do we often experience "the same thing" as wildly different (think of two people who are in the same room, but one is cold and one is not), but even when we think we're experiencing the same thing, we probably are not. Clearly, Jareth and Sarah have a radically different experience of his expression of love.

Consider the following experiment (please try it out!) Fill three bowls with water . . . one cold, one warm and one room temperature. Put your right hand in the warm water, the left hand in the cold water and let them sit there for 60 seconds.

Then, place both hands in the room temperature water . . . *They will report different temperatures!* One hand will tell you that the water is warmer than the temperature the other hand is telling you. So we, even in ourselves, can be divided by the same experience. No wonder Sarah almost seems torn between wanting her brother gone and wanting him back.

It seems to me that it's even worse when it's a matter of color that we supposedly "agree" on. We each have a different brain, and eyes with different numbers of rods and cones. If the number of taste buds help cause the taste we experience (the more bitter taste buds we have the more bitter something tastes) then it only stands to reason that differencing number of rods and cones and "color reporting cells" in the eye would result in a different experience of color (In fact as we grow older, the UV rays that kill those cells in our eyes cause us to experience colors differently. We just don't notice because it is a slow progression). So even though we all point at the fire truck and say "red" that doesn't mean we're all seeing the same "red" we just all learned to call that experience "red" so when we see whatever it is we see we call it red. We don't have a way to compare the experience in our heads with the experience in other people's heads. Just like Jareth tells Sarah in the movie.

> **Sarah:** That's not fair!
>
> **Jareth:** You say that so often. I wonder what your basis for comparison is.

We have no way of knowing what's actually happening in the heads of other people.

In other words, we're alone in our creation of the world. My experience of "red," "bitter," and even "love" is likely different from everyone else's (though maybe similar) even though we use the same words to describe slightly different things. No one can even know what it is like to be me. I am trapped in the creation of my mind, like Sarah, but unlike her, never unable to leave. Though, when you think about it, at the end of the film we're happy to see all of her labyrinthian friends return to her . . . so maybe Sarah really never makes it out.

Dance, Magic, Dance

On a final note, things may not be all that bleak. Perhaps we're alone, but we do have incredible power. Like gods, we actually make the world of our experience. Perhaps it's only our own brains that limit us from having truly amazing experiences . . . just our imagination's wildness that limits us. Perhaps there's something to be said for being a child and not growing up and continuing to experience the amazing, and perhaps self-centered, reality of our own creation. In some ways, it's good that Sarah grows up and leaves that selfish child-life behind. But maybe she should have listened to Bowie-Jared and chosen to be a god in a world of her own creation. It does seem in the way that children are willing to embrace imagination as reality that if it is our minds that make the world, . . . it's the babes who have the power.

Bowie certainly did seem to choose to make the world as he saw fit. Whether through Ziggy Stardust or Jareth the Goblin King, Bowie created surreal worlds of magical possibility. I wonder if, perhaps, though we may be all stuck in worlds of our own creation, music may be one way we can reach out across the void to touch others. Certainly, David Bowie seemed to do so, and, in many ways continues to speak to us across a much greater darkness reminding us, like Major Tom, to never stop reaching out, even if it is only into the dark.[1]

---

[1] This chapter is for Chris.

III

The Bowie Identity

9
When Jumpin' Jack Flash Met Ziggy Stardust

RANDALL E. AUXIER

David Bowie created the persona of the Thin White Duke by adjusting the character of Thomas Jerome Newton, which was the "Earth identity" of *The Man Who Fell to Earth*. That alien visitor was an adjusted Starman, which is who he was before he came to meet us and blew our minds.

The Starman in his turn was the leper Messiah, Ziggy making love with his ego and sucked up into his mind, and of course, Ziggy was Major Tom's return, altered by his existential crisis. After the Duke we have a run of aliens and misfits who pleased us, but by then we knew what to expect. Through the whole run, Mick Jagger was an unsatisfied Jumpin' Jack. He changed costumes and pranced outrageously, but he was always Mick and nothing other—and not just Mick but, more importantly, the lead singer of the Stones, which is about all the public will allow him to be.

It's well documented that between the advent of Ziggy and the time he put to bed the persona of the Thin White Duke, Bowie was, well, pretty close to being psychotic. He was apparently having difficulty in finding David beneath all the characters he played. One thing they all had in common was a lot of drugs. And somewhere in there, just before Ziggy died, he met Mick Jagger in the flesh, having known Mick's persona for many years already. Mick now claims he can't remember when he met David Bowie (see Jagger's

"Tribute" to Bowie), but I think he does. Mick and David had boxed the London compass, keeping tabs on each other since Bowie's real breakthrough in 1972 with the rise of Ziggy. Before that Bowie would not have been so much as a blip on Mick's keen radar. Bowie was chugging in a fleet with Gary Glitter and Mark Bolan and a dozen other Jagger-wannabe's. Mick and his crew had pioneered and perfected the androgyny angle and there wasn't much they hadn't tried in costume and stage sets by 1971.

Mick was dismissive of the whole crew of imitators, and that was fair enough, but Bowie caught his discerning eye, in much the way Mick had caught Andy Warhol's eye a few years earlier. It takes one to know one, you might say. For the youth of America, 1967 was the Summer of Love, but for Jagger and Bowie, the magical interlude was 1973, and it lasted a full year. They were inseparable that year, and like the first dozen Disciples, they held all things in common, including wives, if one can believe what rock journalists and ex-wives say.

It ended, apparently, when Mick bragged to David that the Stones' next album cover art would be done by the new and fashionable Guy Peellaert. Bowie immediately hired the man for *Diamond Dogs* and beat the Stones to press by four months, and with one of the most outrageous covers in Rock history. Bowie claimed in an interview that Mick should have known better than to show him something new. By the time Peellaert's William Blake burlesque appeared on the cover of *It's Only Rock'n'Roll*, it was old news.

This was an interesting and problematic love affair, and instructive.

Street Fighting Men

Let's begin this story with a third party. Angie Bowie has had a good bit to say about this epoch, but I found a different source that is more philosophically interesting. I learned from Keith Richards's autobiography that (Sir) Mick Jagger envied David Bowie. That fact became a sort of embarrassment to Keith. Looking into it, I found that Keith had been harping on this point as early as 1980 (see Alan Cayson's book on Mick). Here's what Keith had to say in 2010:

> Mick got very big ideas. All lead singers do. It's a known affliction called LVS, lead vocalist syndrome. . . . If you combine LVS with a nonstop bombardment of flattery every waking moment over years and years, you can start to believe the incoming. . . . And even if you don't completely believe it, you say, well, everybody else does—I'll roll with it. You forget that it's just part of the job. It's amazing how even quite sensible people like Mick Jagger could get carried away by it. Actually believe they were special. (*Life*, pp. 455–56)

It takes significant ego strength to disbelieve your own press, whether it's good or bad, but perhaps good press is harder to rise above since it feels like you don't *need* to rise above it. Bad press must be met with strength and perseverance by any who endure it, but everyone knows that. Not everyone knows about how praise can destroy a person's sense of perspective and, in the end, also a person's confidence.

The trouble is that whatever modicum of reality you hang onto, it isn't enough to help you take the true measure of either the flatterers or the critics, and those are the only two kinds of people yapping. Some of what they say is true, but how much and which parts? Of course, you *could* trust your oldest friends, but Mick had already discounted in advance anything Keith might tell him and had, in fact, lost respect for Keith, thinking the man simply a fool with a guitar, albeit, one he needed. If Mick underestimated Keith (and he did), he had been given plenty of reason to do so. Why should he be chained to this chump?

But over here was this bright, shiny, beautiful Bowie thing. Keith continues:

> Mick had become uncertain, he had started second guessing his own talent—that seemed, ironically, to be at the root of the self-inflation. For many years through the 60s, Mick was incredibly

> charming and humorous. He was a natural. . . . Somewhere, though, he got unnatural. . . . He forgot his natural rhythm. . . . Whatever somebody else was doing was far more interesting to him than what he was doing. He even began to act as if he wanted to be someone else. Mick is quite competitive, and he started to get competitive about other bands. He watched what David Bowie was doing and wanted to do it. Bowie was a major, major attraction. Somebody had taken Mick on in the costume and bizarreness department. (p. 456)

Far be it from me to question, but I think Keith, so comfortable in his own skin and not feeling the pressure Mick had to deal with being out front, doesn't quite get Bowie and the *why* of this rivalry. What *Keith* saw was "Oh, someone wants to try to compete with you in wardrobe, Mick!" But Mick knew very well that more was going on. Bowie wasn't putting on costumes; he was creating art personas. Mick wanted to do that, or at least imagined he did. Keith finishes the rant thus:

> But the fact is, Mick could deliver ten times more than Bowie in just a T-shirt and a pair of jeans, singing "I'm a Man." Why would you want to be anyone else if you're Mick Jagger? Is being the greatest entertainer in show business not enough? He forgot that it was he who was new, who created and set the trends in the first place, for years. It's fascinating. I can't figure it out. It's almost as if Mick was aspiring to be Mick Jagger, chasing his own phantom. (p. 456)

How can Mick Jagger seriously envy anyone? But the rules of life include the one that says, *whoever* you are, you'll think someone else has it better. But this is more than that. This is about how to hold the top when you're at it. Fame is fleeting—fifteen minutes or so. You have to zig when the rest zag to hold the attention of the fickle public and Bowie was zigging like no one before him, and everyone but Keith Richards knew it.

Mick had to make sure not to zag, and that was his job, not Keith's. In a 1965 interview someone asked Jagger how long he expected to be doing what he was doing. He earnestly answered that he never imagined two years ago he'd still be doing it in the present, and then he surmised "maybe two more years." He was painfully aware of how quickly these things fade. It's easy for Keith to say after fifty years of success, "C'mon Mick, you're the man." It's fair for Mick to point at Bowie and answer "Only because I was paying attention while you, you were just speedballing. . . and you're welcome, *Keith*."

So, Bowie and Jagger became intimates, for pleasure and for utility. But they weren't making common cause. Keep your friends close and your competitors closer, right? This involves not only sharing the same bed, but seeing whether you can dislodge the other guy's favorite lover. Christopher Anderson goes so far as to claim that Bowie himself, and not his wife Angie, was the inspiration for Jagger's song "Angie." There may have been love between Jagger and Bowie. The consensus of the rock rags is that there was almost assuredly sex. For the scandal sheet version of it, see Anderson's *Jagger Unauthorized*, pp. 286–291, or Leigh's *Bowie: The Biography*, Chapter 4.

But it may have been as much a street fight as a love fest.

God Knows I'm Good

It isn't easy to create ethics from an aesthetic, or a series of them. The woes of Oscar Wilde are certainly an instructive case, and the lesson is embodied in his masterpiece *The Picture of Dorian Gray*. Somewhere in some attic is a picture of Bowie that looks like Keith Richards. But he maintained his youth to the end, didn't he?

There are numerous philosophers who have issued stern and lengthy warnings about taking the aesthetic path in life, most famously in Søren Kierkegaard's *Either/Or*, Volume 1, which is the diary of a seducer. But most celebrity artists will not be vulnerable to such moralizing. Why, they will demand, should I not follow the lead of my senses and of what people want and demand of me? Is this not a kind of irresistible "imperative"?

The answer is made more difficult considering that if we had no bodily senses, no capacity for pleasure and pain, how could we ever learn right from wrong? We're animals following our natures. If that isn't the basis of right and wrong, then our Creator has a diabolical twist in fashioning us with such strong drives and then telling us that to be worthy before Him we must not act on them. What sort of morality is *that*, pray tell?

Thus, most who choose the aesthetic path to a moral life do not have any truck with the Western God. Buddhism or various Hindu disciplines are more popular, since the point is to be mindful of your spiritual development and aware of what's beyond your control, to learn compassion, and learn to resign the world. This ethic is easier to grasp from the standpoint of a celebrity artist.

Unfortunately, however, there's not enough guidance here for successful and deep relationships with other people, especially those who, shall we say, live mainly under the veil of Maya. Sometimes this word is translated as "illusion," but my scholar friends tell me that is a bad rendering. They then reject every other suggestion I make about how to translate it and inform me that I'll need to spend the rest of my life learning Sanskrit or Pali or some other language I could never master. You've probably had the same lecture from someone at some point. But I don't think Mick and David can learn it either, if I can't. That doesn't cut out their sense of a spiritual requirement of living that grows from what they do best—cultivate the senses (they are musicians, after all)—and reaches into the sorts of happiness and stable relationships and friendships they crave.

Bowie and Jagger were attracted to Buddhism and evidently variously practiced it. I think we can safely say that Jagger's 1971 conversion to Roman Catholicism was a phase. The danger with passing straight from an aesthetic, a style, a way of approaching pleasure and pain, and straight to spirituality is that the progress, whatever it may be, seems to carry very little in the way of social or political advice. Compassion, yes, but justice? Wisdom of the ages, yes, but aptitude in negotiating interpersonal conflicts? "This too shall pass" seems universally true but not so very practical.

Can't Help Thinking about Me

Is there something more out there that isn't just hackneyed claptrap about "To *have* a friend, *be* a friend" and other pop psychology crap? Yes. There is something worth considering, but it requires that we change our expectations about the relationship between *morality* and *ethics*. These two concepts are not "friends" to one another; they are something closer to mortal enemies, as I will explain. I don't endorse this view, but I find it very difficult to ignore, and very helpful in understanding what happens between people like Bowie and Jagger, with each other and with their intimates, in so far as they have intimates.

The distinction between morality and ethics goes back to Immanuel Kant (1724–1804) who grounded *morality* in "sensus communis," or common sense, that we carry with us on account of being a peculiar kind of sociable being who is *also* deeply unsocial; and, on the other side, *ethics* is the necessity of using our rational powers to recognize those rules and imperatives which conform our *wills* to our *duty*. This is just the sort of thing that led Bowie to write in his very first single with The Lower Third, that he had to leave home, head bowed in shame because he brought dishonor on the family name and the neighbors are talking, so he'll just start walking. This is a relentless wedding of morality and ethics that leaves him trembling in his bed every Sunday night after church. He hates it.

But morality and ethics, are actually fitted to one another, Kant claimed, and they encourage our "autonomy" as moral actors in the world. We give ourselves the moral law and conform, conform, conform. Sounds like Hell doesn't it? Kant also recognized the inevitability of conflict. He saw the conflicts, especially wars and the like, as engines of human moral progress, regrettable but needed, as our common sense gradually rises to the level of our rational understanding.

Don't Lean on Me Man

Simone de Beauvoir (1908–1986) thought this sort of view was, if you'll pardon my French, *merde*. She framed an alternative which casts some light on Bowie and Jagger—I don't say a flattering light, but it has the feel of authenticity. The ethic embraces ambiguity as its central idea—ethical life is not going to become perfectly clear for us when we don't pretend to others and to ourselves about what we really are and what we really want. The effects are pretty far-reaching. As she says, "the concrete consequences of existentialist ethics is the rejection of all previous justifications which might be drawn from the civilization, the age, and the culture; it is the rejection of every principle of authority" (*The Ethics of Ambiguity*, p. 142).

Rejecting every principle of authority seems like the opposite of ethics, but not in Beauvoir's world. Rather, such independence is a condition of living an ethical life. It was a thing back in the day. The paradox of human existence is this: the humans "know themselves to be the supreme end to which all action should be subordinated, but the exigencies of action force them to treat one another as instruments or obstacles, as means. The more widespread their mastery of the world, the more they find themselves crushed by uncontrollable forces" (p. 9). This well describes the dilemma of those who conquer the world aesthetically—the more they love you, the tighter is their grip on your inner being. The life of a celebrity artist is the opposite of free.

Beauvoir was herself a celebrity in the second half of her life. Her friends called her "*Castor*," which means "beaver." The public story is that she was always working. The private story is that the nickname had something to do with sex. But then, that's just people talking, right? She was a highly visible public figure (although "notorious" might be a better word than visible), and she knew a good deal about what that entails. Beauvoir's lifelong relationship with Jean-Paul Sartre posed a problem both to the world and to each of the persons so related. They had *cachet*, to be sure. They were cool intellectuals in a country that makes rock stars of philosophers. As far as I can remember, France hasn't contributed a single popular musician to the rock genre whose name could be recognized in the English-speaking world, but they gave us Foucault and Derrida, and if those aren't pop legends, along with Sartre and Beauvoir, no one is.

Beauvoir and Sartre were almost forty years ahead of Bowie and Jagger, but they did live to see glam rock—Sartre died in 1980 and Beauvoir in 1986. I don't think they noticed Bowie, but I'm fairly sure they would have taken note of the Rolling Stones. The Stones were hard to ignore, and they often lived in France. But Beauvoir and Sartre were breaking rules, and more sacred ones, long before Bowie and Jagger dreamed of androgeny and bisexuality. Beauvoir had a habit of seducing her young female students, and the younger the better, and then passing them to Sartre. She lost her teaching license in France for doing that, and *before* the Second World War at that—not the most open-minded time in history. If Angie and David had a *ménage à trois* on the night before their wedding, well, the Beaver and the Bug-eye were serially deflowering the *parents* of the generation seduced by the Bowies. Beaver and Bugs worked their whole lives to abolish the age of sexual consent in France.

A woman with credentials like this might have something interesting to tell us about the love and rivalry between Jagger and Bowie, especially since she had a similar struggle with the formidable Sartre, which could serve as a measuring rod (forgive the image) for almost any Bohemian intimacies. She says: "Man, Sartre tells us, is 'a being who makes himself a lack of being in order that there might be being' . . . his passion is not inflicted upon him from without. He chooses it. It is his very being and, as such, does not imply the idea of unhappiness" (p. 11).

That is a mouthful. It means that when you hollow yourself out in order to be what you have chosen, don't go making it someone else's problem. If you want to be ethical, own your freedom, accept your own choices and stop blaming the world for your inability to be satisfied. All of this cashes out in two ideas: "bad faith" is the condition of people who keep evading the absolute responsibility of their own choices; and "authenticity" is the condition of those who can own their own freedom, make themselves before others without guilt and without justifying anything to anyone. Such is Beauvoir's ambiguous world, and such is the world inhabited by the likes of Jagger and Bowie. The more powerful they were, the less the world could tell them what to do, and the less power the world had over them, the more raw and free was their encounter with one another. Neither was hollowed out for the world except as he had so chosen, and both knew it in the other.

Queen Bitch

In spring of 1973, and in the springtime of their year of passion, Jagger invited Bowie to the Stones concert in Newcastle, paid for the hotel, with the champagne, the roses, and all the implied control that goes with treating a new arrival on the doorstep of celebrity as your bitch. Bowie went, but not to be subjugated. Christopher Anderson tells the story thus:

> In the middle of "Jumpin' Jack Flash" Jagger noticed a sudden surge in the audience. Looking over his shoulder, he caught sight of Bowie hovering stage left, his trademark orange mane in clear view. Stagehands acted quickly to move Bowie out of sight, and all eyes were once again on Jagger. (p. 288, and see Clayson, p. 127)

That was when Jumpin' Jack Flash really met Ziggy Stardust. Bowie killed Ziggy and fired the Spiders from Mars two months later. It was unimaginable. Mick couldn't do that—as Bowie well knew. And that was when Mick began to speak openly about a solo album.

Philosophers are not journalists. I can't pretend to be a historian or a documenter and purveyor of facts at that level. I don't know these people and I don't know the people who know the people who know them. But how can we not find this relationship fascinating? Surely it means something philosophical from which we can all learn. I suspect that

Mick's failure to extricate himself from the Rolling Stones is his great vexation. Bowie fired his band. And he took on one persona after another. Mick is and always will be the lead singer for the Rolling Stones. He will not be a performance artist, he is to us an outrageous singer and, as Keith rightly notes, the greatest entertainer in the business—but there you have it: "entertainer." He is not an actor, a painter, an artist of any kind. He is, rather, the singer, and I mean *the* singer.

Is that enough? Keith thinks it should be. But Bowie was more, and quite a bit more than a singer. If he fell short of Andy Warhol as an art celebrity, well, he didn't fall short of anyone in rock'n'roll, as an artist. But as a performer, is he Jagger's equal? Never. No way. We may not know Jagger, but we know that *only* he is Jagger. For Bowie, we don't know him, but he is only as good as his next idea, or, in the present, his last idea: Lazarus.

The man defeated Jagger in the rivalry by making his death into a persona. That was authentically Bowie. Jagger had no recourse but bad faith. In his tribute to Bowie in *Rolling Stone* magazine, he represents Bowie as a junior colleague who copied him, the Great Mick Jagger, sometimes. Then Jagger expresses regret that they grew apart. Bowie had said something similar in a number of places. But they really *had to* grow apart.

Hell is other people, and they had caught a glimpse of the faker in one another, if not in themselves, and both were, well, they were much too fast to take that test.

10
David Bowie and Death

MICHAEL K. POTTER AND CAM COBB

Reviewing *Blackstar*, Bowie's last artistic will and testament, Jody Rosen reported that the songs "serve up a veritable Grand Guignol of dread, death, even dismemberment."

Although the context in which the songs were written might suggest to those who don't know Bowie that he was finally forced to confront the inevitable, *Blackstar* was merely the last step in a lifelong lyrical preoccupation. From his very first album to his mature meditation on his own demise in *Blackstar* (2016), David Bowie explored the theme of ambivalence in relation to identity, love, joy, technology, and most consistently, death.

Ambivalence

We experience ambivalence when we simultaneously feel contradictory emotions (or attitudes) toward or about something. We feel torn, pulled in more than one direction, unable to commit to or accept one emotional reaction or the other. In its most noteworthy forms, ambivalence can be a recognition that a situation or phenomenon is too complex to permit commitment to one particular attitude. Sometimes, the more information we have about a situation or person, the more ambivalence we tend to feel.

David Bowie's songs display a deep ambivalence about death. Throughout his career, David Bowie's lyrics explored seven different interpretations of death, as:

an evil to be feared,

a source of social unity,

something to be absurdly defied,

a revelatory event,

an inevitability that must be accepted,

a transition between forms, and

a signifier of human singularity.

Each of these involves different emotions connected to different desires and impulses, some more ambivalent than others. Bowie's approach fits very well with twentieth-century philosopher Bertrand Russell's understanding of these matters. Russell sees ambivalence as the primary psychological force, *the principle of growth*, "an instinctive urgency" leading desires and impulses in "a certain direction, as trees seek the light" (*Principles of Social Reconstruction*, p. 19).

Bowie's first major hit, "Space Oddity" (from *Space Oddity*, 1969) exemplifies the interpretation of *death as an evil to be feared*. In this song, Bowie inhabits the persona of Major Tom, doomed to die alone in space. The song begins hopefully as Major Tom prepares for his trip into the unknown, driven by an impulse to explore. It seems to be creative, a motivation to see and experience new things, perhaps to create new knowledge for the world. After liftoff, Ground Control compliments him on his bravery and newly-earned celebrity. Once he reaches space, however, he is overcome by feelings of helplessness and insignificance that at first resemble awe. Whatever sense of power he may have had in his—and his species's—ability to reach beyond planetary limits, it pales in comparison to the vastness of space.

Awe quickly transforms into apprehensions of doom and loneliness, contradictions not only of the common human desire to feel and be seen as important, meaningful, and powerful, but also of the desire to feel connected to other human beings. This sense of doom seems prescient once Ground Control informs him that there's something wrong with the spacecraft. He is forever alone and will die in space, unable to communicate with anyone back on Earth. And there's nothing he can do?

Or is there? When the Major Tom character is revisited eleven years later in "Ashes to Ashes" from *Scary Monsters* (1980), we are treated to a somber scene of a different sort. As it happens, Major Tom was able to reinstate contact with Ground Control—"They got a message from the Action Man: I'm happy. Hope you're happy, too," he tells them, an odd sentiment that reveals something unsettling about Major Tom's state of mind. The impulse toward love (which Russell characterizes as creative) and desire for human connection seems to have kept him alive, prompting him to use his outward will to overcome whatever difficulties his spacecraft encountered and enter into an unspecified behavior-cycle that would bring him home. Here, as elsewhere (see, for example, "As the World Falls Down" from *Labyrinth*, 1986), love is contextualized in terms of doom, as something that happens when the world is dying and order is disintegrating.

But then we encounter Major Tom after he's returned to Earth. Since then, he has become a wreck, a junkie drowning in despair, unable to cope with the modern world. Despite his best efforts, he can neither kick his drug habit nor the alienation and dread that led him to it. His drugs are the one "valuable friend" he has left, seductively telling him, "I'm happy. Hope you're happy, too." He's consumed by regret, facing his inevitable death alone. The desire for connection was never satisfied, so the suffering that may have motivated Major Tom to keep fighting when he was trapped in space continues, leading to inescapable decline.

In these two songs, we see a complex interplay of desires and impulses at work. Although Bowie returns to some of these in his other interpretations of death, "Space Oddity" is the only song in his catalogue that unequivocally treats death as an evil to be feared—and "Ashes to Ashes" is the only song that deals with the potential consequences of that fear. Fear of death may be understood as the emotional counterpart of a defensive possessive impulse, which leads us to cling to life. At times this impulse is necessary and probably good. But in some cases it merely prolongs or worsens suffering, as it did for Major Tom.

I Never Thought I'd Need So Many People

Yet Major Tom also exhibited a desire for love and connection with others, a desire that Bowie explores from a different perspective in his interpretation of death as a *source of social unity* from his most popular and celebrated album, *The Rise and Fall of Ziggy Stardust and the Spiders from Mars* (1972). The album opens with "Five Years," a prophecy of global destruction delivered by the titular character, Ziggy Stardust.

Upon learning of the impending apocalypse five years in the future, the doomed humans react in disparate and contradictory ways. Mothers sigh, broadcasters weep, some turn to violence, some turn inward. Ziggy observes how death unites people despite their differences, as he and they find some solace in their shared fear.

People still react toward death with fear in "Five Years," which indicates that Bowie still recognizes that the possessive impulse to hold on to life is difficult for human beings to escape. But it is presented in a less straightforward fashion here, for despair is quickly replaced by something more positive, a creative impulse toward celebration and unity. As "Five Years" transitions into the rest of the album, Bowie, in the persona of Ziggy Stardust, treats the death of the world and everyone in it as an excuse to celebrate and live as you wish. We have five years until we're all dead, he rationalizes, so let's enjoy life while it lasts. There also seems to be a desire at work; the desire to enjoy life while it lasts works with the creative impulse toward celebration and unity to control what might otherwise be overwhelming fear. *Ziggy Stardust* ends with "Rock'n'Roll Suicide" in which Bowie returns to the unity and overcoming of difference brought about by impending death, repeatedly crying out: "you're not alone."

Here I Am, Not Quite Dying

The contextualization of love in terms of impending doom, and the emotional response of facing death by committing to life, continue in Bowie's interpretation of *death as something to be absurdly defied*. "Heroes" from *"Heroes"* (1977) combines Bowie's ambivalence toward death with his ambivalence toward love in the tale of doomed lovers who rise to "heroism" (note the scare quotes around the title of the song and album) in an absurd, doomed defiance of their impending destruction.

There is tension throughout the song between irony and sincerity. Although he claims in the first stanza that "We can beat them, just for one day / we can be Heroes, just for one day", the song gives the lie to these claims, at least in a sincere and literal sense. Because the lovers know they're doomed, they can poke fun at what would have been the inevitable decline of their relationship into anomie and bitterness; they will give in to their creative impulse to love nevertheless.

Death is defied in an angrier and more straightforward manner on Bowie's "comeback album," *The Next Day* (2013), which opens with the title track. While defying death, Bowie ridicules the religious authorities who derive power from exploiting the human fear of mortality. Bowie's scream-chant, "Here I am / Not quite dying" becomes the rallying cry of the masses, who, by confronting and spitting in the face of their mortality, alternately participate in a lynching directed by the clergy, then regain their power and self-control, revolting against their theocratic masters.

As it did for the earthlings from *Ziggy Stardust*, death has brought humanity together, this time in defiant rebellion rather than celebration. The creative impulse to love, and the expression of both inward and outward will in service of a desire to determine the courses of their own lives is complicated in "The Next Day" because the impulse is under-controlled. There are indications that the formerly subjugated may have lynched their former masters. Here we see the ambivalence that lies deep within Russell's moral psychology, in the principle of growth itself.

According to Russell, the precise nature of each person's principle of growth is unique, and is the source of whatever potential excellence lies within each person. Although the principle of growth leads each of us toward self-realization, the journey to that destination is fraught with ambivalence, due to the nature of desires and impulses.

Impulses are our most common motivators, unreasoned "erratic and anarchical" instinctive drives toward certain kinds of activities (*Principles of Social Reconstruction*, p. 31). They simply *are*, basic drives that we possess as living beings. Although the principle of growth itself pushes us toward self-realization, it is blind. Consequently, some of our impulses prevent us from reaching our potential, which we don't always recognize.

Desires, on the other hand, are self-interested longings for things we do not yet have, or states of affairs that do not yet exist. The key difference between desires and impulses is that, unlike impulses, desires are tied to a purpose, something that is supposed to satisfy them. These desires can be conscious or unconscious. *Conscious* desires are those states of longing accompanied by true beliefs regarding what will satisfy them. However, *unconscious* desires, accompanied by false beliefs about the purposes or satisfactory ends, are more common (*Analysis of Mind*, p. 76). A moment's reflection is enough to remind us that we are often wrong about what will satisfy us.

Although the people in Bowie's "The Next Day" have made strides toward self-realization by affirming their autonomy and defying death, their emancipation may have necessitated some brutality toward their former oppressors. Seeing this complicates our own emotional appraisal of the principle of growth—and of self-realization as an ultimate end. Is it good? Is it bad? Russell—and Bowie—will not answer for us.

Knowledge Comes with Death's Release

"The Next Day" alludes to humanity's rebellion against God in Eden, when Adam and Eve, by eating the fruit that provided knowledge, defied God's wish to keep them ignorant and under his thumb. Had humanity not rebelled against God, it would always be powerless. Bowie's interpretation of *death as a revelatory event* takes this idea even further, while eschewing the value of self-realization in life. On "Quicksand," from *Hunky Dory* (1971), Bowie writes of death's potential to provide us, finally, with knowledge, and perhaps power. Amidst verses that speak of power, knowledge, and the realization of dreams just over the horizon, the chorus repeatedly tells us, "Don't believe in yourself / Don't deceive with belief / Knowledge comes / with deaths release." This idea appeals to him because he knows, to some extent, that the paths to power he's been pursuing are unpromising, perhaps because they require more from him than he is capable of.

There's some ambivalence toward this power as well ("I'm frightened by the total goal"), perhaps due to the realization that he has sought the selfish sort of power coveted by the people he name-checks in the song: Aleister Crowley, Heinrich Himmler, Winston Churchill, the Nietzschean *Übermensch*, and the ephemeral power of Hollywood's Golden Age stars (such as Greta Garbo and Brigitte Bardot). The desire for power, as we mentioned earlier, is perpetually unsatisfiable, an aggressive, possessive impulse uncontrolled by will and thus contributing to constant suffering. Throughout the song, Bowie is torn and ambivalent; he's aware of the danger of seeking the power he wants, yet his aversion to it is motivated not by consideration of its effects on him and others, but by fear of failure.

He returns to these ideas in "We Are the Dead" from *Diamond Dogs* (1974). The enlightened ones, the people Bowie identifies with in this song, are ostracized and scapegoated. Their lives are difficult, but Bowie urges them to keep fighting. Yet, literally or metaphorically, their enlightenment is owed to death. Does death bring knowledge, does knowledge bring death, or is it both? Bowie will not commit to one answer. Either way, he implies a connection between death and the desire for knowledge.

The desire for knowledge here could be viewed as an uncontrolled expression of a possessive impulse to know, a view of knowledge as something to be acquired and retained. That may be the dangerous approach to knowledge that connects it to death, as opposed to knowledge as a creative impulse to bring new information and understanding into the world. But we may be led astray by our tendency to view death as an evil, which this sort of interpretation presupposes. Bowie may be asserting, instead, that death is a good, whether the reward of enlightenment, or merely the means to it.

The Heart's Filthy Lesson

The most common interpretation of death that we find in Bowie's lyrics is that *death is an inevitability that must be accepted.* Reflecting on the inevitability of death sometimes causes Bowie to cast his gaze backwards to the past, as he does in "Heathen" from *Heathen* (2002), in which he faces the transience of life and inevitability of death with calm resolve, and "Thursday's Child" from . . . *Hours* (1999), in which he reviews his life with regret: "All of my life I've tried so hard / Doing my best with what I had / Nothing much happened all the same." Yet, amidst the regret and disappointment that fills the song, he finds something positive in his memories, notably experiences of love: "Only for you I don't regret / That I was Thursday's child". The love between him and his unnamed partner helps him regain a childlike sense of optimism: "Lucky old sun is in my sky / Nothing prepared me for your smile / Lighting the darkness of my soul / Innocence in your arms."

In the aptly-named "Reality" from *Reality* (2003), he again accepts his fate, this time with an air of emotionlessness. There is a sense, in "Reality," that he wants to approach death without bias, unwilling to allow any emotion to color his understanding.

The art-murder masterpiece *1. Outside* (1995) deals with death in several different ways. "I Have Not Been to Oxford Town," a song presented as funereal chant, returns to the death of the world, a topic we found in "Five Years," "As the World Falls Down," and "Heroes." Its refrain accepts the inevitability of death even as its mournful tune laments and mourns it. There is an element of fatalism in these lyrics. Although it could never have been otherwise, death comes for us because of the choices we have made: "And the prison priests are decent / My attorney seems sincere / I fear my days are numbered / Lord get me out of here." What is this prison in which Bowie finds himself? It is life, or, at least, life in the twentieth century. The death of the twentieth century may not be the death of the world, but rather a transition into a new century that could be better—or worse. This transition, whatever its degree of apocalyptic destruction, is inevitable. "And the wheels are turning and turning / As the twentieth-century dies." The century must die. All things pass.

The lead single and key song from the *1.Outside*, "The Hearts Filthy Lesson," is a sneering condemnation at times, a frantic plea at others. In a promotional film for the album, Bowie explained that "The filthy lesson in question is the fact that life is finite. That realization, when it comes, usually later in life, can either be a really daunting prospect or it makes things a lot clearer." Bowie here is full of longing and regret, contextualized by the album's theme of a detective attempting to solve a case of art-murder. Is it art? Is it murder? Is it artistic murder? There is constant ambiguity.

Although no other album in Bowie's catalogue is as devoutly ambivalent as this one, "The Hearts Filthy Lesson," itself, is rather straightforward: the lesson "falls upon deaf ears", it ends our lives ("if there was only some kind of future"), it imposes itself mercilessly ("I'm already five years older; I'm already in my grave"). Confronting it is a necessity from which we turn away. The song urges us to confront and accept the inevitable, though we may need help doing so. "Will you carry me? Oh Paddy, I think I've lost my way." Later, Bowie attempts to find death in our inevitable destruction: "What a fantastic death abyss . . . Tell the others". If we can find this beauty, let us share it. On "Never Get Old" from *Reality* (2003) he mocks his fears, and the delusions they create when we refuse to face them. Refusing to accept death leads us into undignified delusion.

"How Does the Grass Grow?" recognizes that all growth, all extant life is dependent on death—in the food that sustains us and in the lives that were sacrificed to build our societies. Not only is death inevitable, our dependence on death is also inevitable. Since the present is always dependent on the exploitation of those who once lived, we are all standing on the shoulders of corpses. Reflecting on a graveyard near what was once a battlefield, Bowie contrasts the death and suffering that characterizes the area with the more positive memories he has in the same space. "That's where we made our trysts / And struggled with our guns / Would you still love me / If the clocks could go backwards / The girls would fill with blood and / The grass would be green again." He is even ambivalent about the valor of the dead, in contrast to the popular tendency to glorify the departed: "Remember the dead / They were so great / Some of them."

"You Feel So Lonely You Could Die" wishes death upon someone who has wronged many people in the past, who has so far got way with his crimes. Death is inevitable, Bowie warns. It will come for you—you cannot escape forever. The inevitability of death is the great equalizer. Eventually, all must submit.

The ambivalence within this interpretation of death is complex. Emotionally, it is torn between love, dignity, resentment, contemplativeness, fear, and resignation—and Bowie's confrontation with these emotions relies on acceptance to tie them all together. To accept the inevitable, after all, involves accepting our own responses to it, expressing them, and moving on. If there is a dominant impulse here, it would be the creative impulse to make meaning, an ongoing process from which we can't escape, which is both continually satisfied and never satisfied. We may treat it as a desire as well, in which case we would need to acknowledge that its purpose will never be fully achieved. Any satisfaction we feel is likely to be temporary, readily replaced by more suffering. But that is temporary as well. Endlessly.

Just Like That Bluebird, Oh I'll Be Free

But what is death? This brings us to Bowie's interpretation of *death as a transition between forms*. His final album, *Blackstar* (2016) is an artistic last will and testament in which death is front-and-center. This is obvious in "Lazarus," the final single, which was released two days before his death. "Lazarus" opens with "Look up here, I'm in heaven / I've got scars that can't be seen." Bowie imagines himself dying and floating away, with wry humor and acceptance. He imagines dropping his cellphone as he floats away, adding, "Ain't that just like me". Yet he is unafraid. "This way or no way / You know, I'll be free / Just like that bluebird / Now ain't that just like me / Oh I'll be free / Just like that bluebird / Oh I'll be free / Ain't that just like me."

In "Love is Lost," Bowie appears to be speaking of the transition from one form of life to another. In it, there is the death of one's former self. The first verse implies that he's speaking of the transition into celebrity, as he was twenty-two years old when "Space Oddity" was released: "It's the darkest hour, you're twenty-two / The voice of youth, the hour of dread." And celebrity doesn't banish old fears and concerns; it may even magnify them: "Your country's new / Your friends are new / Your house and even your eyes are new / Your maid is new and your accent too / But your fear is as old as the world." Ultimately, the fear of death is inescapable, and the experience of constant change, even when embraced, is the experience of constant death. What was dies and is replaced by what is, endlessly. "Oh, what have you done?" Bowie repeats as the song reaches its climax, then continues repeating it until it ends.

Here we should look back and remind ourselves of all the different identities Bowie has assumed—not just the outward, named identities that he adopted and discarded during his career, but the identities he assumes in his songs. Bowie usually writes lyrics in the first-person, but often sings from the perspectives of characters in these lyrics. Bowie was constantly playing with this interpretation of death, in other words, inventing identities and killing them off so he could transition into new ones. There was a creative impulse toward self-creation here, and one toward uninhibited exploration of ideas. But what's most remarkable is the lack of a possessive impulse to retain those ideas, except for the period after *Let's Dance* (1983), when he learned that trying to hold on to an identity after it was supposed to die could destroy the creative impulses that led to its inception.

Even "David Bowie" was a character, a meta-character he played for many years who often assumed other identities of his own. David Jones, the human being, remained masked by David Bowie, the celebrity rock star.

I'm a Blackstar

Reflections on celebrity infuse Bowie's final interpretation of *death as a signifier of human singularity*, which is found on Bowie's last two albums. "The Stars (Are Out Tonight)" suggests that through celebrity we can appear to transcend death—"Stars are never sleeping / Dead ones and the living"—but we covet the illusion of immortality that celebrities possess, which leads us to drag the stars down into the gutter. Because that immortality was only ever an illusion, even the stars don't really have it, and we can never attain it. We want the stars to be like us, yet unlike us. "We live closer to the Earth / Never to the heavens / The stars are never far away / Stars are out tonight." Our attitudes toward celebrities are conflicted and ambivalent, tainted by envy and resentment.

The stars reflect on what the public believes about them: "And they know just what we do / That we toss and turn at night / They're waiting to make their moves / But the stars are out tonight." They're afraid. Of what? Of having their own illusions stripped away? "They burn you with their radiant smiles / Trap you with their beautiful eyes / They're broke and shamed or drunk or scared / But I hope they live forever."

Here, clear as day, Bowie lays out the rationale behind David Jones's creation of "David Bowie," even if it's a retroactive rationale. Bowie, celebrity rock star, can bear those envies and resentments, while Jones maintains his distance. Jones himself may count himself among the masses who covet the illusory immortality of celebrity, or who covet the appearance of it.

The title track from *Blackstar* (2016) seems to contain layers upon layers of meaning. At least one of them appears to be a rumination on celebrity and death that continues the line of thought Bowie was pursuing on "The Stars (Are Out Tonight)." Someone is being executed in this song, and as he is, another person has something of a *Spartacus moment*: "Somebody else took his place, and bravely cried: / (I'm a blackstar, I'm a blackstar)." This brave Spartacus-like figure continues to make this declaration as he moves through the crowd. Who is this Blackstar? He is David Bowie, and he is all of us.

One way to interpret this is to think of a Blackstar as an allusion to a black hole, a singularity from which no light can escape, a unique event within which the normal laws of the universe break down. A Blackstar may be a way to describe the uniqueness of each human being—each of us is a Blackstar. And each of us takes in information that, however we try, can never be fully communicated to others, information about our unique experiences and thoughts and emotions that can only be imperfectly suggested. When we die, we take all of that with us. Thus, every death is the death of something utterly unique, the loss of something that will never again be found in the world. Yet we all have this in common, thus we can use a common name to describe this aspect of ourselves: Blackstar.

Bowie contrasts his chosen label of Blackstar with other labels that have been ascribed to him, insisting that he is none of those things: "I'm not a filmstar," "I'm not a popstar," "I'm not a marvelstar," "I'm not a pornstar," "I'm not a wandering star," and so forth. After these denials he declares "I'm a Blackstar." He is a unique human being, with all that that entails. And he has no definitive answers. "I can't answer why / just go with me."

And it is here, in "Blackstar," that Bowie's final interpretation of death finally takes shape as an impulse to individuality, an instinctive drive to be and affirm oneself as a unique being whose essence cannot be captured by titles, labels, or roles. The impulse to individuality is perhaps the purest expression of the principle of growth, the drive toward self-realization and the achievement of one's potential. And it culminates, naturally, in death. How else? In the inevitable extinguishing of each human singularity.

How do we feel about this? How could we feel? Every other interpretation of death that Bowie provided, and every complex and contradictory mix of emotions they entail, constitutes an appropriate way to think and feel about the collapse of our lives into blackstars. No one of them is privileged, or senseless, or wrong. Ambivalence is the appropriate response.

An Honest Response

"Seeing more and feeling less / Saying no but meaning yes / This is all I ever meant / That's the message that I sent," Bowie sang in "I Can't Give Everything Away," the final song from his final album, a parting message as intriguing and cryptic as any other he'd provided over the course of his lengthy career. Ambivalence was woven into his being. And we have considered only a fragment of it here, in relation to one topic. Yet it infuses his lyrics, and his life, so thoroughly that Bowie sometimes appeared to be the very embodiment of ambivalence, an abstract concept made flesh. In a 1980 interview, journalist Angus MacKinnon said to Bowie, "Like many of your lyrics, they're infuriatingly ambivalent." And Bowie immediately responded with a grin.

In Bowie's work, ambivalence is an acknowledgment of duality and complexity, a recognition that nothing is as simple as it seems. Although some interpret this as cynicism, we read it as a refusal to indulge in fantasies or to commit to only the simplest and most obvious emotional responses. After all, his lyrics move beyond mere intellectual considerations, incorporating diverse, often contradictory emotions associated with experiences of ambivalence: confusion, longing, regret, love, lust, fear and resignation. Faced with such complexities, ambivalence represents an honest response to lived experience that is only simple in the abstract.

That Bowie was able to consider and work with so many different interpretations of death opened him up to experiences of ambivalence that not only shaped his lyrics, but prevented him from being boxed into any one reaction. In his work we see a complex interplay between the cognitive and affective domains, where each new interpretation of death complicates Bowie's emotional responses to it, and increases or changes his state of ambivalence. We see the interpretation offered in "Blackstar" as the culmination of each interpretation that preceded it. Perhaps it only appears that way because his life was cut short. Or perhaps he meant it that way, as part of his artfully-managed death.

11
Meeting the Monstrous Self

JERRY PIVEN

David Bowie's imagery is suffused with uncanny and salacious images of demonic couplings, possession, and alienation. Beyond a mischievous taste for vaudeville, pantomime, or the macabre, Bowie's lyrics may suggest an alienated sense of being inhuman, monstrous, sick, or even murdered.

Whether his images of descent into the underworld and confrontation with the inhuman self are existential, archetypal struggles, or whether they are theatrical stereotypes that merely mimic such encounters may be difficult to fathom. Still, Bowie presents us with the sinister idea that our encounters and travails reflect mirror images of our own inner monstrosity, which remains relevant when we find nations and ideologies still locating lascivious evil in despicable others who must be extinguished violently, rather than reflecting on their own terror, dread, and imagination of evil projected on those others.

The Demonic, Alien, and Perverse Within

In Bowie's surreal, sonorous elegy "The Width of a Circle," our narrator uncannily describes happening upon a monster sitting by a tree, and finding that the monster is himself. This is a fascinating concept, and one that may be familiar to students of mythology, literature, and film. Myths as ancient as the *Epic of Gilgamesh* (from over four thousand years ago) describe journeys to the underworld, where heroes meet scary monsters. In some of those stories, the monsters turn out to be companions, components, and reflections of the heroes themselves—as Otto Rank showed in his book, *The Double*.

We have any number of nefarious adversaries who are revealed to be masked or secret selves, whether they are Hydes, Horlas, Hulks, or what have you. Poe's William Wilson turns out to be his sinister doppelganger, and Dostoevsky's "The Double" depicts the horrors of a man encountering his seeming sinister clone, who seeks to replace him in every aspect of his life as the narrator disappears. In many of these tales the self is eclipsed by the evil imposter, but an unnerving current here is the suspicion not only that the apparent self is ephemeral, inconsequential, and illusory, but that the evil other really is the true identity of the self.

Why would Bowie's monster (or any other) turn out to be oneself? Obviously, because the self is really a monster! Is Bowie revealing his own self-repugnance and saying that his outer beauty and costume hide the grotesquerie within? This could reflect Bowie's encounter with his own hideousness, or it could be a revelation about the abhorrence lurking beneath the ostensibly human, beneath all diurnal artifice and appearance.

Let's consider this an insight into our own outer falsity and inner monstrosity. Mr. Hyde isn't just a grotesque aberration, but the real self that emerges after imbibing a potion. It need not be a potion of course. It may just as well be a magical ring, spell, curse, disease, radiation surge, transporter accident, empurpling minion mutator, or whatever. The potion is just a metaphor, a floating signifier that suggests that the tincture, elixir, or magic is only a chimerical thing.

There are all sorts of transmogrifications and accidents that unleash the beasts within. You put on the ring of Sauron and succumb to profligate powers, as if some otherworldly darkness eclipsed your innate goodness. A malignant apparition engulfs the hapless self. But that's a precious mirage, and we cherish it to preserve the fantasy of who we are. What envelops the wretched victim here isn't some alien magic, demon, or disease. What subjugates the self is a malignance secretly lurking within. It was there all along (if only embryonically), even if it seems like an accursed bewitchment by an evil entity beyond.

There are innumerable versions of this motif. We may recall the *Star Trek* episode ("The Enemy Within") where atmospheric interference causes Captain Kirk to be split into benign and malign versions of himself. The fiendish Kirk seems repugnant in its malice, as he skulks, swigs, and even assails a hapless yeoman with some rapacious frottage. But Spock enlightens us. This is no fake. No imposter. The vile Kirk is really a fundamentally real aspect of the self usually imprisoned or leashed, like the hapless human selves that morph into vampires, zombies, werewolves, and wendigos. (Wendigos are malicious, cannibalistic creatures of Algonquin mythology.)

Or like the notorious transformations of putatively beatific beings into Gollum, Mr. Hyde, and the berserk Cú Chulainn. In the early Irish epic, *Táin Bó Cúalinge (The Battle Raid of Cooley)*, Cú Chulainn succumbs to a "riastrad"—distortion or contortion—and becomes so ghastly that foes flee in terror. Where he possessed breathtaking unearthly beauty before, after the riastrad one eye sinks cavernously into his skull while the other drops to his cheek, the cheek peels back to reveal his gullet, his lungs and liver flap within his mouth and throat, and his gnashing teeth spew sparks.

The self really is a monster, but we *hide* it from ourselves in the desperate effort to appear normal, civilized, and sane. We run across it unpredictably, surrealistically, weirdly, when time is out of joint, when things go awry.

Identity itself is the mask, the social construct, the fantasy that we display to others and to ourselves in order to camouflage our monstrosity. This isn't just a cliché about the falsity of social selves or secret identities, but rather the unnerving insight that we aren't what we think we are. We harbor lascivious, salacious, illicit, insidious, infernal entities inside us. We're possessed, but the homunculus is really us, not some foul phantom that invades our souls. That repulsive being must be deemed demonic, alien, subterranean, heathen, or other, lest we horrify *ourselves*. We are consummate liars to ourselves most of all.

And thus when we discover that monster within, we're appalled that it is *us*. That is the horror that Conrad's *Heart of Darkness* reveals, what Bowie unveils with his eerie elegy. (Or even, what Pogo laments sardonically.) For it is not just mythic monsters that are evil and vile, but we who are so malicious, envious, and vicious. Bowie sonorously insinuates that the heart of darkness is the human condition, as much as we wish it were some sinister specter we can compel with a celestial puddle or banish with bursts of magic, like a religious exorcism or Galadriel hurling Sauron across the sky to Mordor. According to Bowie we have met Sauron, and he is not some smoldering introital eye seething somewhere else.

This is the wisdom of so many of these myths and narratives. When Luke Skywalker encounters Darth Vader in the dark swamp, he discovers his own face inside the mask. The notion that evil lurks outside the self is a comfort because it soothes our fear of being wicked and inhuman, but these narratives illustrate that we harbor monstrosity within, and may become beings of death and evil should we disavow our own hidden being. After the first atomic bomb explosion, J. Robert Oppenheimer, who had directed its development, quoted from the *Bhagavadgita*: "I am become death, destroyer of worlds." The sickening realization of what he had done brought home to him that he had indeed become death.

Disavowing the Monstrous Self

At a certain point however, this theme does become a cliché. If you've seen enough movies like *Star Wars*, or read enough comics, or watched enough cartoons, the motif seems obvious and trite. Yes, we have an evil behemoth within and if we don't deal with it we'll split our pants and become joyless green-eyed monsters smashing anything in our path. Ironically, making this mythic theme into a cliché is a way to actually avoid the painful struggle to see the genuinely monstrous within. It loses its incisive, lacerating force when it becomes yet another hackneyed theme. It can even become an ego-deluding, narcissistic posture where you assure yourself that you have looked within and encountered your demons, thus allowing the ego to deceive and inflate itself, to make you feel profound and deep, when the real strife would undermine and rip the ego to shreds.

Is Bowie revealing creepy, rending realization or just riffing on a tired cliché? Fiendish rock dirges have a tendency to devolve into Spinal Tapian caricatures. And indeed, the lyrics of "Width" might be considered farcical Tapenade, perhaps even more laughable and cringeworthy if taken seriously. So which is it here? We might even suggest that Bowie was deliberately being absurd, provocative, and ludicrous. This is why it's so crucial to distinguish, as scholar D.L. Miller says, between an archetype and a stereotype. One becomes a matrix of the self that requires immersion and agonizing discord; the other keeps the ego safe and makes you more conceited. Thus the mythic image often involves the idea of descending into Hell, or the underworld, or an abyss. Encountering the vile self is Hell. It is agony, horror, and terror, death of the ego, not ego-enhancing triumph.

So what of Bowie's perambulating narrator, then? Does he navigate the width of the circle or just dance around the idea of recognizing the monster within? Of course we can't be sure. We know that Bowie was immersed in theater, in images, performance, and so on. It would be an easy thing to simply invoke these images and change costumes before the next number. The descent into Hell could just be another performative mirage and mask. We could mimic or mime the descent into Hell, encounter with the monstrous self, or whatever we want. (Bowie certainly performed mime during his Ziggy Stardust tour concerts.) How do we know it wasn't just fashion? Fad? Identity disorder? The performance of a cracked actor?

We could hypothetically make the argument that acting isn't just about appearance, and that it sometimes reflects a profound existential strife. To quote Zinn's elegant book *The Existential Actor*:

> We shield ourselves from the truth of existence so that we may act – so that we may move forward with agency and without paralysis. All of us throughout our lives cling to our heroic narratives, whether modest or grandiose . . .
>
> The artist, however, must surrender. To be creative the artist must have the capacity to strip away his or her own psychological armor. The actor, in particular, must be able to take on the shape of whatever character she is portraying, complete with all the death-denying armor that character carries around. The most interesting characters, the most challenging, the ones we most want to play and the ones we most want to watch, are those who come to a moment in the narrative when the vital lie is pierced. In that moment the actor must have the capacity to strip away his or her own armor so as to convey the experience truthfully. The actor who can do no more than suggest the shape of that moment and merely present a simulacrum of that experience is, to use a piece of theatrical jargon, just indicating the emotion.

Bowie himself will remain opaque to us. But his lifelong preoccupation with alienation, despair, aging, and death suggest that his artifice isn't mere appearance. People who have worked with Bowie seem to think that he is immensely serious, rather than some shallow glamrocker prancing around egotistically.

So Bowie's "appearances" weren't just glamorous superficial poses or characters he was playing for performance, but reflected the masks worn to both evoke something profound or alien, and perhaps even to illustrate how the appearance itself masks a deeper alienation and monstrosity within. In the manner of a kind of Nietzschean concealment, the appearances are the *Erscheinung*, the shimmering that by its glamour draws attention to something far darker and more painful inside. Bowie's requiems to falling stars, aliens, addicts, those who find themselves decimated or murdered, suggest that the glittering appearances, even the ludicrous costumes and lyrics, signify misery and anguish within.

The Slipperiness of Self-Knowledge (Like Tigers on Vaseline)

However we speculate upon Bowie's own encounters with inner monstrosity, his song itself confronts us with a crucial philosophical question: How can you know yourself? The philosophic maxim "know thyself" has always been a difficult struggle, but Bowie's elegy further poses a crucial epistemological question: How are you really able to know the self if it seems so utterly alien to you? Just because we riff this mytheme to death doesn't mean that we really reveal the insidious intricacies our own inner monstrosity. Again, not only will the monster seem entirely *other*, as if you're being possessed by a ghost or demon, as if the "potion" transformed you into something monstrous—not the real self—but once made fashionable and mimicked and endlessly cloned, it becomes just one more hackneyed cliché. Okay, so the self is an angry monster that wants to smash or murder. We each contain a throbbing heart of darkness or inner Vader. Now what?

One danger, as suggested earlier, is that this inner demon becomes one more thing to inflate the ego. You make it into a superhero. You're secretly riddled by inner fury and aggression, and become Batman or some other tormented, dark knight. That re-mythologizes inner evil and makes it something heroic and admirable. Your inner Vader now becomes an inner Batman. You've made yourself a cool cartoon character instead of confronting the things that terrify you to death about yourself. We need to follow Bowie here. Your self-knowledge might paralyze you, nauseate you, wrench you from the heavens, or render you a corpse. It's not about being a broodingly-suave beacon of justice or wearing a rubber bananasling or trouncing evildoers.

Self-knowledge is slippery, elusive, perplexing, and horrifying. As Nietzsche writes, truth kills. Uprooting our vile, savage, despicable desires sears us to death. It's far easier to lie, rationalize, and deceive ourselves in infinite ways. Our weaknesses are humiliating and painful. To admit that it's not *they* but *we* who are scheming, depraved, or perverse, that is humiliating. Only those vile, repugnant others can be degenerate, stunted, foolish, and odious. But evil is usually a projection, a fantasy that siphons awareness of our own shameful and depraved qualities and maps them onto others. We so seldom know who others are. But we're sure that they are sick, evil bastards.

Consider the history of prejudice. This ethnic stereotype (name the group) is dumb and predatory, and wants to rape our women. That group or gender is inferior, unclean, impure, nefarious, and immoral. That group worships the devil or something so inexcusably vile that we have to smite them in the name of the real (and really good) god. Again as Nietzsche says, "Unbeliever, you have no right to exist."

People have made the most insidious accusations against others, about whom they haven't the faintest knowledge. And they're sure that such iniquitous people are sinful, depraved, and deserving of death. How wonderful that the dynamic of projection could afford them the opportunity to take any self-knowledge of their own shameful perversions, sleazy desires, or homicidal impulses, attribute them to others, and then massacre those others in the name of some other fantastical, imaginary, equally fictitious being who somehow justifies wanton slaughter as a holy or patriotic act. And what's worse, people need to do this, and thrive on it, so that they could make sure they don't know (and then despise) themselves, and then thusly destroy all that evil by torturing or liquidating those evil enemies.

And so, Vamik Volkan could write a book called *The Need to Have Enemies and Allies* and Chris Hedges could write *War Is a Force that Gives Us Meaning*.

Is the Monster Even Evil?

The latter stanzas of "The Width of a Circle" notoriously limn an erotic encounter between the narrator and a seething diabolic entity. While Bowie may have flirted with fashionable satanic images (the fascination with Satanism and dark magic were trending at the time), and while he also dashed off many of his lyrics during recording sessions, some of these improvisations may have revealed some incisively profound ideas.

One final irony in this rumination on monstrosity is that the inner hellion Bowie encounters may not be malevolent or vile at all. It may only appear that way since people are so often assaulted relentlessly from infancy onward with stringent dogmas about what is morally appropriate, dignified, normal, healthy, and good. Once infused with such relentless condemnation, threat, and censure, our own desires may look abominable even to ourselves. The spitting sentry horned and tailed that Bowie describes in his Hellish "Circle" isn't *merely* some satanic fiend undulating above him erogenously, nor his own inner monster. As sentry he's also the wicked observer, the force of evil that voyeuristically presides over perversion in his burning pit of fear. He's the alter ego of the same master earlier blamed first and last, the nebulous body swaying above and both relishing the salacious sin as he consigns us to the inferno. The devil is the alter ego of the super ego, that inescapable, remorseless presence that instills self-condemnation, even when our impulses are not innately evil. To echo Žižek's *The Puppet and the Dwarf* here, the condemning agency doesn't only despise the repugnant act it condemns, but it perversely enjoys inflicting that law, and thus relishes the violation so it may delight in its castigation.

Societies may condemn all manner of desire and propensity, but a wish deemed sick or perverse does not make it so. Societies have condemned all manner of sexuality sinful and worthy of punishment and death. And again that reflects the inner abjection and rage of the persecutor, not the iniquity of the accused. History is riddled with hostile condemnation of "perverse" and "sinful" sexualities, of feminine erotic eruption, of homosexuality, the joyful efflorescence of human eroticism in all manner of disquieting diversity. Bowie's immersion in alienation, alien identities, and deviant sexualities reflects a profound awareness of this condemnation, and his impassioned rebellion against it.

In our current society we have hordes and congregations screaming like harpies about the evil sexualities and sins of others. And even those of us who find such claptrap absurd and stunted may still internalize that invective on some level and deem it sick in ourselves. In *Self-Envy*, Rafael Lopez-Corvo illustrates just how passionately the bitter, jealous, enraged parts of our personality (or the internalized malicious voices of parents and society) can attack the loving and admirable parts of ourselves. This is not mere self-condemnation, but inner objects (the internalized presence of others) who assault other aspects of the personality.

Again, we don't know ourselves, and can even consider our deepest thoughts and love aberrations, and hence refuse to recognize our own reflections. And tragically, it is often those who have internalized that enraged condemnation who come to despise their own inner being, and can only withstand themselves by becoming apoplectic ideologues madly driven to persecute others, so as not to recognize their own repugnance. As Bowie shows us, such eroticism and desire can be sublime, even as we unknowingly condemn and see ourselves as monsters. So indeed, while many of us harbor brutal, murderous, insidious impulses in ourselves that make us monsters, for others it is the relentless assault on *un*monstrous desires deemed vile that brainwashes people to believe they are riddled with repugnance.

It's here that so many monsters are born, not because of those shameful secret desires but because they have been *made* grotesque. The monster here is not a secret wrathful being we submerge and harbor, but the waking ego, which we fantasize is sanctimonious and good even as we inflict that sanctimony sadistically on others. The monster is not hidden within, but is the outer identity we then refuse to recognize as foul while castigating and massacring others in the name of some hallowed delusion of purity.

Some of us do harbor secret lascivious, malign, rapacious selves within, and they would surely appear monstrous to us if encountered. To be human means suffering irrational, passionate, even monstrous impulses. But others have had even erotic, loving, intelligent propensities denigrated viciously, and having been trampled with the idea that their own selves are evil, see their own love and sundry gifts as sinful. And for some unhappy number of those assailed so cruelly, survival means becoming sanctimonious emissaries of that monstrous cruelty rather than its helpless victims. The emissaries need not appear odious or depraved. Many mask their monstrosity angelically. Angelic envoys of malice embody the monstrous but cloak it in devious finery, seeming charming and morally pure so they may inflict their animosity assuming a more blessed or virtuous or patriotic disguise. Some of them may anoint themselves in Crisco and unwittingly make caricatures of themselves as they gurgle echolalic prattle, but they also wear holy vestments or swear on the bible and constitution as they seduce a puerile populace to trample their own rights and cheer for pious carnage. (When erstwhile attorney general John Ashcroft was elected governor of Missouri, he was twice anointed with oil, and after being elected Senator, was anointed with Crisco in resemblance to the tradition of the ancient Kings of Israel, and "Jesus Christ," the Anointed One.)

Bowie and the Dire Necessity of Meeting the Scary Monster

Self-knowledge is not just a cerebral pastime for pretentious philosophers. It's a dire necessity among a race of bloodthirsty hominids who slaughter to avoid knowing ourselves because we fear and detest so much of our own being. And thus the epistemic project of self-knowledge must confront the terror, horror, shame, and disgust of knowing who we are. This is why it kills, and why Nietzsche says that truth requires us to sacrifice everything which our lives, which our hearts depend on.

As Bowie says, it ain't easy. Hence there's no formula or strategy we can simply plug in, no recipe we can follow by rote. We can certainly persevere in our efforts to detect the flaws in our reasoning and discern the fallacies of our logic. We can struggle to become erudite students of reason and read voraciously, following the intellectual reaches of great minds, and subject ourselves to ruthless analytic rigors. But there are no guarantees. Our own terror and anguish block our own efforts to know ourselves. It would be easy if we could just follow some foolproof procedure of locating elusive truths or find them with the right microscope. And some may imagine that they are rational enough and possess enough intellectual clarity to just penetrate the guises and know one's inner workings. That in itself is an absurd, defensive, nearly delusive fantasy, an ego-protecting, ego-inflating consolation and self-assurance.

Thus some few philosophers, and artists like David Bowie, have urged a more agonizing, excruciating existential engagement. Sometimes they look upon us with pity, for after all, we are timid, sad, abandoned, forlorn children who stumble and crawl. Whether Bowie is singing with tenderness or inciting us with sonorous intensity, Bowie cannot shepherd his listeners toward self-knowledge, since he's not a prophet. He alludes to the prophet who pontificates self-knowledge in "The Width of the Circle," with its mention of Kahlil Gibran, author of *The Prophet*.

No one can bestow prophethood upon a self that struggles desperately to un-know its own monstrosity. But Bowie can perform that seismic, lacerating encounter with inner abomination, and try to shake his listeners to the core so they may begin to recognize that inner incubus for themselves.

12
David Bowie's Sincerity

ANNELIESE COOPER

It's not hard to imagine why critics might accuse David Bowie of being "inauthentic": as a performer and a public figure, he was constantly changing his style—from queer extraterrestrial to synth-laced aesthete to blonde and boppy hitmaker, all in just one decade of a half-century career.

Yet some of Bowie's biggest fans find his persona-swapping to be the very source of what makes him meaningful—among them, philosopher Simon Critchley, who argues that "Bowie's genius allows us to break the superficial link that seems to connect authenticity to truth," proving the old camp lesson that even explicit pageantry can be just as affecting, as properly "real," as any more straightforward fare.

By repeatedly reinventing himself, and showing us the seams of that invention, Bowie modeled an "escape from being riveted to the fact of who we are," and thereby demonstrates the power and importance of artistic expression, for rock stars and lonely teens alike (*Bowie*, pp. 41, 54).

But let's get beyond Bowie's authenticity and look at his sincerity—that is, how he conveys, or fails to convey, that authenticity to an audience. Underlying Bowie's choice to sing through characters in the first place, we can detect anxiety: Bowie's fear of being fundamentally disconnected, too alien to be understood. The Ziggy Stardust persona represents, at least in part, a glittering reclamation of that estrangement—his rallying cry of "You're not alone," linking arty misfits the world over. Still, both before and after that infamous phase, Bowie seems fixated on sussing out the limitations of connection through art—the illusory, even deadly powers of fiction, and the particular failings of language to reliably transmit a self.

A Thinker, Not a Talker

Let's start with "Conversation Piece," a 1970 B-side that finds young Bowie singing from the point of view of an unnamed academic—a self-proclaimed "thinker, not a talker" who can't seem to form meaningful human relationships. Though he has considerable academic pedigree and an apartment littered with "essays," he proves worse at chatting than his Austrian neighbor who speaks in "broken English." The song functions essentially as a parable, a reminder of the cruel irony that language itself might be a barrier to communication; as our protagonist admits in the second pre-chorus, "For all my years of reading conversation, I stand without a word to say." A chugging country twang highlights the dissonance between his gloom and the lively world around him, amid the bustle, he walks alone and unknown toward an apparent suicide, his journey blurred with tears.

"Conversation Piece" offers a morbid counterpoint to Ziggy's "Rock'n'roll Suicide," his invitation to "just turn on with me" and thereby avoid loneliness; it's a reminder that your creations, here in the form of "essays," can just as easily preclude connection. Our academic may have more in common with *Space Oddity*'s Major Tom: mediated through a faulty radio, hopelessly ineffectual against blue, blue planet Earth.

What makes "Conversation Piece" noteworthy among Bowie's early tracks is its second life: though originally released to little acclaim, it was among the dozen early compositions revived for 2001's ill-fated *Toy*, which would have featured a few new songs served up on a bed of self-covers. By the time the project morphed into 2002's *Heathen*, however, it had shed all covers but "Conversation Piece," which appears as a bonus track on the deluxe edition. Though it may not be fair to infer any particular meaning from the choice to keep this track over others, the effect of the new recording, as it stands, is striking: an old man retracing his youthful fantasies of age and obsolescence—slower now, and backed by swelling strings. "It all seems so long ago," he croons, a full octave lower, as if weighted down with real years.

The new "Conversation Piece" seems to have gained back some of its sincerity, as the singer is finally old enough to mean what he says: we can believe him when he tells us that his hands shake and his head hurts. Still, the very next line goes inscrutable again, as a world-famous rock star asserts that no one will remember him; it's at once a poignant wink at his teenaged fears of being forgotten, and a genuine hint toward the now-pressing issue of his legacy—all mediated, as per usual, through a persona.

Believable Fakery

For all of Bowie's well-documented obsession with achieving proper vocal tone—from clipped mockney to Scott-Walker-style warbling—you'd be hard pressed to call him a traditionally "sincere" singer, at least insofar as the goal of the "sincere" performer is to turn inside-out on stage, to bare himself emotionally (even biographically) raw. Sure, there are tracks like *Space Oddity*'s "Letter to Hermione," which chronicles Bowie's real-life heartache over losing "his first serious girlfriend, the dancer Hermione Farthingale"—though, according to Chris O'Leary's exhaustive song-by-song Bowie tome *Rebel Rebel*, even that convincing confession may be muddled with artistic intent:

> The reality, Bowie disclosed in 2000, was that Farthingale had resumed contact around the time he wrote the song and "obviously

> we could have gotten back together again." This willful amnesia on his part (he didn't recall receiving her letters for nearly three decades) suggested a deliberate attempt to prolong a state of misery for the sake of a song. (*Rebel Rebel*, pp. 92, 110)

What's often remarkable about Bowie's music is the clash between the overt fakery in play and the believability of his vocals—the more emotive his performance, the greater the intellectual somersault. As Lester Bangs described in a nonplussed review of 1974's *Diamond Dogs*, Bowie's "broken-larynxed vocals" struck him as "so queasily sincere they reek of some horrible burlesque, some sterilely distasteful artifice." For Bangs, even at peak "sincerity," Bowie still comes off constructed.

It's here that the theories of Critchley and others slot in nicely: that artifice doesn't cancel out authenticity—real emotions might live in crafted narrative. But that notion can be as frightening as it is freeing, especially when you consider Ziggy Stardust's game-changing collapse of fact and fiction. By "killing off" Ziggy onstage in 1973, Bowie embodied the fate he wrote for himself in the character's titular song—a rock star destroyed mid-show by his own fame—and after succeeding at self-creation to that almost eerie degree, he was left adrift "like a fly in milk," as he puts it in the 1974 BBC documentary *Cracked Actor*, gliding wan and coke-fed through Los Angeles. "I mean, if I've been at all responsible for people finding more characters in themselves than they originally thought they had, then I'm pleased," he muses:

> That's something I feel very strongly about, that one isn't totally what one has been conditioned to think one is—that there are many facets of the personality, which a lot of us have trouble finding, and some of us do find too quickly.

That final phrase is as chilling as it is vague—too quickly for what?, one wonders—but a sort of reply comes in 1975, during a satellite interview with British TV presenter Russell Harty. When asked whether he'll continue "the glamour-y, glittery Ziggy Stardust thing" in his next tour, Bowie demurs, stutters: "I think the image I may adopt may well be me. I'm sort of inventing me at the moment."

> **HARTY:** You mean reinventing?
>
> **BOWIE:** Yes. Self-invented.
>
> **HARTY:** [*laughing*] From the waist up?
>
> **BOWIE:** Yes. Jolly uncomfortable.

It's moments like these, blank-faced on national television, in which Bowie's penchant for shucking identities starts to seem less like a costume-happy romp and more like an increasingly frantic search for a bottom that keeps dropping out. Even for someone who champions the "finding of characters," the aftermath of such extreme self-escape can be unnerving. Just before Ziggy's arrival, Bowie fretted in "Changes" about "how the others must see the faker"—but what happens when they don't? What happens when you play a part so well and so completely, you make up something true?

When Descartes spiraled down a similar path of self-doubt, afraid of how little in his life could be proved certain—his sensual perception, his ability to distinguish reality and dreams, even God-given facts—he emerged with the foundational understanding that, regardless of all else, "I think, therefore I am." Unfortunately for Bowie's dilemma, consciousness is trapped inside the body; it speaks to authenticity, not sincerity—to self, not self-communication—"a thinker, not a talker," as per the mournful protagonist of "Conversation Piece." One can be secure in one's self-perception and still end up alienated, unable to make that vision real to anyone else, stymied by the faulty conduit of language. Between the "thinking thing" and the outside world lies a formidable gap, across which one can only toss words, images, gestures—a no-man's land of potential misinterpretation.

Saying No but Meaning Yes

There are plenty of times when Bowie, ever the verbose lyricist, seems to relish these tricks that language can play, from 1967's "Maid of Bond Street," which hinges on the homonym of "maid" and "made," to 2003's "New Killer Star," in which Bowie continues a career-long toying with the term "star" by using the title to mirror the word "nuclear"—as pronounced by George W. Bush (*The Complete David Bowie*, p. 174). Even on *Blackstar*—Bowie's knowing swansong of an album, released just days before his death—the repetition of "I'm dying to" on the penultimate "Dollar Days" hammers home a haunting double entendre. Indeed, on his very final track, fittingly titled "I Can't Give Everything Away," Bowie seems to define his whole oeuvre as one long linguistic made-you-look: "saying no but meaning yes—that was all I ever meant." According to Critchley, who penned a touching memorial piece for the *New York Times*, this line is the key that might shed light on a dark, coded discography:

> Within Bowie's negativity, beneath his apparent naysaying and gloom, one can hear a clear *Yes*, an absolute and unconditional affirmation of life in all of its chaotic complexity, but also its moments of transport and delight.

Still, "saying no but meaning yes" underlines once again the gap between what's said and what's meant; words may transport and delight, but they can just as easily mislead or be misunderstood. Bowie sums up this ever-present possibility in the closing moments of "'Heroes'": after five and a half minutes spent painting a love story of near-mythic proportions—kings and queens, guns and dolphins—he finally admits, "maybe we're lying," and the music promptly fizzles. Though often interpreted as celebrating these lovers who strive against impossible circumstance, the song also represents a cautionary tale about the seductive power of stories—the ways in which pretty lies can fool us into chasing a mean, drunk future.

The Man Who Fell

Bowie's career is littered with metaphors for the dire consequences of such misunderstanding—for example, his turn as Thomas Jerome Newton, the alien protagonist of Nicholas Roeg's *The Man Who Fell to Earth* (likely familiar, even to those who haven't seen the movie, as the source of the cover art for both *Station to Station* and *Low*). The story goes that Newton arrives on our planet in hopes of finding water to bring back to his own, but is quickly suckered in by gluttonous Americana—e.g., a wall of televisions—and ends up staying far longer than he planned. When at last he's found out and scientists try to study him, they inadvertently fuse his human-style contact lenses to his eyes, sealing the alien into his disguise, dooming him to a broken, alcoholic end.

The parallels between Newton and mid-1970s Bowie are striking—fused, as he was, to the character of Ziggy, an alien drifting through America, drowning in chemical excess. "I just threw my real self into that movie as I was at that time," Bowie admitted later in an interview for *Movieline*, after copping to using "about ten grams" of cocaine per day at the time. "It was a pretty natural performance. What you see there is David Bowie" (Virginia Campbell, "David Bowie").

And yet, once again, these concerns also precede their extraterrestrial avatar—for example in 1969, when Bowie created a mime routine called "The Mask" as part of a promotional movie for his then-fledging career. In it, he portrays a young man who gains people's applause and praise by putting on a mask—but when he tries to wear it onstage in a theater, the mask sticks to his face and ultimately suffocates him. Bowie would later recall this image in the post-Ziggy "Diamond Dogs Tour," appearing onstage holding a grinning white theatrical mask painted with Aladdin Sane's signature lightning bolt. When he performs the original mime piece, though, there's no prop; the illusion is created by passing his hands over his face and twisting his own features into a manic grin. Which is ultimately fitting: as Bowie reveals in the narration's closing lines, "The papers made a big thing of it. . . . Funny, though: they didn't say anything about a mask." Though perhaps heavy-handed, in *Man* and "Mask" alike, the message is clear: pretending can be stifling, if not deadly, especially when played for an audience.

Homo Superior

It's no surprise that we so often see Bowie conflating performance and death—beginning as early as 1968, with the unfinished musical *Ernie Johnson* (now confined to one lucky collector's four-track tape). The play reportedly chronicles the nineteen-year-old title character as he plans a party at which he will kill himself: one song, titled "Where's the Loo?," has Ernie's guests exclaim upon arrival, "What fabby clothes! Is it true? That after tonight there's no more you? And can we watch?" (*Rebel Rebel*, p. 428).

It's not hard to draw a line from Ernie to Ziggy, whom Bowie did "kill" in public—or even, decades later, to *Outside*'s Detective Nathan Adler, who investigates murders committed in the name of art. In each case, death is a spectacle, complete with "fabby clothes." (One might even add *Blackstar* to this list, in its creative cushioning of an all too real demise.) This recurring theme indicates reverence for the god-making power of artifice, a celebration of its greatest trick.

Gearing up to Ziggy, Bowie makes reference to Nietzsche-inspired "Supermen"—elegizing these "wondrous beings chained to life" on *The Man Who Sold the World*, insisting we "make way for the Homo Superior" on *Hunky Dory*—calling himself "a mortal with potential of a Superman," right before he incarnates himself as a rock god. But his morbid imagery also seems to acknowledge the dark side of such self-creation, the violence inherent in artful estrangement from human consequence—what Walter Benjamin called "self-alienation" and Oscar Wilde called "assuming a pose"—rending oneself from one's image, letting image take over. Meanwhile, there's a way in which these persistent fantasies of "rock'n'roll suicide" hint at a latent desire to spatter the unfeeling theater with blood, to literally spill his guts.

In Ziggy's wake, however, Bowie entered yet another overtly artificial period: the self-proclaimed "plastic soul" phase of 1975's *Young Americans*—a glossy imitation of a genre that trades in emotional, historical, and even religious veracity—hot off his foray into the giddy cut-up lyrics of *Diamond Dogs*. It seems fitting that the surreal, dystopian images of the "Sweet Thing / Candidate / Sweet Thing (Reprise)" suite were created by literally taking scissors to the written word and tossing down scraps in cool-sounding order—that Bowie was so quick to disappear into an established tradition he plainly doesn't quite fit, as if feeding off the dissonance. By doubling down on meaninglessness, as when he sings in a persona, Bowie frees himself from the expectations of sincerity as traditionally understood—an escape not just from some static concept of self, but also from the burden of self-proof. "I've found the door which lets me out," he howls midway through *Diamond Dogs*, "when you rock'n'roll with me, there's no one else I'd rather be."

Through the Gloom

And yet, to echo Critchley's uplifting reading of "saying no but meaning yes," Bowie manages to move past cold postmodernism to offer a new, unexpected kind of sincerity—one achieved, ironically enough, by openly recognizing his own capacity to be insincere: "It's not the side-effects of the cocaine," he reflects on the title track of *Station to Station*, "I'm thinking that it must be love!" Take "Be My Wife," the last verbal hurrah on 1977's *Low* before it breaks down into synth and nonsense syllables. For all the romance promised by its title, it's notably robotic, all clichéd lyrics and dry delivery: "Please be mine," he drones, "share my life." Still, it's almost more poignant in its spareness, straining against the bounds of what's sayable—like a schoolboy's jokey invitation to dance, no less heavy with longing.

On "What in the World," too, a seemingly personal revelation ("something deep inside of me, yearning deep inside of me") breaks down immediately into platitudes ("What in the world can I do? I'm in the mood for your love"). Each one is, essentially, a love song that goes out of its way to underscore the futility of love songs, how easily words can go glib.

And still, Bowie continues—acknowledging again and again the risk, even the impossibility of communication, but pushing ahead anyhow, kicking at expression from all sides. His example, then, is one of audacious optimism—five decades spent relentlessly "talking through the gloom."

IV

Out of Bowie's Mind

13
The Madness of the Musician

MATTHEW LAMPERT

> I go off at the mouth and get very tyrannical and then again I'm very philosophical, with my heads in the clouds. Heads, [*laughs*] now there's the sign of a schizophrenic . . . "got my heads in the cloud" . . . and I want to keep all those. Anyone wants to take those away from me, I'll sue 'em. I'm getting used to suing people.
>
> —DAVID BOWIE, *New Musical Express* (7th March 1976)

David Bowie has often been called the "first postmodern pop star." When I google that phrase in January of 2016, all of the half-dozen or so hits are about Bowie.

References to Dylan Jones's *When Ziggy Played Guitar* pop up, as well as a link to Sean O'Hagan's review of the *Moonage Daydream* coffee table book for *The Guardian*. By the time you Google it, a link to this chapter may pop up as well.

John Savage, in *England's Dreaming*, calls *The Rise and Fall of Ziggy Stardust and the Spiders From Mars* "the first postmodern record," and David Buckley picks up this claim and repeats it in several places, calling Ziggy Stardust "the first postmodern pop star" both in his biography of Bowie and in the liner notes he wrote for the special anniversary edition of the *Ziggy* album.

What does everybody mean by this? (And why is it the Ziggy moment in particular that they tend to focus on when they make this claim?)

"Postmodern" is a complicated—and somewhat contentious—idea, but Pat Aufderhide explains that postmodern art is "marked by several distinctive features. Among them are the merging of commercial and artistic image production and an abolition of traditional boundaries between an image and its real-life referent, between past and present, between character and performance, between mannered art and stylized life." Even this explanation lacks some of the clarity we might have been hoping for. After all, we live in a "postmodern age," when there seems to be little difference between commercial and artistic production left to point to! And if the difference between "image" and "real-life referent" seems less than clear or helpful, it's Aufderhide's reference to the difference between "character" and "performance" that may throw a little light on things: postmodernism seems to efface the difference between "being" a thing and merely "acting like" it, or "truth" and "appearance." As this brief discussion already shows, Bowie long ago put all of his eggs into a postmodern song.

From the beginning, Bowie built his solo career on the inauthentic (pop, commercial) performance of "authentic" (artistic, anti-commercial) forms of music: first folk, then rock, and then soul and R&B—this trend continues right up through *Earthling*, Bowie's pop appropriation of the "authentic" jungle and drum'n'bass club scenes.

Likewise, Bowie's music is highly referential, pulling not only from fine art sources (literature, performance art, philosophy) but also from pop music's own history: his references to other songs and performers, his covers (not just of old blues tunes, the way rock had done, but of his own contemporaries), and of course, more recently, his own self-referentiality (beginning with "Ashes to Ashes," and then really accelerating after *The Buddha of Suburbia*).

Finally, and most importantly, "David Bowie" has always only ever been an "image," and Bowie has adopted a series of such images through his career, *intentionally* effacing the differences between the images and their real-life referent: First David Robert Jones became David Bowie, and then

David Bowie became Ziggy Stardust, Aladdin Sane, Halloween Jack, the Thin White Duke, and so on.

While songs and stories have long been told through narrator characters who are not identical with their authors, Bowie in the 1970s discovers (and shows us) that "acting like" a rockstar is indistinguishable from *being* a rockstar; Bowie may have merely "acted the part" of Ziggy Stardust, but this performance *is* the existence of Ziggy. Likewise, Woody Woodmansey, Trevor Bolder and Mick Ronson (and Mike Garson) were simply "pretending" to be The Spiders from Mars—but in doing so, they *really became* The Spiders; all of our recordings of "The Spiders" are simply (or also) recordings of these men. For Bowie, the intentional confusion went even further: he gave interviews in character; in *Santa Monica '72* you'll hear Bowie introduce "Moonage Daydream" by saying, "This is a song written by Ziggy"; and when Ziggy announced his retirement (during the concert captured in *Ziggy Stardust: The Motion Picture*), it was taken by many to be *Bowie's* announcement of retirement.

As John Savage wrote in November of 1980, Bowie "pushed at the limits, offering himself as Artist, a generalist adopting different roles over a series of brilliant, yet reactive and reflexive albums. Each had a high-profile, visual identity that went with the product: these identities Bowie would live out for the duration of the product's life, to such an extent that the albums seemed to have more life than he did—possession in reverse." David Buckley, in *Strange Fascination*, puts it best:

> Revealingly, by 1973, Bowie was referring to "Bowie" as if it was a media creation like a fan enthusing about a pop star, not a real person talking about himself. 'Bowie' was an abstract, an idea, not a real person at all. Bowie, like Ziggy, was just another character for David Jones to play. The boundaries between all three were dissolving fast. (p. 139)

David Bowie, silver screen: can't tell them apart at all.

Of course it should be said: While the history of pop and rock is yet fairly short (less than a hundred years is short by art standards), certainly all popular music is in some way shaped and informed by that history (look at the development of 1970s rock out of British covers of old blues tunes, for example). And *all* celebrities—and most especially all rockstars—become images that we confuse with reality; likewise, all "serious" rock is sold as a commercial commodity right alongside the most vacuous bubblegum pop.

But Bowie's approach is different. As Bethany Usher and Stephanie Fremaux explain, "Popular music has always supported the creation of personae, both musically through lyrics and through the marketed image." But whereas with other pop stars the audience is supposed to regard the image as at least a projection of the "authentic" self of the celebrity, "This is very different to Bowie's use of personae. He creates fictional characters brought to life through live performance and media interviews." What makes Bowie so "postmodern" is that he doesn't simply *do* these things: he does them *ironically*, and he does them in a way that *shows us that these are merely conventions*. Bowie's approach rejects any notion of "genius" in art (the genius being the divinely-inspired artist who creates new things by channeling some creative spirit), and instead is characterized by a mercenary cobbling together of influences (albeit many of them quite obscure). Notice that, as the faker, the liar, the "arch-dissembler," Bowie is yet totally upfront and honest about his dishonesty. As Buckley explains:

> He was, rather, posing at being a poseur, which is quite a different thing. What many people mistake for shallowness and a lack of substance is in fact an outward manifestation of a very astute customer, of a man adept at dissembling the rock charade. When Bowie told one journalist in 1972 "I lie an awful lot," he was, after all, being brutally honest.

This knowing, ironic, winking performance is what makes Bowie so interesting—and it's also what made him a star. This is John Savage's point when he applies the "postmodern" label: *Ziggy Stardust*, an album about a famous rockstar, also made Bowie a famous rockstar. (Remember too that

Bowie called the first incarnation of The Spiders, back in February of 1970, *Hype*.)

His cobbling together of sources (melodies, looks, and even voices), clever references, and play-acting allowed Bowie to *consciously* craft and sell himself as a pop icon. (Buckley recounts how this same strategy was used by MainMan in the mid-1970s to make Bowie a star in America: they simply pretended he already was one, *and it worked*.) And so, while "postmodern" *is* an excellent way of characterizing Bowie's approach to art and pop stardom, there is another label that seems to fit equally well: cynical.

How the Others See the Faker

An interview with Bowie from the September, 1976 issue of *Playboy* begins:

> He was once a scruffy, honey-haired folk singer. Then the foppish leader of a Beatles-prototype pop band, The Buzz. Then an adamantly bisexual balladeer. Then a spacey, cropped-red-haired androgynous guitarist backed by a band called the Spiders from Mars. Then a soul singer. Then a movie actor . . . and finally, a smartly conservative, Sinatraesque entertainer. David Bowie, it's safe to say, would do anything to make it. And now that he has made it, he'll do anything to stay there.

Bowie's style-chasing chameleon quality, his inauthentic manipulation of image, and his wholesale theft of ideas, melodies, and voices may be what make him such an interesting pop star—but these same qualities have led others to see him as cynical in his single-minded pursuit of fame and fortune. Bowie takes the commercial hype of pop, and gleefully applies it to the rock world in order to make himself a star.

Peter Sloterdijk has literally written the book on contemporary cynicism: his *Critique of Cynical Reason* is the starting point for just about every current discussion of cynicism. Sloterdijk writes that cynicism "arises when two views of things have become possible, an official and an unofficial view, a veiled and a naked view, one from the viewpoint of heroes and one from the viewpoint of valets" (p. 218). It is once the official, heroic view of authentic, anti-commercial rock becomes unmasked in the early 1970s, revealing naked self-interest and commercialism beneath, that rock cynicism becomes possible. In this way, cynicism in rock has the same immediate cause as all other forms of postmodern cynicism: disillusionment after the fallout of late-1960s counterculture. Building upon Sloterdijk's account, Sharon Stanley explains that the cynic "learns to play the game, to thoroughly implicate himself in the very system he has damned."

Thus, cynicism is a strange juxtaposition of several ideas. The first is the judgment that the world (in this case, the rock world) is *bad*, that ideals like authenticity and virtue *would* be good, but that they *are not possible* under current market conditions. The second part of cynicism is the idea that another world is not possible—revolution is a drag, too many snags. And finally, rather than take this as a reason to walk away, the cynic concludes that he therefore must participate in the behavior which he condemns: he must become a manipulator, a faker. Cynicism arises, in the form of postmodernism, in the early 1970s because a generation that is still committed to the ideals of the late-60s counterculture decides that these ideals are impossible to achieve, and that if you can't beat 'em, you might as well join 'em. As Bowie himself put it during the 1990s, "If you're going to work in a whorehouse, you'd better be the best whore in it" (*Strange Fascination*, p. 99).

But Stanley's important insight—and it's where she distances herself from Sloterdijk and most other contemporary accounts of cynicism—is that there is nothing really *new* about this post-1968 "postmodern" cynicism. Its postmodern voice may be new, and its accent too, but the cynical fear—of commodification and the corruption of values by the marketplace—is as old as the world (or at least as old as capitalism). She looks back to the founding figure of Enlightenment cynicism to make her case, the title character of Denis Diderot's *Rameau's Nephew*.

Dirty Boys

Diderot's *Rameau's Nephew* is a dialogue between two characters; contextual evidence identifies them as Diderot and Jean-François Rameau (nephew of the famous composer Jean-Philippe Rameau), though within the text they are merely referred to as *Moi* ("Me") and *Lui* ("Him"). Diderot, in an early echo of Bowie, makes himself a character in the dialogue, but in a way that we're left wondering whether or not the real Diderot fully agrees with the character. That said, it is not with Moi that I believe the most interesting comparisons to Bowie can be drawn, but rather with Lui.

Lui is a struggling musician and a gifted pantomime, who continuously shocks Moi with his bold claims about the nature of (eighteenth-century French) society: Lui claims that we all wear masks, creating "images" of moral selves behind which we calculate and pursue our own self-interest. If Lui—and Bowie—are correct, then *everyone* is in some way like Lui. But what sets Lui apart, as Diderot explains, is something we also see at work in Bowie:

> In this there was much that we all think and on which we all act, but which we leave unsaid. That, indeed, was the most obvious difference between this man and most of those we meet. He owned up to the vices he had and which others have—he was no hypocrite. (p. 111)

In other words, Sharon Stanley is absolutely right to see Lui as an early version of postmodern cynicism; he is the honest liar, the faker who owns up to his own fakery. In comparing Bowie and Lui, I think we can gain two important insights into Bowie's work.

First, by thinking about Bowie's similarity to Lui, I think we can see how Bowie attacks the idea of *genius*, a claim that I had put forward earlier. In the dialogue, Lui tells us early and often that he is not a genius, and is envious of those who are. Painfully aware that he is not a genius, Lui is ultimately terrified of being a "type": "the most frightening of all epithets because it indicates mediocrity and the last stages of the contemptible" (p. 43). A genius is by his very nature a one-of-a-kind—his opposite number is then the "type," one who is indistinguishable from the group. David Jones seems also to have harbored dreams of being "someone else, at the risk of being a man of genius." Bowie, like Lui, is driven to pantomime and imitation, to fakery and the manipulation of images, because he is not *naturally* a genius. Adam Bresnick, in his article "Dialectic of Genius: *Rameau's Nephew*" (*Qui Parle* 5:1, 1991), puts the matter quite nicely:

> As the Nephew would have it, it is better to be a great "good-for-nothing" than to be a mediocre nothing, for at least then you are something. To be mediocre, as the Nephew is painfully aware, is to be nothing at all. The logical upshot of this paradoxical position is that it is better to be something than nothing, even at the cost of becoming a monster or a criminal. (p. 104)

I am not suggesting that Bowie is a monster or a criminal! Nor will you find that Lui is, either. But *Ziggy* certainly became a monster in his own way, as did Aladdin Sane and the Thin White Duke—indeed, David Buckley calls his chapter on the end of the Ziggy/Aladdin Sane era "Killing the Kabuki Monster," and Bowie himself has referred to "his personae as addictive demons from which he needed to free himself." But the more important point is that Lui's pantomime—his great talent for imitating others and pretending to be what he is not—*comes from* the inability to be a genius. The mythic genius, so our long-standing story goes, is one who creates brand new ideas out of nothing. This requires a sort of divine inspiration. Geniuses don't have to pretend or imitate or follow; they are authentic and novel and one-of-a-kind. But those who are not capable of genius, in order to avoid simply being "nobodies," play at roles: it's better to pretend than to be a nobody.

Bowie is an *attack* on the ideal of genius—rather than just an alternative to it—because he's ultimately successful at turning himself into a star. And if Bowie can do it, why not anybody else? Furthermore, by pulling back the curtain, I think that Bowie's work already starts to hint at the ways in which so-called "genius" has always *secretly* operated: *Not*, as we had believed, by creating brand new ideas from nothing, but rather by taking pre-existing ideas and combining them in new ways; as the quote so often (mis?)attributed to Oscar Wilde puts it, "Talent borrows; genius steals." Kirby Ferguson, in the title of his 2011 documentary series, put it this way: *Everything is a remix*. Bowie manages to be both a leading figure in the postmodern attack on genius and yet at the same time a one-of-a-kind star. This is why Bowie is ultimately so important to so many of us: Feeling less-than-genius ourselves, Bowie shows us that we need not let this fact keep us from individuality and stardom.

While well aware of the risks, this is what Savage is drawn to in his article for *The Face*: "That is the promise, the premise of pop and teen fashion: overnight, you can be transformed into something superhuman. Not very pretty, but, to date, necessary. Bowie is the agent of that transformation made manifest and perennial: 'Every man and woman is a star'." Bowie's attack on the idea that genius is a necessary precondition for rock stardom paves the way for punk.

Dollar Days

If you've read *Rameau's Nephew*, you may already have an objection to my comparison. Bowie wears masks because he's trying to be a rockstar; Lui, on the other hand, wears masks because he's part of a nobleman's court. You might object that the two figures are only "the same" in a very abstract sense. Sharon Stanley puts this objection perhaps better still:

> One might wonder, though, what this account of *Rameau's Nephew* has to do with us today. After all, Old Regime France was still a monarchical society rooted in a rigid status hierarchy soon to be torn asunder by emergent capitalism and, more decisively still, the French Revolution.

It's tempting to really drag out the metaphor, here, and to talk about the pop/rock world as a kind of aristocratic universe—after all, wasn't Elvis "The King of Rock'n'Roll"? And well into the 1980s we were still talking about the pop world as having a King (Michael) and a Queen (Madonna). As a metaphor for pop celebrity, then, we could certainly do worse than looking to Old Regime France. But to do this would miss the more important lesson of *Rameau's Nephew*, as Stanley once again shows us; for despite its setting in eighteenth-century France, "the nephew's social universe excludes any authentic source of power like a monarch. *Money* becomes the new sun from which all prestige and status radiate in the nephew's world. . . . Thus, Diderot ultimately satirizes a society driven by the pursuit of money, a pursuit in which all the social classes participate" (p. 395). This is why Stanley is able to read *Rameau's Nephew* as an early version of contemporary cynicism: it is not the corruption of pre-Revolutionary France that makes Lui cynical, but the ways in which the (still emerging) market sets social value. And this, ultimately, is the very issue at the heart of the pop-rock distinction. Rock attempts to distance itself from the commodification and hype of pop, but this distance is only ever imaginary.

In the 1960s, the Golden Age of rock, rock began by defining itself against pop: pop is slick, commercial, *inauthentic*, whereas rock is raw, anti-commercial, *authentic*. Charges of "selling out" are thrown at rock artists who too obviously seek out fame, fortune, and chart success, whereas nobody would ever think of accusing a pop artist of "selling out"; pop stars *are packaged and sold*. But the paradox of rock is that, as Mary Harron so rightly notes, it is defined "through things—records, posters, clothes, drugs—that are bought and sold" (p. 180). As rock grew up in the 1960s, intertwined with the counterculture movement, "rock's anticommercialism became the basis of its commercial appeal" (p. 181). All of the great, "purist" rock bands of the 1960s came up through the corporate structure of the music industry, and each was marketed to appeal to teenaged fans.

Connie de Nave, a publicist who established her reputation marketing teen idol pop stars (like Frankie Avalon and Bobby Rydell) in the early 1960s, was also the one who, in 1964, helped the Rolling Stones invade America; by crafting a press release designed to stimulate parental fears about the bad influence of rock bands, and then helping some teenagers organize a demonstration in support of the group, de Nave created a wave of hype to pave the way for the band's jump across the Atlantic (p. 178). But whether lionized (The Beatles) or demonized (The Rolling Stones), all rock icons were essentially marketed the same way: as idols (and sex objects) for teens. Harron recounts the amusing story of a 1965 issue of teen pop magazine *Fabulous*, in which a young Keith Richards is interviewed about "my kind of girl"!

By the early 1970s, the retrenchment of the Sixties hippie, counterculture movement was revealing just how little had changed; The Who were bitterly vowing, "We won't get fooled again," and The Rolling Stones, facing the decline from 1967's Summer of Love to the violence of 1969's Altamont Free Concert, could only shrug, *Let It Bleed* (after all, "You Can't Always Get What You Want"). Without the sustaining illusion of the ideals of the rock revolution, the rock world was revealed to be what it always had been: a commercial enterprise, in which any message—no matter how anticommercialist—could be marketed and sold for maximum profits.

To enter the rock world, you must go through the music industry: this means becoming a commodity, and being marketed—becoming an *image*, and this image (as two-dimensional) cannot really communicate *the truth* of the artist. A would-be rockstar in the 1960s and 1970s has two choices: Within the marketplace of pop/rock stardom, only (inauthentic) images can appear—but the only alternative to appearing inauthentically is to not appear at all.

Either make yourself a commodity in order to get your message (and image) out, or stay pure and separate from the market system—and then you won't be heard at all. Enter Ziggy Stardust, opportunistic parody of rock. Buckley calls

The Rise and Fall of Ziggy Stardust and the Spiders from Mars "a portfolio of songs which dealt with stardom and how it is manufactured within the entertainment business" (*David Bowie: The Music and The Changes*, p. 11). The song "Star," for example, "reveals the grasping self-promotion that is at the center of most popular music." But rather than merely reject the commodified rock of his day as corrupt, Bowie openly *used* its machinery and hype to promote himself into its pantheon—and told his audience exactly what he was doing while he did it.

Within the constraints of the rock world, dominated by the music *industry*, rock stars present themselves as authentic by *lying*—to us, and often even to themselves—about the crafted images they present. The solution adopted by Lui and Bowie is to find a higher truth in ironic distance: this isn't the real me, it's just a mask I wear. If I am forced to be a liar, then I can still be "true" or "authentic" by being *honest* about my deception, and making it clear that I don't identify any of these masks with the "real me." The "authentic self" is kept separate from each of its masks, and now the faker is free to adopt any position at all, to tell any lie he wants, to become *anyone* for as long as necessary. A perfect example of this can be seen in MainMan's approach to marketing Bowie in the early 1970s; as Buckley recounts in *Strange Fascination*, "MainMan had exclusive rights to Bowie's person and image and could also 'fictionalize' the singer's biography for press purposes" (p. 151); the *Mirabelle* diaries "Bowie" kept from May 1973 to April 1975 were actually written by Cherry Vanilla! But David Robert Jones was free to create any kind of "David Bowie" he wanted—and likewise with Ziggy, Aladdin, the Thin White Duke, and the rest—because all of these images were fictions to begin with.

In a similar vein, we might think about Bowie's much-debated sexuality. In that famous January 22nd 1972 interview with *Melody Maker*, Bowie said, "I'm gay." He was of course already married to Angie by this point! The Thin White Duke was probably better described as asexual (What was "plastic soul," after all, but sexy R&B music with all of the human warmth sucked out of it?)—while Ziggy might have been gay, or at least bisexual. Ellen Willis—a great rock critic, though not much of a Bowie fan—seems yet to have gotten it right when she wrote in her October 1972 column for *The New Yorker*:

> British rock musicians have always been less uptight than Americans about displaying, and even flaunting, their "feminine" side. . . . Bowie's dyed red hair, makeup, legendary dresses, and onstage flirtations with his guitarist just take this tradition one theatrical step further. In any case, Bowie's aura is not especially sexual . . . . What Bowie offers is not "decadence" (sorry, Middle America) but a highly-professional pop surface with a soft core.

In other words, these various characters might be said to have had their own sexualities. The debate about Bowie—"was he, or wasn't he?"—seems *really* to be about the question of David Jones's sexuality. And yet, why does anybody care about that? It's not Jones we're interested in, but Bowie—and as a series of fictitious images, it would seem that we can project any kind of sexuality we want—or none at all—onto them. (I am reminded of the debate about whether or not Bert and Ernie are gay; Children's Television Workshop's very smart answer has always been, "They are neither straight nor gay—they are muppets.")

You could also make the case that Bowie—in his pioneering postmodernism—also begins to show us something important about *all* sexuality: it's a performance! The idea that performing certain acts makes you "gay," or "straight," or "bisexual," or whatever, seems to assume that certain kinds of acts either adhere to, or are direct expressions of, an "essential" identity. Bowie is free to fictionalize, lie about, or recreate his persona because it's only a surface, an image from which he keeps his "true self" at an arm's length. By remaining at an ironic distance from any of the roles, the artist is free to create inauthentic images without *making himself* inauthentic. *If you took an axe to me, you'd kill another man—not me at all.*

But what kind of a solution is this? To keep the self "pure" and ironically remote in this way is to make the "true self" nothing at all. The art, the meaning, and the celebrity all cling to the inauthentic image—all that the artist has left as him*self* is the ironic distance between himself and each of his roles. But isn't this simply to make "the self" *just another role*? All "I" am is "the faker," the ironic actor who's "just playing a role." This is why, in probably the most influential interpretation of *Rameau's Nephew*, nineteenth-century German philosopher Georg Hegel draws a link between the ironic, mask-wearing approach of Lui and *madness*.

It's No Game

For Hegel—who situates *Rameau's Nephew* within a larger story about the development of self and culture within history in his book *The Phenomenology of Spirit*—Lui represents a privileged moment in modern thought. French philosophy, with Descartes's "I think, therefore I am," discovers the self or the "I" as a moment separable from anything belonging to me: I am not my body, I am not my desires or my beliefs or my perceptions; I am the thinking agency separable from all of these things. Lewis Hinchman, in *Hegel's Critique of the Enlightenment* (University of Florida Press, 1984), explains:

> Thus the liberation of the 'I' proclaimed in theory by Descartes becomes in practice the cultivation and manipulation of 'images.' Only the man who has no stable self-identity can adopt and discard any identity as circumstances dictate. (p. 121)

But whereas the Nephew is right to recognize that he can separate himself from each and every one of his masks, this ultimately withdraws the "I" into a moment of absolute negativity: "I" am only that which is separate from everything that I do. This moment of absolute negativity hollows out the self. Having "no stable self-identity" becomes *having no identity at all*, the loss of identity that is the fall into madness.

Referencing Lui's own position as a struggling musician, Hegel writes:

> The content of what Spirit says about itself is thus the perversion of every Notion and reality, the universal deception of itself and others; and the shamelessness which gives utterance to this deception is just for that reason the greatest truth. This kind of talk is *the madness of the musician*. (p. 317, emphasis added)

The language here—typical of Hegel—is dense and oblique, but you will see our central themes emerging quite clearly. This "universal deception" Hegel calls "the greatest truth"; in other words, the faker is telling a greater truth than those who (pretend they) don't fake it.

Hegel—especially in his *Phenomenology of Spirit*—is very much like Bowie in two ways. First, his book is full of references, many of them quite obscure, and Hegel will often speak in other people's voices—without telling you whose voice he's borrowing. Hegel pulls from theater, art, literature, science, and psychology, right alongside philosophy—no field is off limits. Second, much like Bowie, people tend to either love Hegel, think he's brilliant—or think he's a charlatan. From Schopenhauer through Popper, you'll find no shortage of people saying the very same sorts of things that Bowie's worst critics have said: he's all style and no substance, he's a con man, he's a fascist. Would it be going too far to call Hegel "The David Bowie of Philosophy"?

Simon Critchley, in his book *Bowie*, puts the matter much more straightforwardly: "The ironic self-awareness of the artist and their audience can only be that of *inauthenticity*, repeated at increasingly conscious levels" (p. 18). "Art's filthy lesson is inauthenticity all the way down, a series of repetitions and reenactments: fakes that strip away the illusion of reality in which we live and confront us with the reality of illusion" (p. 20).

But:

> Bowie's truth is inauthentic, completely self-conscious and utterly constructed. But it is still right. . . . Through the fakery and because

> of it, we feel a truth that leads us beyond ourselves, toward the imagination of some other way of being. (p. 29)

As Hegel puts it, those who simply dismiss the faker as a liar miss the higher truth; the honest liar "will find in their very frankness a strain of reconciliation, will find in their subversive depths the all-powerful note which restores Spirit to itself" (p. 318).

All the Madmen

So the madness of the musician points the way forward, to a possible restoration of spirit (a return of the alienated self to itself). But this "future reconciliation" does nothing to help the poor madman here and now: to be true in a false world is to be an honest liar, an ironic performer, a madman. This is the ultimate connection between two of the central themes of Bowie's work: fame and insanity. You'll love a lad insane. As John Savage puts it, "Role assumption became loss of identity: crack baby crack."

Bowie has long laid the themes of madness and fame side by side, without calling any attention to their interconnections. Where he has called attention to it, it has seemed that insanity is simply a way of describing the life of a celebrity—what Tennessee Williams called "The Catastrophe of Success." In Bowie's early career—songs like "All the Madmen"—the narrator sees his choice between going out into the world with "the sad men" or remaining with the madmen, who are "all as sane as me." The idea seems to be that "going crazy" may simply be going sane in a crazy (or sad) world.

But whereas this may simply be a larger comment on alienated modern society, the song gets referenced again in "The Buddha of Suburbia," where Bowie calls back the "zane, zane, zane, *ouvre le chien*" refrain. Here, I take it, the idea is that the suburban lad is taking his big plunge into the world of the madmen—the world of rockstars and celebrity. In his late, self-referential period, Bowie seems to draw the connections between insanity and fame more closely. The best example of this, I think, is the song "Jump They Say," off of *Black Tie White Noise*.

Everyone seems to have already noticed that "Jump They Say" references the suicide of Bowie's half-brother Terry. But listen to the song again: each and every line could equally well refer to Bowie's own jump into super-stardom. All of the references, in fact—"he was born again," "he has two Gods," "he has no mood"—seem better descriptions of Bowie's characters than of Terry's schizophrenia.

I'm not saying that this song is really about Bowie rather than Terry, or that it's really about stardom instead of schizophrenia; the song uses schizophrenia as a metaphor for stardom, and the "Terry" Bowie describes is also himself. Having come through the madness of his 1980s pop superstardom and the radical, ground-clearing exercise that was Tin Machine, Bowie in the 1990s begins to look back over his career and more explicitly link stardom and madness.

As we saw with the problem of rock authenticity, however, *recognizing* the problem is not the same as *solving* it. And as a host of Bowie's descendants—from Marilyn Manson to Lady Gaga—should make clear, pop/rock stardom is still a matter of commodification and images. And so the choices would still seem to be the same: either appear inauthentically, or don't appear at all. Those who pretend they are not lying are the worst liars of all—but those who admit that they are lying will find that their "authentic" selves are only empty flights into madness. We have seen this process repeat ad nauseam over the last few years with teen pop stars: when they stop being liars, they go crazy. So what's the way forward?

Bowie's own answer to the problem seems to be a sort of "self-referentiality." Bowie's "authentic" period—emerging during the 1990s—is coextensive with the period where his music doesn't just reference other pop tunes and artists, but increasingly references Bowie's own pop history. "Buddha of Suburbia" references both "Space Oddity" (in the familiar guitar riff halfway through the track) and "All the Madmen."

This trend will continue quietly through the 1990s and early 2000s (remember that *Toy*, Bowie's unreleased album in between *'Hours . . .'* and *Heathen*, was mostly an album of covers—but it was Bowie *covering his own early material* from the 1960s), only to take center stage with *The Next Day*. Here, the album is *about* Bowie's past, with the cover image merely a defacement of the cover of *"Heroes."*

The Next Day is also remarkable for Bowie's own media silence: he gave no interviews about the album, and had limited contact with the media during and following its release. It would seem that the actor, "David Jones," has withdrawn (to exist authentically by not appearing at all?), leaving only Bowie as self-referential artwork to be seen. This is a kind of doubling down on his previous self: rather than simply playing the role of the mask-wearer, "Bowie" is now simply the relation between all of the masks he has ever worn. Usher and Fremaux sum up the new, paradoxical and authentic Bowie like this: "He may have offered several hyperreal simulations of 'David Bowie' to the audience, but this presentation is *who* he really is. Performing 'the other' *is* his authentic self" (p. 75).

But is this "authentic performance of the other" really any different than the cheery, postmodern cynicism of his earlier career? It seems to be merely postmodernism with yet another new face. And in the end, the "content" of the self is still merely the emptiness of self-reference, an attempt at self-certainty. The new "stability" of the schizophrenic seems simply to be the stability of self-contemplation, of turning back upon the self as a kind of picture gallery. And so while Bowie shows us the problem, I don't think it's one he can solve; for this, we must look beyond Bowie, to his inheritors.

A Better Future

A few moments ago I called pop stars like Lady Gaga Bowie's "descendants," but we should distinguish "descendants" from "inheritors." After Bowie, there continue to be those who try to cling to authenticity in rock—most of them are outdated liars from the start, but the most honest and perceptive of them run headlong into the very issues that Bowie exposed. Avoiding Bowie's cynicism at the outset, these honest, simple souls wake up to find themselves victims of a tragedy of their own design (I think of Kurt Cobain, for example, who welcomed his new status as pop star with a cover of Bowie's "The Man Who Sold The World" on *MTV Unplugged*).

Still another group, having learned from Bowie's example, will follow him to become cynics, honest liars. It's no coincidence that New Pop, new wave, and postpunk were all full of former Bowie-boys and Bowie-girls: Gary Numan, Annie Lennox, Siouxsie Sioux, Duran Duran, ABC, The Cure's Robert Smith, The Human League's Philip Oakey, and Bauhaus's Peter Murphy were all avowed Bowiephiles, and in the late 1970s and early 1980s, they all reinvented themselves, crafted new images, and transformed themselves into rock stars. The best of them did so while winking at the audience. They have made some great pop music over the years, and I love a lot of them for many of the same reasons I was first drawn to Bowie. All of these honest liars are Bowie's descendants, Bowie's children.

But Bowie's *inheritors* inherit something more from Bowie than an image and a map to stardom. Bowie's true inheritors are the ones who understand the *problem* that Bowie presents, and try to go beyond Bowie. What would it mean to not simply grasp the problem—the inauthenticity of the rockstar market—but to try and *solve* it? Having caught our clearest glimpse of the problem through Hegel's interpretation of *Rameau's Nephew*, it should not be surprising that Hegel also offers us hints about how to move forward. Having seen through the falseness of the world, the honest liar has recognized the *vanity*—the pretentiousness, you might say—of his fellow (would-be-authentic) rockstars. But the cynical faker has also taken up this vanity himself, acknowledging the power of the very marketplace he scorns. This is the insight that will carry us forward. In the following passage, Hegel is referring to the perspective of the honest liar when he writes "it":

> However, this recognition and acceptance is itself vain; and just by taking possession of power and wealth it knows them to be without a self of their own, knows rather that *it* is the power over them, while they are vain things. . . . In such talk, this particular self, . . . determined neither by reality nor by thought, develops into a spiritual self that is of truly universal worth. It *is* the self-disruptive nature of all relationships and the conscious disruption of them; but only as self-consciousness in revolt is it aware of its own disrupted state, and in thus knowing it has immediately risen above it. (pp. 320–21)

What we have is in fact a two-part process, and by suggesting that we must go beyond Bowie I am in no way denigrating him or suggesting that we discard him! Sharon Stanley is right to see a vital role for the cynic:

> So long as cynicism is not universal, then, cynics may help more politically motivated actors to sharpen their social critiques and achieve a clear-eyed recognition of the forces with which they must content. Cynics can therefore act as provocative gadflies. Lui may refuse to act on his exposure of M. Bertin's decadence and profligacy, but he has paved the way for others to do so. (p. 405)

Bowie plays the necessary "gadfly" role of revealing the way the music industry commodifies and sells off the image of the artist. He then makes the cynical move of commodifying and selling off his own image—and his "children" have been doing so ever since. But those who inherit—and grapple directly with—the problem are those ultimately who are *radicalized* by what Bowie shows us. These radicals realize that we can only solve the problem by changing the system. You'll catch a glimpse of this radical task in the way Mary Harron, in her "McRock" essay, sums up the legacy of Sixties counterculture rock:

> Why attack the music industry when it is yours to run, when it expresses your every thought—or at least as long as those thoughts sell? . . . Only in the early seventies, when the counterculture had

> lost its politics and its drive, would it become clear how little the corporate structure of the music business had changed. Until then it seemed that the spirit of that culture, channeled through its music, would defeat corporations. (p. 185)

Harron follows the cynical story right through the 1970s and into punk; to be sure, Malcolm McLaren was every bit the clever cynic that Bowie was, and the Sex Pistols put this cynicism to good use in their dealings with the record industry. But there is another story we can tell about punk. In the wake of Bowie's glam cynicism, there emerged another, very different response to the pop-industrial complex: DIY.

You Belong in Rock'n'Roll

While there's a certain, cynical layer of pop stardom visible in the punk explosion, there is another layer that directly takes up Bowie's challenge. First, in the punk imperative to *be your own hero* ("Here's three chords; now go start a band"), punk attempts to realize what Savage called Bowie's promise: Every man and every woman is a star. In one sense, this is to destroy the idea of genius by making the star, the genius, the individual into a "type": *everybody* should be a star. *We* can be heroes. But taken seriously, this is also to destroy the idea of "type" once and for all: if *everyone* is the same "type," then there are no longer types—only individuals. By each becoming our own hero, there are no longer heroes and followers.

But second, the DIY punk movement also realizes that Bowie's cynicism is necessary because the music world is dominated by the music *industry*. And so rather than say, "If you can't beat 'em, join 'em," beginning in the late 1970s a group of artists says, "Let's beat 'em." Do-it-yourself is first and foremost an attack on the music industry: you don't need the A&R reps, the record contracts, the expensive producers; you can do it yourself. This DIY spirit is found not just in certain punk quarters (The Desperate Bicycles, Buzzcocks, Minor Threat, Black Flag), but also in the hip-hop movement in the Bronx and Queens and the house and techno scenes in Chicago and Detroit—all springing up around the same time.

The history of the DIY movement would take me too far off topic for this chapter—and the history has already been well told by people like Simon Reynolds and Michael Azerrad. And just as the cynicism of Bowie was "not a final stopping point beyond which there can be no appeal," nor has the indie scene turned out to be one—at the very least, Simon Frith has studied the ways in which the indie scene of the 1980s has been eventually reabsorbed by the music industry (*Facing The Music*, especially pp. 104–114).

Taking Bowie seriously today still means going beyond him; and allowing Bowie to serve as our gadfly means taking up his challenge to become our own heroes, our own rockstars—with the hope of eventually overcoming the need for cynicism and madness.

14
David Bowie's Sadness

CHRISTOPHER KETCHAM

David Bowie's sadness isn't his—it's ours. It's in us as in the high-school football star who stands before his trophy cabinet neatly arranged with fading photographs and tarnished trophies to which he shines a backlight for all to see.

But he's long past his prime with paunch and receding hairline that's no match now for the crew-cut buff figure in full pads, on one knee in the centerpiece. He graduated from high school but has never left. He's gone to every game since, living vicariously through the generations of players that follow, even some into college. The aging footballer is the sadness of what Bowie speaks. It's the cement into which we can seal ourselves, never progressing, never learning, repeating the unrepeatable.

Bowie is part mime, part verbal performer. Through his mime, Bowie's shouting at us with his silent mouth to move beyond where we're stuck. Watch him in his box routine on stage while the rest of the band plays on. He stands in his box, full of himself with puffed out chest until he discovers that he's trapped. He pushes on every wall until he finds the door, opens it, and beckons us to follow him. Will you follow or stay behind? You aren't sure . . . but then you are. See, he steps one step and then he becomes stuck again as if his feet are in cement. He tries to twist himself out of the pose. He can't. Aren't you glad you didn't follow?

You see, that's the problem. Like others: advertisers, employers, co-workers, and friends Bowie is asking you to follow him. You do and immediately become stuck in some other routine that's difficult to get out of. Or, you mill about waiting for something to come along to follow. You follow the fads and you wonder, in the end, Who am I really?

It's the conflicting messages we all get. Wear this suit and become one of the beautiful people. You wear the suit but are shunted to the back of the line in front of the posh nightclub because, let's face it, you ain't beautiful. You're stuck. Let's move on, says Bowie. We're going to give you a new personality just like schizophrenics get from time to time and Bowie is the voice in your head saying follow, follow.

And you do. You grovel at the altar of becoming the fad which soon unbecomes its importance. Bowie is there to help you find another fad even before you know the fad has faded. How does he do this?

Mime or Pantomime

David Bowie studied miming with Lindsay Kemp and others, and has often included miming routines in his stage and video performances (*Strange Fascination*, p. 5). However, his performance genre is more like the English or Christmas pantomime. Mime and pantomime are not the same thing; they're distinctly different.

In the English pantomime the story centers around a fairytale; there's a good bit of singing, dancing, slapstick comedy and cross-dressing. Costumes range from garish to earthy. The audience is expected to sing along and shout out warnings and hiss at villains and taunt jesters. The English pantomime twists the familiar, the fairytale or nursery rhyme into something bawdy, raucous, and then adds a kink of difference to the performance. Difference, yet I can't put my finger on what that difference actually is or what it means.

You can see the same in a Bowie show, the familiar—astronauts—spun into song and choreographed stage antics using the technique of the theater, dance, and rock to emphasize the lyrics. All the while we wonder at the androgyny of Bowie—the *alien* rock star Ziggy Stardust, costumed for the story for the song that is being sung . . . just enough different to wonder just what is this being? The audience sings along, claps and screams in the right places and comes back again to the theater when Bowie does. When they do, it is another Bowie; another fairytale. David Buckley calls him, "supremely mythogenic" (p. 13).

If his show is the English pantomime, Bowie himself is the mime. He's The Who's Tommy—the deaf, dumb, and blind kid—who plays a mean pinball. The pinball wizard is everything but Bowie himself—the silent mime who performs for us, through us, without revealing himself. His chameleon evolves before our eyes and we wonder at the next Bowie we might experience. But are we experiencing Bowie or just his mime? I suggest the mime.

Anatman—No Self

Buckley explains that Bowie studied Buddhism with Chime Youngdong Rimpoche (p. 47). Fundamental to the Buddha's understanding is that there's no separate self or soul. Our minds are continuously seeing, thinking and changing. Our body evolves from youth to old age and we continually create new cells and discard others. We are a system in continuous flux. The Buddha understood this—it's one of the pillars of Buddhist belief. However, this impermanence, while it is a part of everyday existence, also produces *dukkha* or what many call suffering. Wait a minute. There's no one self? Are you saying that we're all schizophrenics, running from one self to another? If we can't hang on to—cling to—that which we are, is this not madness? So said Bowie, the sad men roam free but they die. I'd rather be with the madmen ("All the Madmen," *The Man Who Sold the World*, 1970). Fine, you say, be with the madmen. But schizophrenics have wiring problems. You're wired okay, you say. So be it. So, if you are wired okay, where does this schizophrenia come from?

Schizophrenia

Freud didn't like Schizophrenics because they resist "becoming oedipalized" (So say Deleuze and Guattari in *Anti-Oedipus*, p. 23). Remember, Freud had boys lusting after their mothers like the Greek Oedipus who even married his mother. It's all about sex, sex, sex. Freud didn't like schizophrenics because they didn't quite fit the mold and didn't respond well to the therapy Freud created, called psychoanalysis.

Why not? Well, there are three concepts that Deleuze and Guattari say are common to schizophrenia. First of all, they dissociate—they're not quite connected to the world so the therapy just doesn't get through. They also demonstrate autistic behavior, specifically: being stuck in a particular routine like, for example, head banging, or repeating an action over and over again. Third, they distort space-time (p. 22). We never know whether they're here or somewhere else.

According to Deleuze and Guattari, schizophrenia is embedded in our capitalist society. Produce, produce, produce. But when profits fall, find something new to produce. Send those who buy on spending sprees to buy more and then stop them with a new voice—the new voice of advertising to purchase something different. Find those most likely to purchase what you are selling and get them to buy and buy again. Go into debt to buy more and then find a better job to earn more to buy more and pay down the ever mounting debt. When profits fall, do it to us all over again.

But wait a minute, you just said that it's the schizophrenic society, the one without a self, that's running from one personality to another that is the cause of my schizophrenia . . . even though I maintain that I am wired okay.

Certainly, you speak the truth. But isn't that part of the problem—being stuck in trying to become something you can't become, but at the same time trying to remain stuck in who you are or once were like our nostalgic footballer? You're caught up in the wave of production, reeling from fad to fad while at the same time you're trying to keep from becoming unglued. Sometimes, like the footballer, you stop and then what happens. You get stuck. To get unstuck you have to go back out there, back into that roller coaster called society.

Think about it. Bowie unveils new personalities with each new routine—he never goes back. He progresses even though it is probably wrenching to him and certainly for you and I who have to figure out this new persona and what it means. Perhaps that is what Bowie is trying to say about the no-self. Get over it and become. But become in your way, not what society wants you to be.

A Problem with Time

The issue associated with time, psycho-phenomenologist Eugene Minkowski concluded, is that in relationship to becoming, time is both succession and duration. He called this *lived succession* and *lived duration* (*Lived Time*, p. 26). We are both being and becoming. We have *élan vital*, meaning that we're constantly looking forward. Minkowski offered that if the *élan vital* is impaired by schizophrenia, for example, we do not become—we remain stuck in a mode of being that isn't forward-looking. He describes one patient as becoming more and more withdrawn (autistic), retreating further and further into himself in order to not have to experience the blows of life (p. 411). This pathology of abbreviated time Bowie addresses in the title of his song, "Love You Till Tuesday" (1967).

Bowie's own half-brother became schizophrenic and mental illness stalks his family. Bowie's sadness isn't about his family; it's about the mechanized schizophrenia that Deleuze and Guattari wonder about. Sure you're wired okay, but is society? Everyone wants you to be like them—wear their suits, drink their booze—it's the best, the highest, the most wonderful! But then they bring you the new and improved model. You reel from one high to another, never touching ground. But you do touch ground when you crash in between because all of that psychic energy you built up to be what they told you ought to be has just been let out like a hissing balloon (*Anti-Oedipus*, p. 34). The yo-yo of the capitalist structure seeks both higher limits of production and to repress them at the same time when something new comes along. Think about it: just like the competing voices of the schizophrenic. Giving but withholding, says Bowie: "She will be your living soul . . . But she won't stake her life on you" ("Lady Grinning Soul," *Aladdin Sane*, 1973).

Bowie's Magical Worlds

The schizophrenia which Bowie is reacting to, and in good measure displaying for us through the magical world of production, is the schizophrenia that territorializes—puts us like the mime into the schizophrenic's box without a place to escape, while at the same time society wants more and more from us. Bowie's generation, says Buckley, was the first to understand the American import of capitalism as sterile and imperialistic (*Strange Fascination*, p. 15). The madness of voices yelling both stop and start at the same time produces not a raving lunatic we associate with the psychotic schizophrenic, but the robotic moving autistic schizophrenic who does the same thing over and over again because it is comfortable to do so.

As Buckley points out, the media has a hand in this by creating, "a 'false' notion of community," through the sameness of being—being one with the other; the other with the one (*Strange Fascination*, p. 17). Bowie reacts by fashioning the stage, the song, the act, and the dance as a community to which we are invited to engage. Then he snatches it away with his next album and invites us into a different community.

Bowie continually escapes from the box of how we want to see him. To do so, Bowie delves into the magical world of production, steeping himself in it with the most elaborate costumes, sets, and special effects he can find. The transformation is never complete for the change is but temporary and the true mime that he is, we never see his insides. As Buckley says, "Some of the musicians who have spent months and months on the road with Bowie have little idea of what he's really like" (p. 7).

We hear the schizophrenic; we see the schizophrenic, but the schizophrenic is foreign because the schizophrenic resists becoming shoved into the psychoanalytic box, just one box of many required by societal production. However, says Bowie, it's a slow burn, where we're led on and on and on in a terrible little town: the box of it all ("Heathen," 2002).

Bowie's British pantomimes come from the fairytales of society—spacemen, plastic soul, heroes, golden years. He usurps them for his own end through the grotesque and sublime, leading us into his dressing room where all we see are costumes, wigs, makeup—but he doesn't let us see what the mannequin underneath really is. He has disabused us of the self, the soul, gender, and he emphasizes the being of production that wants ever more, but he closes the stage door before we can pin a marquee on it. Then he's gone, dancing away from the stage door never to return the same again. He leaves us wanting more. Even so, "He's a quadrophonic . . . he's got more channels" ("Station to Station", 1976). Yes, he's over the top. Why? Well, doesn't that capitalist society want you over the top—select all the car options, the bigger house, the longer yacht? He's just giving us what society says we should have. Yet society keeps us in our place through the realities of the two percent annual raise and the persistent lack of opportunities for minorities.

Anon, the Dance

We're unnerved by madness, Say Deleuze and Guattari, not by its extreme but because the mad seem so innocent, and, "If schizophrenia is the universal, the great artist is indeed the one who scales the schizophrenic wall and reaches the land of the unknown, where he no longer belongs to any time, any milieu, any school" (*Anti-Oedipus*, p. 88). For Bowie, its Minkowski time, both duration and change. He has endured, but like Deleuze and Guattari's great artist, he resists any moniker, label, or genre. Nor has there been another like him; perhaps there never will be.

Claire Colebrook asks, But what of the dance and dancer? The traditional Aristotelean view is that we are a species of norms ("How Can We Tell the Dancer from the Dance?" p. 5). The dance then is constituted towards the meaning of the norms of life, right? Wrong. The dance is both duration and change. It's also production and movement. Says Colebrook, "The dance is the end itself; at each moment in the dance we are fully dancing, and we do not have to complete the dance to say that we have danced" (p. 8). The dance is the means and the end to life itself. The dance moves us out of our complacency; but not into the schizophrenic norm of society ever wanting more and more but denying it to us at the same time. Rather the dance is all about the dancing—it's living, damn it!

Bowie uses the dance to dance himself from moment to moment. He doesn't stop, as life itself never stops; life just keeps dancing until the end of time, the end of being itself. The dance isn't the body. It's the potentiality of the body, says Colebrook, "it is the present without thickness, the present of the actor, dancer, or mime—the pure perverse 'moment'" (p. 11). Perverse because it's outside of the box. It's movement, not stasis. The dance flows past the body, overcomes the body—it sings the body transcendentally.

Colebrook looked at the dance in relationship to the schizophrenia of our society. Each dancer sets out a territory. They may come together now and again, but there is distance between them for the most part. Is the dance an endless flailing about without any choreography to guide it, or is it a negotiation of, "The chaos that always threatens to introduce too much difference" (p. 12). We try to maintain our sanity even in the world of chaos which tells us to strive for more is what you should do, but less is all you can get. This is the schizophrenia of which Deleuze and Guattari speak . . . and which Bowie exemplifies by: going around and around the garage again at high speed, but he is "always crashing in the same car" ("Low," 1977).

However, is the dance of the mime, Bowie's dance, one of spacing, of territorializing . . . or is it the dance that seeks to uncover the edges of the box, the prison, the catatonic grasping onto the sameness that covers the chaos of our everydayness? The mime wants out; the mime seeks to find ways to become from being territorialized for too long. It is the mime who sees beyond the box but confines being within that box, grasping and holding the viewer to the same. We become frustrated as is the mime. Then the mime lets us go and we are once again free to think, to move, to dance our own dance.

Bowie's mime centers and decenters at the same time. We come to see the last Bowie who no longer exists. He makes us prisoner to the new Bowie and then disappears again, leaving his songs behind only to reappear guised as something foreign to any of the Bowies we have come to know before. He's dancing through us, you see, while he's also dancing past us, beckoning us to come along to dance with him, better yet, to create our own dances even to overcome him, to pass him by on the road to our own potentiality. Don't just listen; don't just sing along; dance and dance some more: "Let's dance . . . let's sway . . . in this serious moonlight" ("Let's Dance," 1983). Ah, the schizophrenic moon that is both romantic and hides monsters in its eerie light. Don't stop dancing or love might capture you; don't stop dancing or the bogeyman will catch you.

Paying the Price

The schizophrenia of capitalism's bipolar production, seeking ever higher goals while putting limits on the same produces a society that becomes stuck in that paradigm as a steel rod does between two opposing magnets. The cost of breaking out of the magnetic vice is sanity itself. Standing still is difficult to pull off, for sure, but at the same time one becomes invisible, a fixture in the world—nobody bothers the statue-you. Sanity as stasis has its own price and that is the inauthentic being. Here's what I mean.

Martin Heidegger called the others, the other beings in your world *the they*. You want to be like the they. Granted you may be different from the they, but you are all in the magnetic vice together. It's easier to be a they than an I. Being the I, the different being, the anti-oedipal who doesn't conform to what is considered the norm is what Heidegger called the being towards death. The one who is frozen in the path of death is the one we worry about. You, the other (the well-wired one) cares about the world and at the same time understands that for you, the world, this world now and the time remaining, is all the time that there is. You who becomes a me outside of theyness becomes an authentic you, albeit an authentic you towards death.

While Heidegger speaks of death in the sense of being no more, death is also the systematic destruction and re-creation of you from moment to moment. Being in the moment and re-creating yourself in a forward looking manner—dancing the dance of life, is frightening and unnerving. Bowie explains, "Let me dance . . . And I'm gone . . . Like a dead man walking" ("Dead Man Walking," *Earthling*, 1997). I am dancing unto death, but please, don't let me stop dancing.

As Minkowski says, our own dance is a complexity involving time, lived distance, and goals. Minkowski compares the normal concept of distance to lived distance. Lived distance is either the dancing you, or the stuck you. If you dance your lived distance, you go from here to there to achieve a goal, which is something more than just distance and place. Not only are you moving in time, but you are traversing space (*Lived Time*, p. 402). What can you do to maximize your lived distance? Don't stop dancing. But understand this: "Time may change me; But I can't trace time" ("Changes," *Hunky Dory,* 1971).

Major Tom slips from the bonds of Earth to travel among the stars. His technology fails, but Major Tom continues on, watching the blue of Earth, seemingly without care. He has escaped the bonds of everydayness and he's a being towards death but in the moment, the moment of mindfulness of being all that he can be—even though he is tethered to a dying spaceship: "No one here can see you . . . No one here can beat you . . . Dancing out in space" ("Dancing Out in Space," *The Next Day*, 2013). His lived distance has become a dance, a dancing out in space. What a delightful end!

No less are the demon monsters of everydayness. The tearing down and building up of authentic you towards death can and does take a toll. Peter Sellers suffered for his many personas. He experienced depression but at the same time played raucous comedic roles like Inspector Clouseau, and Dr. Strangelove. Robin Williams seemed always to be in role, which left the casual observer believing he left little of himself for himself. David Bowie on the other hand over the years has seemed comfortable in his different roles, but made this revealing comment in 1976: "Bowie was never meant to be. He's like a Lego kit. I'm convinced I wouldn't like him, because he's vacuous and undisciplined. There is no definitive David Bowie" (*Strange Fascination*, p. 1). He's not the everyman because the everyman is foreign to him. He's like Ralph Ellison's *Invisible Man* who says from his basement home, "Whence all this passion towards conformity anyway?—diversity is the word. Let man keep his many parts and you'll have no tyrant states. Why, if they follow this conformity business they'll end up forcing me, an invisible man, to become white, which is not a color but the lack of one" (pp. 435–36). Isn't the invisible man the product of the same schizophrenic society, becoming what they want, which isn't becoming someone at all, but becoming no one.

So, how do they get you to buy into it? Conditioning and subtle changes—the same but with a twist. You can choreograph a dance and perform it again and again. Likely it will be only slightly different from time to time. However, given new choreography, the dance, even to the same music, may become quite different. What Bowie grapples with (as did Sellers and probably Williams) is where the choreography ends and the dance begins. Finding new steps, rhythms, and moves isn't an easy process. It requires more thinking, more being, more dancing than repeating the same old moves over and over again.

We've been lulled into George Balanchine's *Swan Lake*. We've seen it again and again. Difference is frowned upon, but we like the higher throw or the more graceful pirouette—exaggeration, not difference. The schizophrenia of the Balanchine Swan Lake production is that it must soar to new heights while maintaining the consistency of the moves—the Brand Balanchine.

Bowie the mime has no such franchise. He soars; he suffers. He becomes the in-act then the also-ran act. You see, there is nothing anyone can pin on him. As David Buckley says, "Bowie was living proof that our personalities are constantly in flux, constantly being made and remade, not fixed in stone by age, class or gender" (*Strange Fascination*, p. 7). Like many entertainers, even his name is flexible. He began life as David Jones and in 1965 became David Bowie, his first real change of persona (p. 27).

Nor is his mime pure. He's taken the mime of Buster Keaton and Charlie Chaplain from the silent movie era and let loose all of the cacophony that the talkies would unleash upon the world. His is no mute mime like Marcel Marceau, asking us to believe what we see, not what we hear. Rather a Bowie performance asks us to fill the silences of the wordless mime with the music of the world, creating a ballet, of sorts, with full orchestra. Then he tears himself from his mime and becomes once again the musician and singer. He informs us with his performance not to expect, but to anticipate, to dance with him, not to lag behind or dwell in what just was or has been.

Faddishista

David Bowie's sadness isn't just his own internal struggle with identity but with his seemingly endless transformations of his persona through this or that element of pop culture that seems to grasp for purchase without ever finding any. He's led us, running from this fad or fashion to the next on an incessant trying on with no intent to keep it for long. "There's what I was yesterday; that is now sitting in the consignment shop where maybe someone will want it; but it is no longer for me, or mine, or of me." This or that fad-full persona has been shed like a butterfly's cocoon. "There I am, pretty again, but it will not last because literally I have no stomach, no stomach at all to keep this going for very long." He reveals the schizophrenia of Deleuze and Guattari's production, always wanting more and more, putting it on and ripping it off at the same time. And remember, I'm "Getting my facts from a Benetton ad" ("Black Tie White Noise," 1993). Society has convinced you that Benetton is the authentic you, you most want to be.

The sadness of David Bowie is also in the superficiality he's so good at showing us about our fad-full selves and shoving it in our faces. Bowie exposes our cultural bipolarity: raging popularity one moment only to commit violent suicide the next as we reel from one vacuous high to another listless low, hoping for the next high to be even higher. The swings loosen our bearing and mooring along the way, serving only to have us bob up and down with the tide, as so much flotsam in the sea of society that would just as soon flush us into the bay as carry us along with it.

It isn't the popular culture that is to blame, but the investment by some in it. The caution is with Sellers and Williams in mind and even with Bowie's own denial of his own identity, that there is a cost to becoming totally invested in the faddish moment. What worries the faddishista most is at what moment of continuous metamorphosis will I awake like Franz Kafka's Gregor Samsa in *The Metamorphosis* and become a bug, unsavory to all and what is worse, myself? How much can I enjoy before I crash and burn? Said Bowie, "It's all deranged, no control" ("No Control," *Outside*, 1995).

Beyond the Pleasure Principle

Pleasure is the release of excess excitation, so said Freud (*Beyond the Pleasure Principle*). At the same time our ego tries to limit the stimuli that produce too much excitation, by a being towards death, tamping, even stomping on stimuli to release the tensions of excitation.

Simon Critchley rightly states that Freud needed to go beyond the pleasure principle because "The psyche is not oriented towards the fulfillment of wishes that result in pleasure. Rather, the psyche is organized in relationship to a trauma. And, "To go beyond the pleasure principle is to assent that what trauma yields is compulsive repetition, and the compulsion to repeat overrides the pleasure principle" (*The Problem with Levinas*, pp. 69–70). Are we locked into this compulsive repetition? Is the trauma of being towards death the only option?

Bowie reveals the trauma of the psyche by changing over and over again. He takes the being subdued by the ego towards its own repetition and reveals the pleasure of excess, the surplus of being more and more without ever repeating. He's asking us to maximize. We are Heidegger's being towards death, but we are also the mindful Buddha, living in the moment without dwelling in the past. The surfeit of emotion which Freud tried to tamp down by going beyond the pleasure principle isn't a death wish for Bowie, but a release of the tension of being in the schizophrenic world of production. However, with his own comments and that of others who jump from role to role, we realize he's askance to a society that requires us to follow what production tells us to do rather than our own way, and this does take its toll.

Heidegger suggests that the authentic being is a challenge because we must buck the they to get there and we are but beings towards death anyway which must be turned around from a death wish to a life wish in the face of death. What Bowie has done is to proclaim that we can become authentic in spite of the pressures to conform, to product, to repeat, to stay, doggie stay. But with this authenticity comes cost which many are not willing to pay.

15
Aladdin Sane or Cracked Actor?

SIMON RICHES AND ANDREW WATSON

When David Bowie was asked by BBC television chat show host Michael Parkinson about his relationship with his mother, he quoted Philip Larkin's famous line:

> They fuck you up, your Mum and Dad
> They may not mean to
> But they do.

Bowie mentions his family history of mental health problems on several occasions: "Everyone says, 'Oh yes, my family is quite mad.' Mine really is" (quoted in *Bowie: Loving the Alien*).

Several members of Bowie's family received treatment for mental health problems. Perhaps this preoccupation with mental health reflects Bowie's own fear of becoming unwell. In the following passage we see how self-aware Bowie was about his vulnerability to losing his grip on reality:

> My family's nuts. They're all pretty crazy. There's quite an amount of insanity within any family I think. I think we just got more than our share. But it's better to kind of recognize the angels and devils within oneself, I think, and that prevents true insanity. I'm no more insane than the next man but I keep making myself aware of how flighty I am and what a grasshopper I am and how my moods

> change such a lot, so drastically and even more my persona changes quite a lot. There's one minute I can be quite verbose and articulate and the next I feel like a stumbling philistine. (*Jarvis Cocker's Sunday Service*)

Bowie was particularly troubled by the illness of his step-brother, Terry, who had a diagnosis of paranoid schizophrenia, eventual committing suicide due to the condition. It was Terry who first introduced Bowie to popular music, playing him his vinyl collection at an early age. Many believe Bowie did not cope well with the tragic death of Terry, who then featured in several of Bowie's songs. "The Bewlay Brothers" is a notable example.

Ideas of madness were formative on Bowie's outlook and featured in much of his work. Despite his concerns about his own vulnerability, there is evidence from Bowie's songs that he struggled with inner conflict. On "Oh You Pretty Things," Bowie sings about a crack in the sky. Discussing this song in a BBC interview, Bowie connects his own experiences to what he terms a 'kind of schizophrenia' or an 'alternating Id':

> A lot of the songs do in fact deal with some kind of schizophrenia or alternating Id problems and "Pretty Things" was one of them. The sky, the crack in the sky is always . . . according to Jung . . . to see cracks in the sky is not really quite on. And I did, you know, the sky for me representing something solid that could be cracked and I still had a dome over the world which again I found out was just my own repressions. I haven't been to an analyst, my parents went and my brothers and sisters and my aunts and uncles and cousins and . . . they ended up in a much worse state so I stayed away. I thought I'd write my problems out really. (*David Bowie at the BBC*)

Here Bowie alludes to the fact that he deals with his inner turmoil by writing about it in his songs. So much so, in fact, that if we consider passages from Bowie lyrics, they appear to show that he often blurs the distinction between his imagination and his perceived reality. This blurring often allows his imagination to transition into hallucination and become what he considers to be his reality.

In considering mental states of this kind, we might think of the symptoms of serious mental health conditions such as psychosis. People with a diagnosis of psychosis often feel disconnected from reality and experience delusions and hallucinations that distort what appears real to them.

Some of Bowie's songs, like "Space Oddity," have an otherworldly, distant quality: a symbolic representation of him leaving our world or our reality. Bowie was very interested in exploring the unconscious, as can be seen from his interest in the Swiss psychoanalyst Carl Jung. Jung was the originator of many now-popular psychological concepts including the archetype, extraversion and introversion and the collective unconscious—all prominent themes in Bowie's work. Bowie mentions Jung in several interviews and songs, including "Drive-In Saturday." His reference in this song to "Sylvian" perhaps refers to the "Sylvian fissure" (also known as the lateral sulcus), a prominent structure of the brain, which many believed to be associated with auditory hallucinations, a typical symptom of psychosis.

We might consider this apprehension of reality in psychosis to be fragmented, and this can often be very distressing for those who experience it; and yet there can be a sense in which Bowie also embraces this fragmentation. One way he embraced the fragmentation of reality was in the "cut up" writing style that he borrowed from Beat Generation writer William Burroughs to construct some of his songs and develop song writing ideas. This appears to be a deliberate attempt to fragment reality.

The various alter egos that Bowie brings to life (Aladdin Sane, Ziggy Stardust, and the Thin White Duke) might be said to constitute manifestations of these hallucinations and of this fragmented conception of reality. Speaking about the birth of the character Ziggy Stardust, Bowie stated:

> I didn't know who to be when I got out there, that was the big struggle . . . I was wondering if I should try and be me or, if I couldn't

> cope with that, then make up some people and would I be them easier and it was much easier to be somebody else and so I was somebody else and then it worked better . . . so I said I was an actor and came up with all these different guises and that seems to be how it's evolved really and now I seem to be finding it much easier to get nearer to some kind of me. . . . but I wonder, though. . . . I don't know, I don't think so. . . . maybe I'm still acting up there. I wanted to be anybody but me, I think. And that's how Ziggy got started, you see. . . . I thought, well, if I don't like being David Jones, then we'll think of somebody else to be for a bit and we came up with Ziggy. (*David Bowie at the BBC*)

In this statement we see that even Bowie himself is unclear about when he is playing a character and when he is himself. In constructing this range of characters and apparently bringing them to life, Bowie's understanding of reality raises metaphysical and epistemological questions about what's real and what's merely imagined, and how we can tell the difference.

We might think of the uncertainty raised by these questions in much the same way that the seventeenth-century French philosopher René Descartes observed that dreams could often be mistaken for reality:

> I am in the habit of sleeping, and representing to myself in dreams those same things, or even sometimes others less probable, which the insane think are presented to them in their waking moments. How often have I dreamt that I was in these familiar circumstances, that I was dressed, and occupied this place by the fire, when I was lying undressed in bed? At the present moment, however, I certainly look upon this paper with eyes wide awake; the head which I now move is not asleep; I extend this hand consciously and with express purpose, and I perceive it; the occurrences in sleep are not so distinct as all this. But I cannot forget that, at other times I have been deceived in sleep by similar illusions; and, attentively considering those cases, I perceive so clearly that there exist no certain marks by which the state of waking can ever be distinguished from sleep, that I feel greatly astonished; and in amaze-

> ment I almost persuade myself that I am now dreaming. (*Meditations on First Philosophy*, Meditation I)

Descartes put forward this argument in the context of a methodology of radical skepticism about the external world. Descartes was aiming to understand what could be known with absolute certainty and found that a lot of what he thought he knew could, in fact, be subject to doubt. It is this kind of radical skepticism which lies at the heart of philosophical ideas in popular culture, such as we find in *The Matrix*.

Descartes was making a point about the nature of *knowledge*. A key philosophical question is to consider how we can *know* what's real and what's merely imagined. Bowie's constructed reality casts doubt on how he, and indeed, we, can know what's real and what's imagined.

In the case of Bowie, the reality of the newly created characters appears to be convincingly maintained through a complex web of delusions. For instance, the depth of Bowie's delusional belief that he is Ziggy Stardust is exemplified in the fact that Ziggy is a wholly-formed creation that takes over Bowie's entire existence. In the BBC film *Cracked Actor*, filmmaker Alan Yentob described Ziggy Stardust as "A parody of the archetypal rock star and an extension" of Bowie's "own personality."

In adopting these characters and making them an extension of his personality, Bowie is potentially deluded that he actually is these characters (or that they are actually him). Some philosophers have argued that this kind of delusion is undesirable. Consider for instance the view of twentieth-century British philosopher Bertrand Russell: "It is not by delusion, however exalted, that mankind can prosper, but only by unswerving courage in the pursuit of truth ("The Pursuit of Truth").

Perhaps this concern about delusion underpins Bowie's cry, "Who'll love Aladdin Sane?" And yet there's also a sense in which Bowie's numerous identities, maintained by a network of delusion, appear to provide Bowie with a therapeutic catharsis. Perhaps these characters are an escape from his internal conflicts. However, in the end, Bowie abandons each delusion, killing off his characters, such as Ziggy with his rock'n'roll suicide, in order to return to his true self. In his later years Bowie becomes more comfortable being 'David Bowie', perhaps indicating the fruition of a psychological process that began with the demise of David Jones and the creation of new selves.

Turn and Face the Strange

An alternative way of looking at Bowie is that he deliberately questions what it means to be 'sane'; exploring and challenging the societal norms and expectations of rationality. For instance, on *All the Madmen*, Bowie describes his affinity with what he terms 'the madmen': "For I'm quite content they're all as sane as me."

This could mean that all the 'madmen' he speaks of are, in fact, 'sane'; or it could mean that Bowie considers himself to be one of the 'madmen'. However, on either interpretation Bowie appears to be casting doubt on the cogency of the distinction between madness and sanity.

Compare this interpretation of Bowie's work with the view of French philosopher and social theorist Michel Foucault who highlights the historically-relative, socially constructed elements of the distinction between madness and sanity:

> The constitution of madness as a mental illness, at the end of the eighteenth century, affords the evidence of a broken dialogue, posits the separation as already effected, and thrusts into oblivion all those stammered, imperfect words without fixed syntax in which the exchange between madness and reason was made. The language of psychiatry, which is a monologue of reason about madness, has been established only on the basis of such a silence. (*Madness and Civilization*)

Consider also the views of American psychiatrist Thomas Szasz, who wrote the following in 1973: "If you talk to God, you are praying; If God talks to you, you have schizophrenia. If the dead talk to you, you are a spiritualist; If you talk to the dead, you are a schizophrenic" *(The Second Sin)*.

Elsewhere, Szasz writes:

> By pretending that convention is Nature, that disobeying a personal prohibition is a medical illness, [psychiatrists] establish themselves as agents of social control and at the same time disguise their punitive interventions in the semantic and social trappings of medical practice. (*The Manufacture of Madness*, p. 167)

In espousing these views, Szasz was challenging assumptions about mental health and psychiatry in America in a fundamental and radical way. Szasz was doing this around the same time as Bowie was challenging similar assumptions about rationality and identity in his music.

In many ways, both men were writing in the spirit of the times. This was a highly politicised era: there was heightened awareness about civil rights, an anti-authoritarian stance towards the Vietnam War, feminism, and most pertinent to the discussion at hand, the antipsychiatry movement, exemplified by such thinkers as Szasz, R. D. Laing, David Cooper, and others. What these movements had in common was a move away from the powerful subjugating the oppressed towards a more equal society.

Such an interpretation of Bowie as a thinker who is challenging our basic assumptions and categories in order to make a political point towards a more equal society is supported by the fact that he challenged societal norms in many other areas as well as that of mental health. Take, for instance, the topics of gender and sexuality, two themes that recur throughout his work. In "Oh you Pretty Things" he famously sings, "Don't you know you're driving your Mamas and Papas insane?" and concludes: "You gotta make way for the Homo Superior."

Just as a few years earlier Bob Dylan had warned parents that "The Times They Are A-Changin'." In "Oh You Pretty Things" we find Bowie in similarly assertive mood, showing that the categories of sexuality and gender identity are changing in radical ways that will challenge the establishment. And it's clear from Bowie's lyrics that this change will and *must* occur. This change needs to be confronted. We must: "Turn and face the strange."

Bowie's exploration of androgyny is one of the defining aspects of his image, his lyrics, and of his influence on the music industry. It spans his entire career. Much is made of the effect of Bowie's androgynous image on the public during his early television appearances. Perhaps most notable are his cavorting with Mick Ronson on their 1972 performance of "Queen Bitch" on *The Old Grey Whistle Test* and his famous 1972 performance of "The Jean Genie" on *Top of the Pops*, footage of which was later lost and only recovered by the BBC in 2011. This latter song was a homage to the work of French writer Jean Genet who himself was very politically active after the events of Paris 1968 and wrote extensively about homosexuality.

Bowie's exploration of androgyny is often seen as foreshadowing glam rock. However, Bowie's treatment of this topic is deeper than just the elaborate costumes. Bowie was rebelling against the conventions of the time. He rejected the traditional notions of identity and sexuality, despite the fact that at this time homosexuality was still viewed by some as a mental illness. This point is emphasized in "Lady Stardust." Bowie argues for continual changes in personality and image. He did not want others to copy him; he wanted them to find their own identity. According to this view, Bowie was making an intellectual point about the disunity of human character and the undesirability of this ideal. In an obituary of Bowie in the *New Musical Express* we find the following description:

> His shape-shifting nature—which Bowie himself put down to restlessness and boredom—laid the blueprint of what a pop star should be: chameleonic, enigmatic, seductively alien and constantly challenging society's accepted boundaries of personal freedom and expression.
> (www.nme.com/blogs/nme-blogs/david-bowie-obituary)

Again the fragmentation of the Burroughsian cut-up technique might be said to apply here. This fragmentation challenges the boundaries of sense and of rationality, and goes against a strong tradition in philosophy.

The ancient Greek philosopher Aristotle argued that what's distinctive to humans is rationality, and that humans are to be judged as better or worse insofar as they fulfill the principle of rationality (*Nicomachean Ethics*, Book I, 1098a).

In contrast to the Aristotelian approach, Bowie suggests that we need not aspire to the narrow conventions of rationality. Instead, we can reject conformity in favor of complete freedom of expression. In "The Jean Jeanie" he sings: "He's outrageous, he screams and he bawls / Jean Genie let yourself go!" In "Heroes", he describes how we can escape from the confines of oppression and just be ourselves: "We can be us, just for one day." In "Cygnet Committee" we find a cry of freedom: "I want to believe / In the madness that calls 'Now' / And I want to believe / That a light's shining through / Somehow."

The characters Bowie creates might be thought of as satirical constructions that allow him to highlight the fragile mask of human performance: the apparent madness he exhibits (the "cracked actor") highlights the absurdity of this pretense.

Where Are We Now?

Bowie is chameleon, comedian, Corinthian, and caricature. We've looked at two interpretations of his relationship to madness and identity.

The first is that Bowie has lost contact with reality; the second is that Bowie thinks that the rest of humanity, with its narrow and restrictive conventions, has lost contact with reality. On either interpretation, Bowie has allowed people the freedom to feel more comfortable with their true selves and their unconventional ways.

Bowie was a unique performer. No other artist has ever written his own obituary in the form of an album release, just days before his death: "Everybody knows me now."

Is it true that everybody knows him now? Bowie's illness was known to very few people. To the very end, Bowie embodied the unconventional and the contradictory. With a career spanning six decades, the extent to which Bowie's identity was a reality or statement remains unknown. As Bowie also asserted on his final album: "I can't give everything away."

References

Anderson, Christopher. 1993. *Jagger: Unauthorized*. Delacorte.

Anderson, Walter Truett. 1989 [1979]. *Open Secrets: A Western Guide to Tibetan Buddhism for Western Spiritual Seekers*. Tarcher.

Aristotle. 1994 [350 B.C.E.]. *Nicomachean Ethics*. <http://classics.mit.edu/Aristotle/nicomachaen.html>.

Aufderheide, Pat. 1986. Music Videos: The Look of the Sound. *Journal of Communication* (Winter).

Azerrad, Michael. 2001. *Our Band Could Be Your Life*. Little, Brown.

Bangs, Lester. 1996 [1974]. Swan Dive into the Mung. In Thomson and Gutman 1996. Originally published in *Creem* (August 1974).

Beauvoir, Simone de. 1948. *The Ethics of Ambiguity*. Citadel.

Benjamin, Walter. 2006. The Work of Art in the Age of Mechanical Reproduction. In Morra and Marquard 2006.

Botz-Bornstein, Thorsten. 2010. What Does It Mean to Be Cool? *Philosophy Now* (80).

Bowie, David. 1967. *The Laughing Gnome*. <www.youtube.com/watch?v=xZ_Wbjz8JTc>.

———. 1969. *The Mask*. <http://www.metacafe.com/watch/9932508/david_bowie_the_mask/

———. 1975. Interview with Russell Harty. <www.youtube.com/watch?v=G4_0bVgIRjg>.

———. 1999. BBC interview with Jeremy Paxman. <www.youtube.com/watch?v=FiK7s_0tGsg>.

———. 2016. David Bowie at the BBC. <www.bbc.co.uk/programmes/b06z19rx>.

Bowie, David, and Mick Rock. 2013 [2005]. *Moonage Daydream: The Life and Times of Ziggy Stardust*. Genesis.

Buckley, David. 2012 [2005]. *Strange Fascination: David Bowie—The Definitivwe Story.* Virgin.

———. 2015 [1996]. *David Bowie: The Music and the Changes*. Omnibus.

Campbell, Virginia. 1992. David Bowie: Bowie at the Bijou. *Movieline* (1st April) <http://movieline.com/1992/04/01/david-bowie-bowie-at-the-bijou/2>.

Carson, Tom. 1992. David Bowie. In DeCurtis, Henke, and Warren 1992.

Cocker, Jarvis. 2016. Jarvis Cocker Pays Tribute to David Bowie with Two-Hour Radio Show. <www.nme.com/news/david-bowie>.

Colebrook, Claire. 2005. How can we tell the Dancer from the Dance? The Subject of Dance and the Subject of Philosophy. *Topoi* 24:1.

Cayson, Alan. 2005. *Mick Jagger: The Unauthorized Biography*. MPG.

Conze, Edward. 1967. *Buddhist Thought in India: Three Phases of Buddhist Philosophy.* University of Michigan Press.

Critchley, Simon. 2014. *Bowie*. OR Books.

———. *The Problem with Levinas*. Oxford University Press.

———. Nothing Remains: David Bowie's Vision of Love. *New York Times* (11th January).

Crowe, Cameron. 1976. David Bowie: The *Playboy* Interview. *Playboy* (September).

Danto, Arthur C. 2009. *Andy Warhol*. Yale University Press.

DeCurtis, Anthony, James Henke, and Holly George Warren, eds. 1992 [1976]. *The Rolling Stone Illustrated History of Rock-'n'Roll*. Random House.

Deleuze, Gilles, and Felix Guattari. 2000. *Anti-Oedipus: Capitalism and Schizophrenia*. Penguin.

Descartes, René. 1999. *Discourse on Method and Meditations on First Philosophy*. Hackett.

Devereux, Eion, and Aileen Dillane, eds. 2015. *David Bowie: Critical Perspectives*. Routledge.

Diderot, Denis. 1966. *Rameau's Nephew*. Penguin.

Doggett, Peter. 2012 [2011]. *The Man Who Sold the World: David Bowie and the 1970s*. Harper.

Egan, S., ed. 2015. *Bowie on Bowie: Interviews and Encounters with David Bowie*. Chicago Review Press.

Ellison, Ralph. 1952. *Invisible Man*. Random House.
Feuerstein, Georg. 1992. *Holy Madness: The Shock Tactics and Radical Teachings of Crazy-Wise Adepts, Holy Fools, and Rascal Gurus*. Penguin.
Foucault, Michel. 1988. *Madness and Civilization: A History of Insanity in the Age of Reason*. Vintage.
Freud, Sigmund. 2010. *Beyond the Pleasure Principle*. Pacific.
Frith, Simon, ed. 1988. *Facing the Music*. Pantheon.
Gethin, Rupert. 1998. *The Foundations of Buddhism*. Oxford University Press.
Gibran, Kahlil. 2015. *The Prophet*. Albatross.
Greif, Mark. 2015. *The Age of the Crisis of Man*. Princeton University Press.
Guenther, Herbert V., and Chogyam Trungpa. 2001. *The Dawn of Tantra*. Shambhala.
Harron, Mary. 1988. McRock: Pop as a Commodity. In Frith 1988.
Hedges, Chris. 2014. *War Is a Force that Gives Us Meaning*. Public Affairs.
Hegel, G.W.F. 1977. *The Phenomenology of Spirit*. Oxford University Press.
Heidegger, Martin. 1959. Aus einem Gepräch über die Sprache: Zwischen einem Japaner und einem Fragenden [A Conversation about Language between a Japanese and an Inquirer]. *Unterwegs zur Sprache.* Tübingen: Neske.
Hinchman, Lewis. 1984. *Hegel's Critique of the Enlightenment*. University of Florida Press.
Humphreys, Christmas. 1998. *Zen Buddhism*. Diamond.
Jagger, Mick. 2016. Mick Jagger Remembers David Bowie. As told to Patrick Doyle. *Rolling Stone* 1254 (Bowie Tribute Issue, February 11th).
Jones, Dylan. 2012. *When Ziggy Played Guitar: David Bowie and Four Minutes that Shook the World*. Preface Publishing.
Jung, Carl G. 1989. *Memories, Dreams, Reflections*. Vintage.
———. 2006. *The Undiscovered Self*. Signet.
Kuki, Shuzo. 1997 [1930]. *Reflections on Japanese Taste: The Structure of Iki*. Power.
Leigh, Wendy. 2014. *Bowie: The Biography*. Simon and Schuster.
Ling, Trevor. 2013 [1973]. *The Buddha: The Social-Revolutionary Potential of Buddhism*. Pariyatti.
Lopez-Corvo, Rafael. 1977. *Self-Envy: Therapy and the Divided Internal World*. Aronson.

MacKinnon, Angus. 1980. The Future Isn't What It Used to Be: David Bowie Talks about Loneliness, Insecurity, and Myth. And the Dangers of Messing with Major Tom. *New Musical Express* (13th September).

Marx, Karl H. 2014. *On the Jewish Question*. CreateSpace.

Miller, D.L. 2016. *World Peace: The Influence of the Unconscious*. Unpublished manuscript.

Miller, John J. 2006. Rockin' the Right. *National Review* (26th May).

Minkowski, Eugene. 1970. *Lived Time: Phenomenological and Psychopathological Studies*. Northwestern University Press.

Morra, Joanne, and Marquard Smith, eds. 2006. *Visual Culture: Critical Concepts in Media and Cultural Studies*. Routledge.

Nietzsche, Friedrich. 1974. *The Gay Science: With a Prelude in Rhymes and an Appendix of Songs*. Vintage.

———.1977. *The Portable Nietzsche*. Penguin.

———. 1996. *Human, All Too Human: A Book for Free Spirits*. Cambridge University Press.

O'Connell, Grace. 2013. Special Feature: How to Read Like Bowie—David Bowie's Top 100 Books. <http://www.openbooktoronto.com/news/special_feature_how_read_bowie>.

O'Hagan, Sean. 2003 review of Bowie and Rock, *Moonage Daydream: The Life and Times of Ziggy Stardust. The Guardian* (12th January).

O'Leary, Chris. 2015. *Rebel Rebel*. Zero Books.

Orwell, George. 2013 [1949]. *Nineteen Eighty-Four: The Annotated Edition*. Penguin.

Pegg, Nicholas. 2011. *The Complete David Bowie: New Edition—Expanded and Updated*. Titan.

Rank, Otto. 1989. *The Double: A Psychoanalytic Study*. Karnac.

Rawls, John. 1999 [1971]. *A Theory of Justice*. Harvard University Press.

Reynolds, Simon. 2005. *Rip It Up and Start Again*. Penguin.

Richards, Keith, with James Fox. 2010. *Life*. Little, Brown.

Roszak, Theodore. 1995 [1969]. *The Making of a Counter Culture: Reflections on the Technocratic Scoety and Its Youthful Opposition*. University of California Press.

Rosen, Jody. 2016. David Bowie's 'Blackstar' Is Filled with Songs about Death and Doom: Album Review. <www.billboard.com/articles/review/6836029/david-bowie-blackstar-album-review>.

Russell, Bertrand. 1916. *Principles of Social Reconstruction*. Unwin.
———. 1921). *The Analysis of Mind*. Routledge.
———. 1949. *The Scientific Outlook*. Second edition. Routledge.
———. 1993. The Pursuit of Truth. In *The Collected Papers of Bertrand Russell*. Routledge.
Sandford, Christopher. 1998 [1996]. *Bowie: Loving the Alien*. Da Capo.
Sartre, Jean-Paul. 2007. *Existentialism Is a Humanism*. Yale University Press.
Savage, John. 1980. David Bowie: The Gender Bender. *The Face* (November).
———. 2008 [1992]. *England's Dreaming: Anarchy, Sex Pistols, Punk Rock, and Beyond*. St. Martin's Press.
Sloterdijk, Peter. 1987. *Critique of Cynical Reason*. University of Minnesota Press.
Stanley, Sharon 2007. Retreat from Politics: The Cynic in Modern Times. *Polity* 39:3.
Stein, Murray, ed. 2010. *Jungian Psychoanalysis: Working in the Spirit of C.G. Jung*. Open Court.
Szasz, Thomas S. 1973. *The Second Sin*. Doubleday.
———. 1997. *The Manufacture of Madness: A Comparative Study of the Inquisition and the Mental Health Movement*. Syracuse University Press.
———. 2001. *Pharmacracy: Medicine and Politics in America*. Praeger.
———. 2003 [1961]. *The Myth of Mental Illness: Foundations of a Theory of Personal Conduct*. Harper.
———. 2008. *Psychiatry: The Science of Lies*. Syracuse University Press.
Thomson, Elizabeth, and David Gutman, eds. 1996. *The Bowie Companion*. Da Capo.
Trynka, Paul. 2011. *Starman: David Bowie—The Definitive Biography*. Hachette.
Usher, Bethany, and Stephanie Fremaux. 2015. Turn Myself to Face Me: David Bowie in the 1990s and Discovery of Authentic Self. In Devereux and Dillane 2015.
Volkan, Vamik. 1988. *The Need to Have Enemies and Allies: From Clinical Practice to International Relationships*. Aronson.
Warhol, Andy. 1975. *The Philosophy of Andy Warhol: From A to B and Back Again*. Harcourt.
Wrbican, Mark. 2016. A Modest Memoir of a Cultural Giant, David Bowie. <http://blog.warhol.org/museum/a-modest-memoir-of-a-cultural-giant-david-bowie-2>.

References

Wilcken, Hugo. 2005. *David Bowie's Low (33 1/3)*. Continuum.

Yentob, Alan. 1975. *Cracked Actor: A Film about David Bowie*. <https://www.youtube.com/watch?v=FsPVrsZcbZU>.

Zinn, Jeff. 2015. *The Existential Actor: Life and Death Onstage and Off*. Smith and Kraus.

Žižek, Slavoj. 2003. *The Puppet and the Dwarf: The Perverse Core of Christianity*. MIT Press.

Authors Who Fell to Earth

Theodore G. Ammon drives a 1956 Dodge Coronet Lancer, with two-speed automatic push-button transmission and a V-8 with dual exhausts, to Millsaps College in Jackson, Mississippi, where he has taught Philosophy for more decades than he's willing to admit. He loves to teach. But he has published some stuff, in the areas of philosophy of logic, history of philosophy, and aesthetics. In fact he is the extremist of the department: he teaches logic and aesthetics. He would like his audience to know that he kept his vinyl, has a new turntable, and routinely plays it.

An obscure but earnest graduate student created the persona of **Randall E. Auxier** in Atlanta back in the late 1980s. He toured in that persona to places like Hastings, Nebraska (where he was almost hired), and eventually a number of towns in South Dakota and Virginia and Tennessee, where he was almost an administrator. To avoid stagnation, he fired himself as an Oklahoma philosophy professor in 2000, and then re-invented himself as a different and more successful philosophy professor at Southern Illinois University Carbondale. Unsatisfied with this role, he became "Randall E. Auxier, pop culture writer," in 2004. He has been riding that roller coaster for a while, so he is working on his next identity, which he will reveal to the world when the time is right.

Thorsten Botz-Bornstein is a German philosopher trying to be slightly funnier than Kant. He studied philosophy in Paris, and received his PhD from Oxford University. As a post-doctoral researcher based in Finland he undertook extensive research on Russian formalism and semiotics in Russia and the Baltic countries. He received his 'habilitation' from the EHESS in Paris in 2000. Being attracted by everything that is virtual, stylish, playful, and dreamlike, he has been drawn towards things Japanese. He has found much of the desired dreamlike atmosphere in classical Japanese and Chinese philosophy but has also elaborated on profound parallels between the design of the new Mini Cooper and traditional Japanese pottery and provided philosophical reasons why some Asian subjects tend to use the English language as a "linguistic air-guitar." The continuation of his research takes place in a setting not less unreal than Japan: Kuwait.

Cam Cobb is an Associate Professor in the Faculty of Education at the University of Windsor. His research focuses on such topics as social justice in special education, narrative pedagogy, and co-teaching in adult learning contexts. Over the past few years his work was published in a variety of journals including *Per la Filosofia*, *Cinema: Journal of Philosophy and the Moving Image*, the *F. Scott Fitzgerald Review*, the *British Journal of Special Education*, the *International Journal of Bilingual Education and Bilingualism*, and the *International Journal of Inclusive Education*.

Anneliese Cooper is a freelance writer living in Brooklyn. She has written extensively for Artinfo.com and other arts publications. Currently, she's working on a collection of essays in which performance, gender, and David Bowie play defining roles. She has a degree in film studies from Columbia University, where she received the Andrew Sarris Memorial Award for Film Criticism.

R. Kevin Hill is Associate Professor of Philosophy at Portland State University. From 1994 until 2001 he taught in the Philosophy Department at Northwestern University. He is the author of *Nietzsche's Critiques: The Kantian Foundations of His Thought* (2003) and *Nietzsche: A Guide for the Perplexed* (2007); he's also editor and co-translator of *Nietzsche's The Will to Power: Selections from the Notebooks of the 1880s* (forthcoming).

CHRISTOPHER KETCHAM earned his doctorate at the University of Texas at Austin. He teaches business and ethics for the University of Houston downtown. His research interests are risk management, applied ethics, social justice, and east-west comparative philosophy. The sadness isn't just saying goodbye to David Bowie, but it's saying goodbye to new characters he was thinking about that we will never see.

MATTHEW LAMPERT has a PhD in philosophy from the New School in New York. By the time he got to New York, Matthew was living like a king—but then he used up all his money on graduate school. So now he lives in Queens and teaches at several colleges in the area. His recent work includes essays on business ethics, critical pedagogy, and the work of Louis Althusser and Jacques Rancière.

GREG LITTMANN does not live on his back, is ambivalent about chimney stacks, and is associate professor of philosophy at Southern Illinois University Edwardsville. Outrageously letting himself go, he's published on metaphysics, evolutionary epistemology, the philosophy of logic, and the philosophy of professional philosophy, as well as writing numerous chapters for books relating philosophy to pop culture, including volumes on Black Sabbath and The Who. He refuses to believe that Ziggy Stardust and the Spiders from Mars are never getting back together.

NICOLAS MICHAUD teaches philosophy and English in Jacksonville, Florida. Often lost in his own thoughts, he identifies with Major Tom—though others tell him that he's more reminiscent of Sir Didymous.

MARTIN MUCHALL teaches in the Philosophy and Theology Department at the Royal Russell School in South Croydon, which is quite close to Bromley and Beckenham, two of Bowie's old stamping grounds. His previous publications include an article on *Groundhog Day* and the Buddha. He has also contributed to some Buddhist-themed side projects undertaken by *Philosophy Now* magazine. One result of his present research into non-radical Islam (especially Islamic punk rock or 'taqwacore' music) is that he does not agree with Donald Trump's view that we are all going to get killed by Muslims.

Jerry S. Piven has taught at Case Western Reserve University, the New School for Social Research, and New York University, where his courses focused on the philosophy and psychology of religion, existentialism, death, and evil. He is the editor of *The Psychology of Death in Fantasy and History* (2004) and *Terrorism, Jihad, and Sacred Vengeance* (2004), and author of *Death and Delusion: A Freudian Analysis of Mortal Terror* (2004), *The Madness and Perversion of Yukio Mishima* (2004), and numerous articles on philosophy, religion, psychology, and history. His latest work in progress is *Slaughtering Death: On the Psychoanalysis of Terror, Religion, and Violence*.

Michael K. Potter is a philosopher by temperament and education—employed as a Teaching and Learning Specialist in the Centre for Teaching and Learning, University of Windsor—whose research focuses on applications of pragmatist, anarchist, and nihilist philosophy in higher education. The author of *Bertrand Russell's Ethics* (2006), most recently he was co-editor of a special issue of *The Canadian Journal for the Scholarship of Teaching and Learning* on the importance of the arts and humanities.

When he saw him perform on Broadway in *The Elephant Man*, **George A. Reisch** was very young and not exactly sure who David Bowie was. But after seeing the video for "Ashes to Ashes" a few years later, his brain began to hurt, a lot. This could only be soothed by listening to *Scary Monsters* close to every day during college. Since then he has taught philosophy and history of science at Illinois Institute of Technology and Northwestern University and has published research on cold war intellectual history and philosophy of science. He's currently managing editor of *The Monist* and Series Editor for the Popular Culture and Philosophy series.

Simon Riches is a researcher and trainee clinical psychologist at the Institute of Psychiatry, Psychology and Neuroscience, King's College London. He previously taught philosophy at University College London and Heythrop College, University of London. He holds a PhD in philosophy from University College London and has also studied philosophy at the University of Southampton and psychology at the University of East London.

His research interests lie in epistemology, virtual reality, and the intersection between philosophy and psychology. He is editor of *The Philosophy of David Cronenberg* (2012) and has contributed chapters to many volumes on popular culture, including *Leonard Cohen and Philosophy* (2014), *The Philosophy of David Lynch* (2011), *Dune and Philosophy* (2011), *Dexter: Investigating Cutting Edge Television* (2010), *101 War Movies You Must See Before You Die*, and *101 Gangster Movies You Must See Before You Die* (both 2009).

Andrew Watson is studying for a PhD in cognitive neuropsychology at University College London. He holds an MSc in Neuroscience from Imperial College London and has previously studied psychology at the University of Essex. He has formerly held posts in psychology at the Institute of Psychiatry, King's College London, and in the Department of Medicine, Imperial College London. His research interests lie in mental health and wellbeing, particularly in relation to cognitive processes. He is a contributor to *The Philosophy of Neil Young* (forthcoming).

Index of Nothing and Everything